THE SONG OF THE
PARTISANS

KATHRYN GAUCI

First published in 2022 by Ebony Publishing

ISBN: 978-0-6487-144-4-6

Friend, do you hear the dark flight of the crows over our plains?
Friend, do you hear the dull cries of our country in chains?
Hey, Partisans. Workers and farmers, this is the warning.
Tonight, the enemy will know the price of blood and tears.

"The Song of the Partisans"

*This book is dedicated to the bravery of the
men and women of the Resistance during
WWII, and to all those who give their lives
in pursuit of freedom.*

CONTENTS

CHAPTER 1

Paris. First Week of April, 1944

IT WAS POURING with rain when Simone arrived back at 68, rue Octave Feuillet with only five minutes to spare before curfew. She pushed open the heavy door and shook her umbrella in the darkened hallway before taking the elevator to the fifth floor. From there, she walked the last flight of stairs to her apartment in the pitch dark, cursing her landlady for not fixing the light. In the silence of the night, she was acutely aware of her footsteps on the tiled floor, and a soft rustling sound as she fumbled in her bag for her key. When she unlocked the door to her apartment and switched on the light, her eyes fell on a thin sliver of light coming from underneath the closed kitchen door at the end of the hallway. Pulling the gun from her bag, she slipped off her shoes and cautiously tip-toed towards the door. With her body pressed tightly against the wall, she listened for a few seconds until she heard a clink of glass. At that moment, she kicked open the door aiming her gun at a man in a dark suit sitting at her kitchen table drinking a glass of wine.

'You can put that thing away,' the man said. He picked up a half-empty bottle of wine and poured her a glass. 'Come and join me.'

'*Merde*, Jacques! You gave me a fright. I never expected to find you here. I thought you were in Marseille?' Knowing he was an expert lock picker, she didn't even bother to ask how he got in.

'I was, but something important came up.'

Simone took off her wet overcoat, shook it, and hung it up to dry. 'Well, it must be something important to bring you here in this weather.' She sat down at the table with him, lit a cigarette and raised her glass, toasting his return. '*Santé!* Now maybe you can tell me what is so urgent that you needed to see me at such a late hour and frighten the living daylight out of me into the bargain.'

'I have an assignment for you.'

'Go on, I'm listening.'

'How long have I known you, Simone?' Jacques didn't give her time to answer. 'Three years, two months, one week to be precise.'

'Oh my, that's impressive.' Simone smiled. 'You always were one for fine details.'

'Exactly,' he replied, 'which is why I'm entrusting this assignment to you.'

The way he said it puzzled her. Since joining the Resistance, Jacques had given her many assignments. In fact he'd trained her.

'I can't tell you too much at this point, but what I can say is it comes from higher up.'

'You mean de Gaulle?' Simone leaned back in the chair and crossed her long legs, trying to read his face, but Jacques was a man who rarely let his emotions show.

'It appears to be an Anglo-French affair, so I imagine de Gaulle is certainly involved in this one too. They appear to have put aside their distrust of each other for the moment and become more co-operative.'

'Is it somewhere in Paris?'

'No – it's Reims.'

'Champagne country! How long for? A day or two like the other jobs outside Paris?'

'I'm afraid not. This assignment means that you will have to relocate and live there for a while. I have no idea how long for, but it will be at least a few weeks, maybe even a couple of months.' His facial expression still gave little away. 'I realise you aren't familiar with the area, but with the right contacts and a map, it shouldn't take you long to acquaint yourself with your surroundings. That's not the main reason I'm sending you. It's because we urgently need a woman to work alongside one of the Special Operation Executive's network chiefs – a woman with brains.'

'You flatter me, Jacques. It's the first time I've heard such praise. In fact I can't recall you ever saying more than a "Well done".'

Jacques shifted uncomfortably in his chair. 'I don't praise people for a variety of reasons. The first is that I never know how long they will survive, and the other is because I want my men and women to stay grounded. Praise could go to their heads and catch them off guard. No room for egos in this business.'

Simone suppressed a smile. She wanted to tell him that there were enough egos in the people she worked with to wreak havoc on the Resistance if they chose to – including Jacques himself. After all, one had to have a strong belief in the moral right, or few of them would be putting themselves at risk at the drop of a hat. In her opinion, a good dose of ego went a long way. It fuelled the adrenaline and made them do things they never would have imagined.

Jacques headed a large Resistance network of several hundred in Paris, and Simone wondered why he'd chosen her. In the early days of the Occupation, her work consisted of covertly dropping leaflets around Paris. After that she was given courier work, delivering messages or aiding the Resistance to move escapees and weapons to safe houses. Over the past year this work had proved to be extremely dangerous as the Gestapo had eyes on every street, mostly in the form of collaborators, and quite a few of the networks had been caught and their members executed. Where once, Simone had been rather naïve, she soon learnt to keep her wits about her. Jacques drummed it into her that once caught, that was it, there was no second chance.

'I'm curious; why me?' she asked. 'There are plenty of other operators in the group who are far more experienced than me, especially when it comes to working with the Special Operations Executive agents. Besides, if it concerns the British, why doesn't SOE get one of their own female agents to do the job? Surely they already have women in the field.'

'Due to the urgency, there is no-one London can send at the moment. All other agents are occupied elsewhere and waiting could jeopardize the mission. This is why SOE turned to us. I will level with you, Simone, they *did* have a woman working in the circuit, one working closely with the network chief, unfortunately something went wrong and she was caught – along with their radioman. They were brought here to Paris and after interrogation in Fresnes Prison, "disappeared". We believe they have been sent to Germany. Whatever the case, the trail has gone cold. Jacques paused to assess Simone's reaction before continuing. 'I don't need to tell you that this operation is highly dangerous. If the Gestapo even suspects you are connected with the Resistance, they will have you tailed. If this happens, you must adopt another alias. At all costs, you must stay one step ahead of them.'

'Nothing complicated then,' Simone said with a smile.

Jacques raised an eyebrow. 'This is certainly not a joke. You will be in danger from the moment you get there. I am being honest with you when I say this; if you last the distance you will be damn lucky.' Simone's cheeks reddened. It wasn't exactly what she'd expected to hear but she thanked him for his honesty. 'We already have resistants in the area – good ones at that – but my colleagues and I think you are perfect for the job. You've been a fearless courier; you are cool and calculating, and I have seen how good you are in the field, *and* you speak German. More importantly, I trust you. In many ways, you are just as good as some of those agents SOE send over. You've already been on several assignments with some of their agents, so you understand their ways.

Jacques poured out the last drop of wine and asked if she had another bottle. Simone could see it was going to be a long night and pulled out a bottle of cheap red wine from the kitchen cabinet, apologizing that she had nothing better. She also prepared them a bowl of leftover soup – lentils laced with vegetables and slivers of dried sausage.

'You say I am not one for compliments,' Jacques said, 'but this soup is delicious.' He polished it off quickly and asked for seconds. 'I can't say the same about the wine though. Still, where you are going to, you won't have to worry about bad wine.' After finishing the second bowl, he lit up a cigarette and continued. 'Now, where were we?'

'Will I be acting as a courier for the circuit – or will there be other tasks?' Simone asked.

'I cannot give you precise details, but it's highly likely you will be asked to do things you've not done before. I think you know what that means – possibly eliminate someone – it will depend on the circumstances.'

Simone couldn't believe her ears. He spoke in such a detached, matter-of-fact way that it took her a few minutes before the gravity of his words sank in. 'So far, I've never killed anyone, Jacques. I don't know how I would feel if it came to that point. The thought appals me.'

'My dear girl, the thought appals us all. The first kill is always the worst. After that it gets easier – if you keep your wits about you. Don't worry, you won't be going out there entirely untested.'

She wondered what on earth he meant. 'Can I ask if I know the leader of this circuit? After all, as you said, I've worked with quite a few agents.'

'You helped him move to a safe house when he came to Paris a year ago. At the time, he was recovering from shrapnel and bullet wounds to the shoulder, chest, and stomach – the result of a German ambush. When he recovered, you and Victor took him to Poitiers. From there he returned to England.'

Simone's eyes widened. 'You mean Pascal! Well, well, this is a surprise.' She shook her head. 'I don't know if that's good news or bad. After all, if I recall correctly, he'd already lost a few of his men in the ambush – the result of not being careful enough. Now you're asking me to put my life at risk and work with him in the field?'

Jacques expected this reaction and was prepared for it. 'The ambush was the result of bad intelligence from the Resistance – not from his men – so I think we owe him, don't you? Anyway, he praised you for helping nurse him back to a full recovery. He trusts you. I gather it was Pascal who personally asked if F Section could use you, and Buckmaster agreed.'

Simone thought back to the time she and three other resistants picked him up after the ambush. Pascal was lucky to be alive; one bullet almost penetrated the aorta. They moved him to a safe house in the middle of Paris, right under the noses of the Germans, and it was there that she and Victor took it in turns to care for him. When they said goodbye in Poitiers, she never expected to see him again.

'As I've indicated,' Jacques said, 'this is a dangerous mission so it's imperative that you work together and cover each other's backs. Trust me on this, Simone. It's not for the faint-hearted.'

There were a few awkward minutes of silence while the enormity of the task ahead sank in. She apologized for seemingly being flippant when in reality she felt a mixture of fear and excitement.

'Have you forgotten I'm a nurse and needed here?'

His reply was swift and to the point. 'Resign. Tell them you're going to look after a sick aunt – make up something. This is where your clear thinking comes in.'

By the time they'd finished the second bottle of wine, Jacques managed to quell any doubts Simone might have had about being up to the job and she readily accepted, even though she wasn't quite sure what she was getting herself into.

'Excellent. I knew I could rely on you. Now, to more practical things, can I sleep on the couch tonight? We'll discuss this more in the morning.'

Simone fetched him a couple of blankets before retiring to bed herself. She lay awake for a while, rerunning their conversation in her mind. Of all the people he could have asked, he chose her and she was flattered. She had a lot of admiration for Jacques, but until now never quite knew how highly he thought of her. One thing she was sure of though, she would not let him down.

CHAPTER 2

It was the smell of fried onions wafting through the apartment that woke Simone up. The next minute, there was a knock on the bedroom door.

'Get up,' Jacques called out. 'It's not often I cook breakfast for people, so don't let it go cold.'

Simone rubbed her eyes and looked at the clock. It was six-thirty and after a sleepless night thinking about her "dangerous mission", all she wanted to do was go back to sleep. When she entered the kitchen, Jacques was just plating up a mound of fried potatoes and onions.

'There you are,' he said, pushing the plate towards her. 'Get something substantial in your stomach. You've got a busy day ahead of you.'

He cut up a few slices of one-day-old bread and poured them a cup of ersatz coffee before sitting down to join her.

'I didn't know you were a chef too,' Simone said. 'First compliments and now breakfast, whatever next.'

'It's the best I could do under the circumstances. You don't have much food in the cupboard. You can't live on lentils, onions, and potatoes, you know.'

Simone assured him she wasn't starving as she was fortunate to eat one good meal a day at the hospital.

'Have you had any more thoughts about last night's little chat,' Jacques asked, scooping up a mound of fried onions with his bread. 'No change of heart?'

'I confess, I did have a rather sleepless night, but I will do my duty for my country. After all, what I have I got to lose, but my life?' Simone realised her reply sounded rather noble, but given the circumstances, it was probably true.

'The right attitude.' Jacques gave her a wink. 'Now eat up.'

After finishing their breakfast, Jacques informed her that she needed to resign immediately.

'So quickly; I thought maybe you would give me a couple of days.'

He shook his head. 'Sorry. It has to be done now. I will accompany you and wait while you hand in your notice, and then I want to take you on a little journey.'

'Do you mind if I ask where to?'

'You'll find out soon enough. Now, be a good girl and get ready. We must be at the other rendezvous by 10:30.'

Simone lived alone and wasn't used to being told what to do in her own apartment. Nevertheless, she did as Jacques asked. Fifteen minutes later, they left the apartment together and hailed a taxi.

'The 10th arrondissement,' Jacques said to the driver. 'Lariboisière Hospital.'

When they reached their destination, Jacques paid the driver and told Simone he would wait while she handed in her resignation. 'Be snappy about it,' he said. 'We must get a move on or we'll be late.'

He sat on the low wall and watched her until she disappeared through the grand archway, noting for the first time, the words, *Liberté*, *Égalité*, and *Fraternité*, engraved into the stonework at the top of the arch – words fundamental to the values that defined French society and for which he was prepared to lay down his life. Last night's rain had cleared and it was another beautiful Parisian spring day. The trees were in blossom, women had shed their winter clothes for prettier attire, and all seemed normal, apart from the German armoured vehicles which passed by frequently. There were even German soldiers stationed near the hospital entrance.

When he saw Simone return, he jumped up, stubbed out his cigarette and asked how it went.

'As well as can be expected, I suppose. The matron was sorry to see me go as they are short staffed at the moment, but she wished me well and hoped to see me back again sometime soon.'

'What did you tell her?'

'That I'm going to nurse a sick aunt as she has no-one else because her two sons are in Germany.'

Jacques smiled. 'You see, making up little white lies is not that difficult is it?'

Simone threw him a dirty look. 'Where to now?'

'All in good time.'

They walked to the nearest Metro and caught a train to an industrial area on the outskirts of Paris. When they exited at the other end, one of the resistants who Simone knew well, was waiting with a car.

'Hello Simone, how are you?' Maurice asked, opening the passenger door for her.

'I'm fine, thank you, but I'll feel a lot better when I know what this is all about.'

Maurice glanced at Jacques who gave nothing away. They drove for about ten minutes until they reached an old industrial area bordering the Seine and stopped outside a large double-gated entrance to what was once an old disused brick factory. Another resistant, with a Sten gun slung over his shoulder, unlocked the gates and waved them through. The car slowly made its way towards the back of the dilapidated building and parked in a courtyard filled with rubble and overgrown weeds where they encountered more resistants sitting outside smoking cigarettes and keeping watch.

'Well,' Jacques said to the men as they piled out of the car. 'Has he confessed?'

One of the resistants nodded solemnly. Jacques, Simone, and Maurice entered the building accompanied by all but two of the men who stayed outside to keep watch. Simone recognized the place. She'd been here twice before for clandestine meetings and it didn't take her long to realise what was going on.

They walked through the shell of the building, stepping over mounds of rubble and navigating pools of water where the previous night's downpour had entered the building through the partially ruined roof, until they reached one of the few intact rooms. There they found a bloodied and bruised man shackled to a chair. He had been stripped naked except for his underpants which were drenched in a mixture of sweat, blood, and urine. A putrid, cloying stench filled the room. Twelve resistants were gathered around him, staring at the unfortunate man with cold hatred. Simone bit her lip at the distressing scene.

The man's head lolled listlessly to one side until Jacques grabbed it by a clump of wet hair and pulled it up, forcing him to look at them.

'So, it was you who ratted to the Gestapo about the safe house?' Jacques said. 'How much did they pay you, filthy *mouchard*? Whatever it was, it wasn't worth your life.'

The man had a broken jaw and nose, and had lost several teeth in the beating. He could barely speak, but he did manage to ask for forgiveness, saying he did it to feed his family. Jacques told him it was too late. He took out his gun from his belt, cocked it, and handed it to Simone. 'Finish him off,' he said, matter-of-factly.

Simone stared at the gun for a few seconds and then at Jacques. He remained stony-faced but his eyes penetrated deep into her soul. They were the eyes of a wild animal on the hunt – kill or be killed. Her throat went dry and she was aware of her heart beating loudly in her chest. *So this is what he meant when he said she wouldn't be sent away untested.* All eyes turned towards her, waiting to see what she would do. No-one said a word. The room was filled with expectation, the silence magnified in the humid atmosphere. Somewhere outside she heard the cawing of a crow through a shattered glass window and the rhythmic dripping of water from a nearby broken pipe.

Seeing the man's plight, she did not want to be the cause of prolonging his suffering any more than necessary. Her heart thudded at the thought of being his executioner, but she had to do it. Now was not a time for a discussion. The men had found him guilty, he had betrayed the Resistance, and he must pay. She took the gun, took several deep breaths, and aimed at his heart. Then she took one long breath holding it as she fired. A split second later, he was dead. The impact had knocked him backwards and he lay, still tied to the chair, on the floor in a steadily seeping pool of blood, his eyes staring emptily at the ceiling.

Maurice took his pulse and checked the point of entry. 'Bullseye – a perfect shot through the heart.'

Jacques took the gun from Simone but her fingers were clenched so tightly that he had to prise them open to release it. She stared at him with a vacant look for a few seconds and then hurriedly left the building to get some fresh air. After a few minutes, he came outside and joined her. He offered her a cigarette and for a while, neither of them spoke.

'Did you really need to test me like that?' she asked, her legs still feeling like jelly.

'I'm afraid I did. It's one thing to be a good shot in training, but it's quite another to kill in cold blood. I trained you and I wanted to be around to see your first kill.' He touched her arm gently. 'I knew it would be difficult, but I told you, this assignment is dangerous, and I needed to be sure you could keep your cool.'

Maurice joined them and Jacques suggested they go to a nearby bar run by another of the resistants while the men took care of the body.

The bar was empty when they arrived and they sat near the window where they could keep a watch on the street. 'Drinks are on me,' Maurice said. 'What will you have?'

The enormity of what she'd just done was starting to sink in and Simone began to shake uncontrollably. 'Bring us a Pastis,' Jacques replied. He squeezed her hand and told her she would be fine.

Maurice placed the small glasses of anise-flavoured spirit on the table along with a jug of water. After she'd taken a long sip, Simone asked Jacques what the dead man had done.

'We were about to move a group of escapees from Belgium who had been hiding in a safe house. The *mouchard* lived across the road. He spotted one of our men taking them packages of food on a couple of occasions and thought it unusual as the place was supposed to be empty. He notified the Gestapo and when they raided the place, they found the escapees – a family of Jews – a man and his wife, a young girl and her older brother, and a grandmother. They were taken away and the Gestapo lay in wait for our man to return. As he neared the house, his instincts told him something was wrong. He scanned the street and noticed the man peeping from behind a curtain. Smelling a rat, the resistant kept walking and then slipped into a doorway to hide. Half an hour later, he saw the man leave his house and meet with several plainclothes men in the street, who he surmised were Gestapo. A car drew up and the plainclothes men left. Waiting until after midnight, the resistant cautiously returned to the house and discovered the family had vanished. Their suitcases were gone, but several items of clothing lay strewn about the room.

'The resistant notified us straight away and our sources confirmed a Gestapo raid. Suspecting this had something to do with the neighbour, we followed him for a few days. On one of his return trips, we kidnapped him and brought him here, where he confessed.'

Throughout the time Simone had worked for Jacques, the Resistance had ordered the killing of quite a few traitors, but she had never been present at any until now. She always prided herself on being extremely cautious, and despite several narrow escapes, so far had managed to avoid being caught. A good dose of luck always played a big part. All the same, she often carried her gun, but had never needed to use it.

Jacques asked Maurice if he had the papers ready. He took a brown envelope from his inside jacket pocket and handed them to Jacques, who cast his eyes over them and slid them across the table to Simone.

'Your new documents,' he said. 'You'll be leaving in two days' time.'

After what she'd just experienced, Simone was prepared for anything Jacques threw her way. She picked them up and was about to take a look when he put his hand on them, telling her to put them away. She could check them later.

'Your new Identity Card, travel pass, ration book, and a first-class ticket to Reims.' Simone felt as though she was being swept along on a tidal wave and was about to be hurtled on to the rocks. 'From the moment you leave Paris, you will no longer be Simone Guillot, you will be Martine Dumont. Memorize the details of your new identity.

It won't be that difficult, it's mainly a change of name and address. You will still use your nursing skills. You answered an advertisement in the newspaper for a position of live-in nurse and companion to an elderly woman in the wine village of Verzenay. Her name is Madame Marie Legrand and she is a strong supporter of the Resistance. She and her family are completely trustworthy.'

Simone raised her eyebrows. 'Legrand! You mean of the famous Champagne house?'

'That's right. So you see, there will be perks to this assignment – excellent Champagne.'

Maurice looked at her and smiled. 'Lucky girl, Simone. We get to drink what the Germans don't want.'

The light moment soon turned serious again. 'Madame Legrand is aware you will be going to care for her,' Jacques continued. 'Naturally, your new identity entails a new family – both your parents are dead. You father died of cancer ten years ago, and your mother died of a heart attack one year before the Germans occupied France. No siblings. I don't want you to use your existing address so your new one is 50, rue du Landy, Clichy. Just in case you are questioned about your domicile by the Gestapo, there are two churches nearby. The smaller Église Saint-Medard and the larger Église Saint-Vincent-de-Paul. I live nearby and will keep a lookout should anyone try and check you out. Across the road from the entrance to Saint-Vincent-de Paul is a kiosk. The owner is with the Resistance. We'll speak more about that before you depart. Any questions?'

Simone's head was spinning. 'I'm sure there will be plenty once I've digested the situation.'

'Good. You will see from the ticket that your train departs from Gare de l'Est at 7:00 p.m. in the evening. There's a café two blocks away from the railway station. It has a yellow awning. I'll meet you there at 5:00 p.m. sharp to give you your final details. After that, you will board the train to Reims.'

Jacques ordered one more Pastis before they left. It was a sombre meeting and there was no more mention of the execution or the upcoming trip. Maurice dropped them both off at the Metro and they all went their separate ways. As Simone descended the steps to the Metro, she felt a nauseating surge of panic and steadied herself against the wall to stop herself from fainting. A passer-by stopped and asked if she was alright. She waved him away.

She began to wonder if she was capable of carrying out whatever it was she was supposed to do. Last night she had felt confident, now she wasn't so sure. She took a deep breath to steady her nerves and returned to the apartment.

CHAPTER 3

AFTER A NERVOUS two days, mostly spent studying a detailed map of Reims and memorizing her new cover story, Simone, attired in a smart smoky-grey wool flannel suit and carrying a small suitcase, arrived at the café at 5:00 p.m. sharp. Jacques was already waiting for her. She placed her suitcase next to her seat and sat down opposite him where she had a good view of the room. She noticed the way he looked at her. He seemed most impressed. After all this time, it was as if he'd only just noticed she was a woman.

'Allow me to say how charming you look,' he said. He cast his eyes around the room. 'The most beautiful woman in the room by far.'

His comment eased the tension and made her smile. 'Another compliment, Jacques. You're continuing to surprise me. Thank you.' He grinned and ordered her a drink. 'As I'm travelling First Class, I thought I'd better make an effort,' she added.

Simone noticed he didn't miss a thing. He commented on her matching nail polish and lipstick which she'd just purchased with money from her last pay packet – a treat to herself for agreeing to an assignment shrouded in mystery and from which she might never return, and he approved of her Chanel No 5 perfume. It was the last comment about the perfume that threw her. Most men wouldn't know what perfume it was, but he did. He was a dark horse.

She had just turned twenty-five. Of medium height with a slender figure and shoulder-length dark hair, styled off her face in soft curls, she possessed a vibrant and energetic personality which showed in her expressive and large dark eyes. For all her beauty and charm, she had only ever had one love affair, a doctor – Pierre – who was sent to Germany soon after the German Occupation for voicing his outrage

23

against the Germans and Vichy government. She hadn't heard from him since and had no idea where he was and if he was alive or dead, but it was Pierre who had taught her to stand up for what is right, and he was the main reason she had joined the Resistance.

As for Jacques, she realised she knew nothing at all about him. She didn't even know if he was married or had children, or where he was born. In fact, she even doubted if his real name was Jacques. He said he was an engineer with a large company near Lyon before the Occupation. What he did in Paris, apart from running their Resistance group, she was never quite sure. When the Compulsory Labour Laws were implemented in 1943, he managed to obtain an exemption by producing a doctored X-Ray showing a large ulcer. Tall and well-built with dark brown hair, a clean-shaven, strong-boned face with high-cheek bones, and hazel eyes, he was viewed by the other resistants as a serious, no-nonsense character. He rarely smiled, but when he did, it showed a warmth and vulnerability which Simone guessed he preferred to hide. In fact she'd seen him smile more during the last two meetings than at any other time before. There was, however, one thing she'd learnt from their last conversation – that he lived somewhere near the address in Clichy.

Jacques looked at the clock on the wall and said they'd better get down to business as she didn't have much time. 'When you arrive in Reims, make your way to the Hôtel De La Cathédrale in the centre of the city. Give the password to the hotel manager and he'll look after you. I want you to wait there until someone collects you and takes you to your final destination. Because of Madame Legrand's family connection to the grand Champagne houses, I think you'll find you'll be able to move about a little more freely. Pascal will contact you there. From that point, you will be under his direction.'

'Why can't I go straight to Madame Legrand, especially if it's not far from Reims?'

'Security: in case you're followed.'

'Will you be in contact with me at all?' she asked.

Jacques shifted in his chair, a gesture which made her think he was unsure how much more to tell her. 'Maybe, but if you need me, try to get a message to the owner of the kiosk opposite L'Église Saint-Vincent-de-Paul as I mentioned the other day.'

Simone told him she'd already checked it out. He looked surprised but pleased.

'I stopped by on my way here,' she said. 'I thought it better to familiarize myself with my *new* address, just in case I'm questioned. I even checked out the surrounding streets and the two churches nearby. I spotted the kiosk and bought a newspaper in order to make a note of the owner's face. It's an elderly woman.

'Her son works with us. His mother allows us to use the kiosk as a dead-drop.'

'Don't you have any way I can contact you directly in Reims itself?'

'Let's just say that I will be keeping an eye on you, so don't worry. Except for Pascal, who you already know, you are going there "blind". The less we are in contact, the better. One day, when it's all over, we can discuss it over a glass of wine.'

Simone smiled. 'Hmm, let's hope we both survive until then.'

'You'll be fine. Just keep your wits about you. The Allies will be here soon and there is still much to do. The Germans know this and are stepping up their hunt for us. Paris is a nest of spies and collaborators at the moment, so you may even be better off away from here. Has that crossed your mind?' He reached into his jacket pocket and pulled out an envelope. 'A little money to keep you going for a while. Now drink up, I think it's time to get going.'

A trickle of patrons left the bar at the same time, all making their way towards the Gare de l'Est.

'Do you have your pistol with you?' Jacques asked.

Simone told him it was safely hidden in a secret compartment in her suitcase.

Just before they reached the railway station, he stopped abruptly and told her it was time to say goodbye. He shook her hand and wished her good luck. It was an awkward moment for both of them and neither knew what to say. Simone stood in front of him almost expecting that at any minute he would say it was all a big joke – that he'd just been testing her loyalty. But it wasn't the case. His friendly smile disappeared and he reverted to his old self – the serious, no-nonsense person she was used to.

'Go on,' he said, jerking his head towards the station. 'The queues are starting to form. I don't want you missing the train.'

She picked up her suitcase and walked away, her legs almost buckling from her nervousness. *Pull yourself together*, she said to herself. *Or you won't even reach Reims.* As she mounted the steps, she turned and looked back. Jacques had vanished. *This is it. Martine Dumont, you are on your own now.*

The station was packed with German troops and civilians, and fortunately Simone was used to this from her previous courier jobs. The men she particularly needed to be aware of were the plainclothes Gestapo, the hated Milice, and the ever-present informers who lurked in the shadows like deadly spiders in crevices waiting to pounce on their unsuspecting prey. The Resistance had a long memory when it came to all of them, particularly, the latter two groups. After showing her papers, she headed to the First Class compartment where three high-ranking Wehrmacht officers and an aristocratic-looking German in a smart, well-cut suit were also boarding. They politely bade her a good evening and stood aside to let her board. One of the officers offered to help her with her suitcase. It turned out that they would be sitting in the next compartment. The officer kindly placed Simone's suitcase on the rack in her compartment and wished her a good journey. She gave him a charming smile, took off her jacket and sat down next to her other three travelling companions – an elderly couple and a middle-aged man in his fifties. The carriage was hot and stuffy, and the elderly woman asked her husband to pull down the window to give them some air. Simone didn't know which was worse, the stuffy compartment, or the shouts and whistles on the platforms and the choking stench of locomotives belching out steam as they prepared to depart. Not wanting to enter into conversation, she pulled out a book from her handbag and settled down to read.

The journey to Reims passed without incidence but when the train pulled into Reims, the same officer appeared to help her with her suitcase again. Casting aside the cool expressions on her travelling companions' faces, Simone thanked him. His chivalry did have a fortunate side to it as he offered to carry it for her and they quickly bypassed the long queues of people showing their documents. When they exited the station, there was a commotion as a group of people were being led away by the Gestapo. It was an ominous start. The man handed her the suitcase while his companions piled into a waiting car. He asked if they could give her a lift.

'That's quite alright,' she said, hoping he wouldn't pursue the matter. 'You've been very kind as it is, and I don't have far to go.'

'Bruno Albrecht,' he said, offering her his hand. 'Oberstleutnant Bruno Albrecht.'

It was clear he was waiting for Simone to give her name. 'Martine Dumont,' she replied.

'Well, Mademoiselle Dumont, it was a pleasure to meet you. Perhaps our paths will cross again. Reims is a small city.'

Like Paris, Reims was an elegant city and the cafés and restaurants were filled with people. The short walk through the park along the tree-lined boulevards to the hotel cleared her head after the stuffiness of the train compartment. It was good to breathe in the scent of blossoms in the balmy night air; it helped lift her anxiety. The Hôtel De La Cathédrale was a small and well-appointed building surrounded by several other hotels and cafés. It had a view of the cathedral and the Square du Palais de Justice. A rotund, middle-aged man was at the reception desk giving directions to an elderly couple.

'Good evening, Mademoiselle. Do you have a booking?' the man asked, when the couple moved away.

'Uncle Pierre sent me. He asked to give you his regards.'

The man scrutinized her over the top of his glasses and smiled. 'Ah, yes. Mademoiselle Dumont. How is your uncle? Fine, I hope.'

Having acknowledged the password, the manager said he had reserved a room for her on the first floor. He picked up a key along with two freshly laundered towels from a cupboard near the desk and asked her to follow him. There was no elevator and they walked up the flight of stairs.

The room was at the front of the building, giving Simone a clear view of the square. 'This room is always reserved for our special guests,' he said, placing the towels on the bed. 'Breakfast is served in the dining room opposite the reception desk.' He paused for a moment. 'If you need anything, just let me know.'

Simone thanked him and said she wasn't sure how long she would be staying.

'No need to worry. You will find us most accommodating here.' He patted the towels and turned to leave. 'But I must warn you that we do have German guests staying here too, so please be careful.'

After he left, she looked around the room and opened the window to take in the view of the square. Except for a handful of Wehrmacht uniforms, you wouldn't have known there was a war on, although the base of the cathedral was protected from bombing raids. Her room was small, with a single bed, rudimentary furniture including a bedside table with a reading lamp and a box of candles in case the electricity was cut. There was no bath, only a white marble sink in an alcove. The walls were covered with heavily embossed green wallpaper, making the room appear even smaller and somewhat claustrophobic, but at least it was clean and comfortable and she was among friends. She placed her suitcase on the bed and took out most of her clothes, leaving it open with only a few items of underwear draped over it. It was a ruse she often used when travelling around for her courier work. If ever there was a raid and the Gestapo saw an open, almost empty suitcase with delicate underwear, they didn't look so closely.

When she picked up the towels to hang them on a rail near the sink, a note dropped to the floor. It read: *Someone will pick you up at 10 o'clock tomorrow. Be ready.*

She screwed it up and set it alight in the ashtray. Afterwards, she emptied the charred remains out of the window.

CHAPTER 4

Simone rose early the next day and took a short stroll through the streets surrounding the cathedral to get her bearings, before joining the other guests in the breakfast room. From their accents, she could tell most were not locals. One couple was Belgian, another Swiss, and there were three Germans, one accompanied by his wife. The atmosphere seemed quite convivial. They were all chatting or reading newspapers, apart from a bald-headed man in a dark grey suit sitting alone in the far corner. He appeared to be studying the other guests as much as Simone. A folded French newspaper lay on his table. After half an hour, the room began to empty. The bald-headed man was the last to leave and he bade her good day as he exited the room. Simone was sitting by the window and noticed that he left the hotel and went to a kiosk in the square. He appeared to buy something, but it was too far to see what it was, perhaps cigarettes or matches. Then he went to sit in an outdoor café.

Her senses alert, she had a tendency to suspect everyone until proven otherwise and wondered what he was doing. Maybe he was a collaborator surveying the area to report someone to the Gestapo for a few thousand francs. When she got up to leave, she noticed he'd left his newspaper on the chair. She picked it up and took it to the reception desk.

'Good morning, Mademoiselle Dumont,' said the manager. 'I trust you had a good night's sleep.'

'Thank you, yes,' Simone replied. She put the newspaper on the desk. 'I think the man who just left forgot his newspaper. Maybe you'd like to keep it for him.'

The manager picked it up and put it in the guest letter slot. 'The Monsieur is always forgetting things,' he said, with a shrug. 'It's normal.' There was a room number but no name and she didn't want to ask his name.

It was almost ten o'clock and she said she would wait in her room until the person she was waiting for came to pick her up. The hours ticked by and no-one arrived. By five o'clock she went downstairs and tactfully mentioned something to the manager.

He didn't seem at all concerned. In a whisper, he told her this sort of thing happened all the time and that she shouldn't worry. But Simone did worry. She had been trained never to stay too long in a hotel as the Gestapo made regular checks on the guests and often carried out searches. Unfortunately, there was little she could do but wait. By eight o'clock the next morning, there was still no sign of her contact and she went down to breakfast again. Most of the previous day's guests had left, but the man sitting alone was still there. He bade her good morning and started to read his newspaper whilst waiting for his breakfast to arrive.

She had just finished eating when she saw a *gazo*, one of the wood-burning cars park outside the hotel. The driver got out and entered the lobby. Moments later, the manager came to tell her she had a visitor. She quickly finished her tea and went outside to greet him. The middle-aged man, with the strong physique and tanned looks of a woodcutter, introduced himself as Baptiste.

'Good morning, Mademoiselle Dumont. I am here to take you to your aunt.'

The manager nodded all was well and Simone went to collect her suitcase. As Baptiste put her bags in the car, she noticed the bald-headed man watching her from the breakfast room.

'Do you know that man?' she asked.

Baptiste glanced towards the window. 'No.' He saw the worried look on Simone's face. 'I wouldn't be too worried. There are lots of new faces in Reims. He's probably as curious about us as you are about him.'

They drove away and Baptiste apologized for not picking her up earlier. 'We had a little upset,' he said. 'Pascal will explain later.'

The car drove south of Reims towards the Montagne de Reims. In the distance, as far as the eye could see, was an undulating landscape of vineyards; vineyards that produced the grapes to make the world's most prestigious sparkling wine. Tiny villages nestled among them, their simple church towers topped with spires, peeking out over clusters of trees.

'It's beautiful countryside,' Simone said.

He agreed but warned her that because of its prestige in the production of Champagne, there were always plenty of Germans around, especially the *Weinführers* who plundered whatever they could lay their hands on. 'Thankfully most of them stay in Épernay or Reims, but some have requisitioned villas and they occasionally pay us surprise visits, so it's not quite as peaceful as it looks.'

Simone wanted to tell him that, after Paris, where they confronted the Gestapo and Milice on a daily basis, this looked like heaven.

The car pulled into the driveway of a charming *maison bourgeoise* on the outskirts of the picturesque village of Verzenay. Built during the middle of the 19th Century, it was a large, shuttered house lying in the shadow of the village church, with a well-kept garden and a flowery terrace shaded by lime trees. An elderly white-haired woman, sitting in a white wicker chair with a black Labrador lying on a mat beside her, was waiting for them. When the car stopped, the Labrador jumped up and bounded towards them, enthusiastically wagging his tail and running circles around Baptiste, happy to see him. The woman stood up, and with the aid of an elegant walking stick, took a few steps across the terrace. Baptiste put Simone's suitcase on the steps leading to the terrace, doffed his cap and wished her good day, saying they would meet up again soon. He told Simone he would be in touch and drove away, with the Labrador running after the car until it turned out of the driveway.

'You must be Martine,' the woman said, extending her hand. 'I am Madame Legrand but please call me Marie. I trust you had a pleasant journey.' She picked up a small silver bell sitting on the table next to her chair and rang it. A woman wearing a black maid's outfit, with a starched white apron and small white cap, appeared. Mme Legrand asked her to take Simone's suitcase and put it in her room.

'Now my dear, come and sit down and we'll have a drink and a chat. Afterwards, Lucie will show you to your room.'

The Labrador, who was introduced as Ulysse, sniffed Simone with great curiosity. When he was satisfied she meant no harm, he flopped back down on his mat and continued to watch her with his expressive, intelligent eyes. Lucie soon reappeared carrying a tray of sandwiches, real coffee, and a glass of Champagne. She set it down on the table next to vase of pink tulips. She also refilled Ulysse's water bowl, which he slurped thirstily.

Mme Legrand picked up her glass of Champagne and wished Simone a happy stay. Simone, still awestruck at finding herself drinking Champagne so early in the day in such beautiful surroundings, had to pinch herself that all this was real. It had been a couple of years since she'd sipped Champagne, and combined with the beauty of her surroundings, she didn't feel at all as if she was on an assignment. After Paris, this was like a dream. It wasn't long before Mme Legrand brought her back down to earth again.

'Firstly, I want you to know that you are among friends here,' she began. 'Lucie is one of us so you don't have to worry. She lives with her mother in the village. My son, Claude, whom you will meet soon, lives in Épernay, where he oversees our Champagne house. He is a friend of both Jacques and Pascal.' She paused for a moment to offer Simone another sandwich. 'My house is a safe house. Quite a few people have passed through here since the Germans arrived, including influential associates of the French and Polish government in exile. I do my best to help people, but not everyone is lucky to leave France alive. I gather from Jacques and Pascal that you have been an excellent and trustworthy courier for quite a while now. You will know what I mean when I say not everyone makes it to freedom.'

Simone put down her sandwich. 'I can honestly say that when I helped people escape out of Paris, I rarely got to hear what happened to them. There were others who were given far more dangerous assignments. Jacques doesn't say much and I don't pry.'

Mme Legrand eyed her carefully and smiled. 'Don't underestimate yourself. From what I've been told, you're very smart.'

Simone blushed. These days she was wary of strangers, but she'd taken an instant liking to this extremely gentile, elderly lady who retained a great deal of aristocratic charm for her age. She still maintained a slender figure and would have been extremely beautiful in her youth. Simone noticed she wore make-up; just enough to look natural – a little blush on the cheeks and a hint of amber eye shadow highlighting her natural light olive, and still youthful, complexion. Her white hair was swept back in a loose chignon, reminding Simone of the Greek and Roman statues she'd seen in the Louvre, and she wore a simple pale green cotton dress with open-toed sandals. Most importantly, it was her smile that Simone warmed to. She displayed kindness and empathy.

'I gather you looked after Pascal when he was in Paris,' Mme Legrand continued. 'He speaks highly of you.'

'I just took care of him while he was recovering and then helped him get to Poitiers. As a nurse, I've taken care of a few injured people hiding from the Germans.'

'That could not have been easy. I know how difficult it is for the Resistance in Paris these days.'

'Did you know the woman who was working with Pascal before me – the woman who was caught and taken to Fresnes Prison?' Simone asked.

'Ah, poor Sylvie, I met her once with Pascal. She didn't stay here. She was living somewhere in Reims. I don't know what took place the night she was caught, but I do know that Pascal and the Resistance were most upset about it. It was because of her arrest that Pascal asked if I could put you up here. He thought you would be safer in this village. He also knew I needed a nurse as the other lady I employed moved away to be with her family in Bordeaux. The advertisement I put in the newspaper was merely a front in case we were questioned and your background as a nurse fitted the bill perfectly. This way, you can care for me *and* help Pascal and the Resistance at the same time.'

Simone asked about Mme Legrand's health and what her duties entailed.

'I had a heart attack around the time the Germans arrived and was hospitalized for a while. Unfortunately, it left me with a weak heart.

The doctor has prescribed medicine, but there is little that can be done, and if I exert myself I am likely to suffer another heart attack, which is why I now have the walking stick.' She gave a little half-smile, one of resignation rather than sadness. 'No-one has told me, but I know I only have a few years left. My son asked me to move in with him, but I value my independence. I grew up in this house. It's my home. Then there's the vineyard. I have a manager and together we keep an eye on it. That alone keeps me busy. I would be bored in Épernay.' She laughed. 'Your duties here will be light; just keep an eye on me and make sure I take my medicine, that's all. Apart from that, you are free to come and go. Along with overseeing the vineyard, my main preoccupation is to see that the Germans leave.'

'I have to admit that it was a surprise when I was asked to come here,' Simone said. 'I thought London might have sent one of their own to help Pascal.'

Mme Legrand shrugged. 'I am afraid he will have to answer that himself.'

The conversation drew to a close and Simone was shown to her room. 'I'll leave you to settle in and afterwards you can join me in the sitting room and we can talk further. I do hope you will be happy here. If there's anything you need, please let myself or Lucie know.'

Simone surveyed her room. Never in her wildest dreams had she expected to find herself living in such salubrious surroundings. She sat down on the soft double bed, covered with a blue toile de Jouy coverlet, and looked around. The bedroom was large, filled with tasteful antiques, and had a beautiful view towards the back of the house where the church nestled behind a cluster of trees and bushes. Whatever her assignment entailed, she was certainly happy to be here. She hung her few clothes in the armoire, placed her book on the bedside table, and saw that someone – probably Lucie – had thoughtfully left a few chocolates in a small cut-glass crystal dish for her– a luxury unheard of these days. She popped one in her mouth and closed her eyes, savouring the sublime sensation of a chocolate covered praline. Sheer bliss.

Mme Legrand was waiting for her in the sitting room. Sensing Simone's unease, the old lady patted the couch. 'Come and sit down. I'm glad I will be spending time with you. To be frank, a younger woman around the place will do me good.'

'You mentioned your son lived in Épernay,' Simone said. 'Do you see him often?'

'Not as often as I'd like but he calls me whenever he can. He's very busy. The German hierarchy has a thirst for fine Champagne, as you can imagine, and that necessitates him travelling all over France and occasionally to Germany. He knows you are here and has helped to arrange for an *Ausweis* with the relevant authorities so that you can drive the car and travel about quite freely under the pretext of needing to take me to Épernay and Reims for doctor's appointments or to get medicines. As we are known in the area, this is a genuine request. A forged *Ausweis* could get us into trouble.' Mme Legrand saw the look of astonishment on Simone's face. 'You do drive don't you?'

'Yes, but it's been a while now. Since petrol rationing, I've managed to get about by train or bicycle. I'm afraid Jacques never mentioned I would be driving a car.'

'When the Germans arrived, they requisitioned many cars, especially, the good ones. The family car – a beautiful Mercedes – was one of them. Fortunately, they left the old farm-truck and the Peugeot after Claude protested we needed them for the business. My manager, Monsieur Charpentier, is the only one who drives now, but he prefers the old truck or the horse and cart – they attract less attention. We have an *Ausweis* for the truck, but not for the car, which is harder to get these days. Now, let me show you around the rest of the house and grounds. You'd better familiarize yourself with the place if you're going to be living there.'

The house had two sitting rooms and two dining rooms, one of which was only used for formal occasions, and each room had a large fireplace. The smaller dining room was more intimate and used on a daily basis. Upstairs were four bedrooms, including Simone's, each with a bathroom, and wonderful views. The rooms were spacious with touches of grandeur such as chandeliers or exquisite drapes, and the walls were hung with artworks and family photographs, many featuring Champagne events. Despite its size, the house had an intimate charm and welcoming atmosphere.

Mme Legrand particularly wanted to show Simone the outbuildings where the Champagne was made. They went into the back garden and walked along a narrow path skirting the manicured lawn until they reached a hedgerow with a small wooden gate separating the garden from a group of sheds on the edge of the property. One of them housed a tractor, the truck, and the Peugeot. The largest shed was where the wine-making took place and contained large vats, presses, and barrels, along with all the other paraphernalia used by winemakers: baskets, cutting implements. A streak of sunlight from the open door captured tiny flecks of dust dancing in the midday sunshine, highlighting a long wooden table at the far side of the building, behind which hung faded family photographs of wine harvests. It reminded her of Leonardo da Vinci's Last Supper, but without the disciples. Simone was amazed at the scale of the operation.

'This is where the grapes are brought after harvesting,' Mme Legrand said. 'At this time of year it's quiet, but at the end of summer, when harvesting begins, it's a hive of activity. I can honestly say it's the happiest time of the year – or it was until the Germans arrived. Thankfully, not all my workers were sent to Germany when they brought in the new labour laws, but we've still had to cut back. The Germans have no respect for the countryside, driving their vehicles through the vineyards and destroying vines. As if that wasn't bad enough, they confiscated all the fertilizers. Some vignerons have stopped producing, while others, like me, try to keep on the right side of them, even if they are Nazis.' They walked towards the table. Mme Legrand ran her hand over its smooth surface. 'We've had some good times here. During the harvesting, I have a chef prepare food for the grape pickers. It's a tradition. All the vineyards do it. These days, we make a feast with whatever we can lay our hands on. Let's hope we will be free by the time the next harvest comes around.'

Simone realised the grape harvest was almost six months away and she had no idea if she would still be here then. Mme Legrand continued, 'Behind that wall are tunnels – the *caves*. The Germans know we keep the Champagne down there, as we do in Épernay, but what they don't know, is just how many tunnels there are. They are approached through that door.' She pointed to the far side of the wall where a row of baskets and grape-pickers' panniers and straw hats hung. The double wooden doors were in full view, near a wine press. She then waved her hand towards the opposite side. 'The other thing they don't know is that there is another tunnel over there.'

Simone looked and couldn't see anything, except for a devotional statue of the Virgin Mary cemented into a niche in the wall. Two enormous wine barrels topped with white candles stood either side. Mme Legrand laughed. 'We vignerons are a superstitious lot, but it's not because of that we keep a statue of Our Lady in here. This particular tunnel is approached from behind the statue and is used by the Resistance. We built it when we got wind that the Germans would attack. Come, I will show you.'

Mme Legrand slid her hand behind a decorative stone rosette at the side of the niche, and the statue, which at first appeared attached to the wall, swung aside revealing a narrow doorway. She pushed it open and told Simone to take a look. A gush of cold air momentarily took her breath away. As her eyes became accustomed to the darkness, she saw a set of stairs leading into the bowels of the earth. Mme Legrand smiled. 'I'm showing you this because, as a trusted member of the Resistance, it's highly likely you may need to use it – as many others have.' She closed the door and slid the statue back in place. 'Such a hiding place is essential. In fact there are quite a few such places all over the countryside. My family may have connections with the Germans because of the Champagne, but that doesn't stop them treating us with suspicion. Several owners of Champagne houses are already under suspicion.'

Simone spent the rest of the day alone on the terrace, studying maps again or reading a book. She had no idea when Pascal would turn up. In the evening, she took a stroll through the village, meandering through the *parcelles* of vines, making a note of which belonged to which family from the markers at the side of the road. By the time the sun set, painting the sky a deep magenta, she made her way back to the house, joined Mme Legrand for a drink, and after the evening meal, read her book in the sitting room, enjoying the peace and tranquillity of her surroundings while she could.

CHAPTER 5

TWO DAYS PASSED before Pascal arrived at the house and when he did, it was after midnight. Mme Legrand knocked on her door to inform her he was waiting for her in the kitchen. She quickly dressed and went to meet him. Mme Legrand left out plenty of food for them before returning to her room, leaving them to talk alone.

'Hello, Martine. It's good to see you again.' Simone noted that he now called her Martine and not Simone as he had known her in Paris. She also noticed he look tired and drawn. 'I apologise for not being here to greet you earlier, something urgent cropped up.'

She wanted to tell him she was getting used to waiting now. It not only irritated her, it frightened her too. Lateness often signified something was wrong.

'I confess you did have me worried, especially after what happened to the other woman – Sylvie,' she replied.

He cut a thick slice of bread, spread it with rabbit terrine, and devoured it hungrily. 'How have you been? You look as pretty as ever.'

'I'm fine, but let's not beat about the bush shall we? What are you doing back here and why on earth did you ask Jacques for me? This is hardly my territory.'

'It's not mine either,' Pascal replied sharply. 'I was sent here to liaise with the Resistance, and in particular the Maquis in the area, in readiness for D-Day. I need all the help I can get. I would rather have a seasoned Resistance woman than F Section send me someone half-trained, which is what they proposed. We are working closely with de Gaulle's Free French too, and I know you and Jacques helped some of them get to England where they have been training. Quite a few of them are back here, working in the field. I also want a woman because you know as well as I do, women are able to move around easier.'

'Are you going to tell me exactly what I am required to do?' Simone asked.

'Well let's just say you will not be resting here too much, so don't let Madame Legrand's beautiful surroundings lull you into a false sense of security.'

Simone was incensed at his curt reply. 'Don't take me for a fool, Pascal. At least tell me something or I will go back to Paris, even if it offends you all. This is my neck on the line as well as yours, you know.'

Pascal laughed. 'That's the spirited woman I remember during those days when I could barely walk. That's why I suggested you.' His laughter faded and his voice took on a serious tone. 'Over the next few days you will understand what it is we are tasked with doing. For the moment, I have more urgent things on my mind. Two days ago, we were supposed to receive a new radio operator and more ammunition for the Resistance, but the drop zone was compromised and the drop cancelled. I have been without my own operator for over a month now. The last one was sent elsewhere just before Sylvie was caught. Since then I've been sending messages via the Resistance in Troyes. I've located a new drop zone, but I need the co-ordinates relayed to London urgently. I can't do it myself because I have urgent work with the Maquis. The problem is, if we don't get this message through immediately, we'll have to wait until the next moon.'

'Troyes! That's over a hundred kilometres,' Simone blurted out.

Pascal continued eating his bread and terrine and, after a few minutes passed in which neither spoke, Simone understood what he was trying to say.

'You want me to go to Troyes. Is that it?'

Pascal nodded. 'That's right – and I want you to leave straight away.'

'Madame Legrand said her son was arranging to get me an *Ausweis*. Maybe I could take the car, it's quicker.'

'That's not possible – for two reasons. One of the conditions of you staying here is that Madame Legrand is seen to be friendly with the Germans. If you go against their rules, it will have consequences for the family and their Champagne house and their vineyard will be confiscated. Arranging a genuine *Ausweis* will take a few days as you need to go to the offices yourself for them to check your identity. By then it will be too late. The other problem is that the Germans have started implementing further restrictions and the *Ausweis* will only cover you for the area between Épernay and Reims. Troyes is too far. Madame Legrand has a bicycle on the premises. You can use that. I know you've ridden long distances for Jacques, so I'm sure you'll manage it.'

Simone knew it was no use arguing about the distance or whether she could go by bus or train. She had to do as Pascal asked and travelling by bicycle was the safest and easiest option.

'All right, what is it you want me to do?' she asked with a sigh.

Pascal pulled out a map and paper and pen from his pocket. He circled an area to the west of Reims on the map and wrote down the co-ordinates for her. 'This will be the new drop zone. Give these co-ordinates to a man called Gilles.' He wrote down another address – a farm on the Épernay/Troyes road a few kilometres south of Troyes near the village of Charmont-sous-Barbuise. 'You will see the signpost for the farm just as you near the village. Study this and destroy it.' He paused while she looked at the notes. 'Can you remember the co-ordinates too?' he asked. 'If you are sure you won't make a mistake, destroy these too.'

'Did you tell Madame Legrand all this?'

'Yes. Now, the thing is, do you think you can cycle to Troyes and back in a day?'

Simone's eyes, widened. 'You're asking a lot aren't you? Averaging fifteen kilometres an hour, it should take me just over six hours. Don't you think it's better if I stay overnight?'

'No!' Pascal's reply was sharp. 'I want you to wait for a reply from London and come straight back. It's imperative this drop takes place tomorrow evening and I want you with me. There's too much to do and an extra pair of hands will be helpful.'

'Fine. I'll do my best.'

'I am asking London to time the drop for the early hours of the next day – around 01:00 a.m. Baptiste will come and pick you up. I want you to meet some of the men.'

Simone looked at the clock on the dresser. It was 02:30 a.m. 'I will leave in an hour. It will give me a head start before curfew ends.' She watched him finish his meal. 'I'd better prepare something to eat on the way. I hope Madame Marie won't mind.'

'Thank you,' Pascal said. 'I know I'm asking a lot, but I wouldn't do it if there was any other way. I simply cannot risk missing the moon period. Are you sure you're fine with cycling at night?'

Simone cut a chunk of bread and a slice of the leftover rabbit terrine, and wrapped them in paper. 'I'll be fine. It's not the first time I've cycled long distances at night.'

'They'll give you a good meal when you reach the farm,' he replied.

'They'd better, or you'll be in trouble.' She laughed. 'It's a good job I had time to study those maps. My relaxation period didn't last long, did it? I thought it was too good to be true.'

Simone went to her room to prepare herself for the long journey ahead. She wore a flared skirt and knitted top. It was too warm for a jacket, but she took it anyway, making sure her gun was securely hidden in the lining. Pascal left the house with her and they parted ways at the gate. He headed north towards Reims and she headed south to Troyes. It was a cool evening and the waxing gibbous moon cast silvery ghost-like shadows over the undulating, vine-laden landscape. Simone rode for two hours before stopping to sit under a tree at the side of the road for a bite to eat, just before dawn.

Over the past few years, she'd made many journeys through the countryside in the middle of the night for Jacques, and although it was dangerous, she actually relished being alone. The silence of the night, broken only by the creaking sound of her bicycle, the occasional hoot of an owl, and her own breathing, was soothing to her. It gave her time to think. *What would life be like when the war ended? What happened to those she'd helped?* A flock of waterfowl flew from the reeds of a nearby stream, flapping their wings gracefully in the blue-tinged morning light. It was times like this she cherished the most. In such moments, there was no war.

Simone approached the village of Charmont-sous-Barbuise just before midday. There was hardly anyone about and she found the farmhouse without any difficulties. It was set back from the road by the edge of a wood. An elderly woman wearing a brown scarf was herding cattle through a gate and stopped to ask what she wanted. Simone gave the password, asked for Gilles, and the woman indicated for her to go to one of the sheds. A thin man in his late forties appeared at the door and introduced himself as Gilles.

'I have an urgent message from Pascal. He needs you to send these new co-ordinates to London immediately.'

He invited her inside. Three more members of the Resistance were there too, including the farmer himself and his daughter, Sonia, who offered to get Simone something to eat while Gilles immediately started to prepare the radio for a transmission. Simone sat opposite him watching as he carefully coded the message to London. When he'd finished, he took off his ear-phones and told her they would have to wait for a reply.

Sonia returned carrying a steaming hot bowl of chicken soup. 'You must be starving,' she said watching Simone devour the food. 'Pascal is crazy, sending you all this way and then expecting you to return straight away.'

'I'm used to travelling long distances,' Simone replied, tipping the bowl up and scooping out the last drop of soup.

Sonia picked up the bowl and left the shed. Several minutes later she reappeared with more food – sausage, cheese, two eggs, and bread. 'Eat whatever you want. The rest you can take back with you.'

After the meal, she asked one of the men to prepare a place for Simone to lie down while they waited for a response from London. Simone protested but the man ignored her. He removed a rolled up mattress from the hayloft above the rafters, and laid it out on the stone floor.

'Get some sleep while Gilles waits for them to get back to us,' Sonia said. 'It will do you good.'

Having cycled on adrenaline, Simone felt wide awake, but she knew Sonia was right. If she didn't grab a little sleep now, it could slow her down later. Sonia handed her a blanket and sat down next to her. 'Let me massage your legs. It will help.'

Simone closed her eyes while the young woman deftly pummelled and massaged her legs from the thighs and calves to the soles of her feet. She was obviously used to doing this. Within a few minutes, she drifted into a deep sleep.

Two hours later, Sonia gently shook Simone's shoulder. 'Wake up. We've received a reply.'

Simone rubbed her eyes, slipped her shoes back on, and sat back at the table where Gilles was packing up his equipment. 'London says it's on for tonight. Pascal is a lucky man. A day later and it might have been a different matter.'

'Thank God.' She was relieved. 'Now, if you will excuse me, I'd better get going or I won't be back in time.'

Gilles smiled. 'Not so fast, Mademoiselle. We've arranged for you to go part of the way by van. That way, we can be sure you won't wear your pretty legs out.' He glanced approvingly at Simone's shapely legs, the result of cycling over the past three years. She blushed.

'I'm fine, really I am.'

'Not another word.' He shook her hand and wished her *bonne chance*.

The other men escorted her outside, where she found a waiting bread van. A rotund man wearing a beret and smoking a cigarette was opening the back doors. 'Put the bicycle in here,' he said to them. 'And cover it up with those empty flour sacks.'

He told Simone to get in the passenger seat. Sonia handed Simone the wrapped package with the rest of the food for the return journey and wished her a safe journey. 'Say hello to Pascal for me and tell him to take care.'

Minutes later the van was back on the main road heading north.

'Where are we going?' Simone asked the van driver, as they drove away.

'I'm taking you half-way there. It's as far as my *Ausweis* will allow, but it will save your legs. That way you will get back well before curfew.'

Not long after the van driver and Simone parted ways, her bicycle chain came off. She was in the middle of the countryside with no house in sight. '*Merde*,' she said to herself as she dragged it onto the grass embankment and set about trying to fix it.

At that point, a German patrol passed by, and seeing that she had her hands covered in oil, they stopped. Two men got out of the vehicle and approached her. In German, they asked if they could help. She had no other option but to appeal to their kindness and hope they didn't decide to search her and discover her gun or knife. One of them gave her his handkerchief to wipe her hands and offered her a cigarette while the other fixed the chain. They spoke only a few words of French and she smiled innocently at them, appealing to their German ideas of women being the weaker sex who needed protection. Not letting on that she spoke German, she understood every word the two said to each other. One wished she was his girlfriend, and the other made remarks about French women being out alone putting their lives in danger.

'*Jetzt ist alles gut, Fräulein*,' the soldier said. 'You should be fine now.'

'*Merci, vous êtes des messieurs*,' she said with a smile as she waved them goodbye. 'You are gentlemen.' She was relieved to see them go.

CHAPTER 6

'MARTINE, WAKE UP.' Mme Legrand's soft voice woke Simone from a deep sleep and for a moment she wondered where she was. When she realised she'd fallen asleep, fully clothed on the bed, she apologised.

'What time is it?' she asked, drowsily.

'Almost midnight. Baptiste's waiting for you. You have fifteen minutes to get ready.' She walked out of the room leaving Simone still trying to pull herself together.

'*Mon Dieu*,' she mumbled to herself as she headed to the bathroom to tidy herself up. 'I can't believe this is happening. All this time as a courier and now I am shoved into the thick of it – a parachute drop of all things.'

She leaned over the sink and peered closely at herself in the mirror. She looked awful! With a heavy sigh, she filled the basin with cold water, reached for the lavender oil that Mme Legrand had so kindly left out for her, and splashed a few precious drops into it. She pulled her hair back, soaked a facecloth in the scented water and bathed her face for a few minutes. It had the immediate effect of reviving her. After running a brush through her thick hair, she changed into a pair of dark trousers, put on a pair of sturdy shoes, and went to join Baptiste in the kitchen. He was sitting in the same spot as Pascal the night before with Ulysse at his feet. The aroma of real coffee filled the air, mingling with the scent of lavender oil.

'Everything all set to go?' Baptiste asked, scratching Ulysse's head. Simone nodded. 'Good, then let's get going.'

'Wait a minute,' Mme Legrand said. 'Let the girl have a bite to eat and something to drink first. She's had a hard day; another five minutes won't hurt.' She poured Simone a large cup of coffee and cut her a slice of honey cake. 'There's hot milk if you want it,' she added.

'Wonderful, just what I need.'

Simone savoured every drop and Mme Legrand poured them all another cup. 'Knowing a few Germans does have its perks,' she said. 'Real coffee being one of them – real coffee in exchange for Champagne.'

'I hope I didn't wake you when I returned,' Simone asked. 'It was eight-thirty and as I didn't see you, I presumed you'd gone to bed early.'

'I was in my room, but I kept an ear open for you returning. Ulysse heard you first. He gave a low growl but when he realised it was you, he quietened down. He's an excellent watchdog. I heard you go straight to your room and didn't want to bother you. I hope everything went smoothly. No hassles on the way?'

'A couple of checkpoints and a problem with my bicycle chain, but nothing I couldn't handle. At least I got a few hours' sleep.'

Baptiste looked at Mme Legrand and grinned. 'You see, Madame Marie, that's why Pascal wanted her. She's made of stern stuff.'

Mme Legrand looked Baptiste up and down and scoffed. 'Maybe you should take a leaf out her book and cycle that far a bit more often. You might lose some weight!'

'Ah, dear Madame, remember, I have diabetes.' He grinned and told her how good the cake was. 'Besides, I am not as good-looking and would not be able to charm my way out of difficulties as easily as Mademoiselle Martine.' He wiped his hands on a lace-edged napkin and declared it was time to leave. 'Come on, no cycling this time, I've got the car.'

'Take care, Chérie,' Mme Legrand said to Simone. 'Don't let your guard down for a second.'

It took less than thirty minutes to reach the drop zone. Baptiste drove off the main road and along a dirt road into a wooded area where the car couldn't be spotted by passing German trucks. They walked the rest of the way on foot, clambering through the trees and bushes until they came to a fence bordering a field. Someone from the Maquis armed with a Sten gun was keeping guard and waved them on. Minutes later they were met by Pascal and a group of maquisards.

47

'Did London give you a time?' Pascal asked anxiously.

'Around 01:00 a.m. Gilles said you were lucky. Another day and it would have been too late.'

Pascal gave a sigh of relief. 'There,' he said to the men. 'I told you she was reliable.'

The men crowded around her, each one personally wanting to welcome her into their group. She had been ready to give Pascal a piece of her mind for not asking how she was after her marathon journey, but the men's welcome made up for it. It was probably for the best as there was too much to do to be self-indulgent. Happy that they hadn't gathered for nothing, the men retreated to their hiding places in the woods around the field. Pascal sat under a tree and patted the earth, indicating for Simone to join him.

'We may as well make ourselves comfortable while we wait,' he said. 'By the way, I want to thank you for undertaking that task yesterday. I know it was hard, and I don't want you to think I didn't factor in the risk. It's been a difficult few months and I'll be asking a lot more of you. That's why I wanted someone tough.'

Simone thought about the traitor in Paris. 'Were you aware that until just before coming here, I'd never actually fired a gun except for shooting practice?' she asked.

'No, although I knew you were a crack shot. Jacques told me.'

'I've known him for a while now, yet in reality, I know nothing about him except that he's a good Resistance leader. He puts on a tough face and expects everyone else to do the same. A few days before I came here, he actually put me to the test and told me to execute a man they had interrogated; a *mouchard*. The test was for this job – to test my mettle.' The memory still haunted Simone.

'And did you kill that person?'

'Of course! I was under orders. If I'd said no, Jacques wouldn't have sent me here, and I'd probably have been seen as a liability to the organisation. I couldn't risk that.'

'How did you feel – about the killing I mean?'

'How do you think? I've tried to block it out.'

Pascal threw her a concerned glance. 'Don't do that, Martine – at least not until this war is over. You need to remember that the Germans have also been instructed to kill. I imagine many of them don't want to kill either. That's war and you can't afford to be sensitive or sentimental.' He paused for a moment. 'Tell me something, when you knew that person was a traitor, what would you have done if you'd come face to face with him under different circumstances, for instance, if you'd caught him in the act of telling the Germans about the people in one of our safe houses?'

'I would have shot him,' she replied without hesitation.

'There we have it. Given that it's your life or the traitor's, the answer is easy.'

Simone leaned back, her head resting on the gnarled tree trunk. 'By the way, a young woman at the farm asked me to give you a message. Her exact words were, "Say hello to Pascal for me and tell him to take care."'

'Ah, Sonia - she's a good woman.'

'A good woman who has a soft spot for you.' Simone couldn't resist. 'Have you been breaking hearts? I recall that when I took care of you in Paris, you told me you were married.' Pascal chuckled to himself but didn't reply and she changed the subject. 'What exactly happened to Sylvie? Did someone give her away to the Germans?'

'We never found out. A few weeks earlier, she told us she thought she was being watched and we moved her to a new safe house. Enquiries with her new landlord led us to believe it might have been a random search as all the houses in the street that night were searched and others taken into custody at the same time, all of whom had nothing to do with us. Her arrest still haunts me, even more so when I know what she must have endured, yet she never revealed anything about our network.'

'How can you be sure?'

'Because they would have caught us by now. We all went into hiding for a while. Then we heard she'd been sent to Germany. She was very brave.'

'*Was?* Do you think she's dead?'

Pascal looked at her with sad eyes. 'Your guess is as good as mine. I can't afford to get sentimental about it. All I know is that her papers were in order and she was a good courier – fluent in French and careful in everything she did. Believe me, I've gone over and over that night in my mind, but cannot think why she was the only one to be sent to Fresnes prison when the others were allowed to go free the next morning.'

'If you went into hiding, does that mean you didn't search her apartment after she was taken?'

'The landlord packed up her belongings and gave them to us when the heat died down.'

Simone looked at him incredulously.

Pascal saw the look in her eyes. 'Why are you looking at me like that? What are you thinking? Spit it out.'

'Surely there had to have been something. Maybe you missed it by not looking yourself.'

'So I'm a fool am I?' he replied sarcastically. 'The landlord said he thought all seemed to be in order when he packed up her belongings. There's no time for us to make thorough searches every time someone is taken into custody. We could have been watched.'

'Now who's being sensitive?'

Pascal rolled his eyes. 'Jacques didn't say you were an amateur sleuth as well as a good shot.'

Simone looked at her watch and changed the subject. 'What are you expecting tonight?'

'A new wireless operator for a start; ammunition, money, and a few tins of food for Maquis. They're demoralized at the moment as they expected the Allies to have landed by now. I understand their frustrations, but there's little I can do except give them something to tide them over while they wait.'

At that moment the low drone of an approaching aircraft could be heard in the distance.

'*Dieu merci!*' Pascal said, jumping up and grabbing his gun. 'Come on, let's get ready.'

They headed towards the perimeter of the field where he flashed a light to the others. Several men appeared out of the woods, scurrying into position in the field ready to flash the landing signal. The humming sound grew louder and seconds later a low flying aircraft resembling a huge dark shadow of a bird of prey, flew overhead, dropping its precious cargo into the field – twelve containers and Pascal's radio operator. The Maquis ran to collect the containers, but the radio operator veered off course towards the northern edge of the woods.

'*Putain!*' Pascal cried out. He made a dash to the area where the man would land. Simone and Baptiste followed him.

Their eyes quickly scanned the brooding dark shadows until they spotted him hanging from a tree, moaning in agony. 'I can't move,' the man called out. 'I've broken my leg.'

'That's all we need,' Pascal said, despondently. After checking the injured man was indeed the person they were waiting for, he and Baptiste took out their knives and cut him down. He let out a howl of pain forcing Baptiste to clamp his hand over the man's mouth.

Simone checked the leg. 'It's bad. His right femur bone is broken and we're likely to injure him more if we're not careful.'

Pascal and Baptiste attempted to pull the man up but he yelled in pain. Without a second thought, Pascal brought his arm back and struck the man on the chin so hard, he passed out. 'Welcome to France, Jean-Yves.'

Simone was aghast. 'Was that really necessary?'

'There was no other option.' Pascal replied. 'Now we can move him. Let's bury this parachute and get out of here, before the Germans come snooping around.'

After checking the rest of their comrades had safely left the landing zone with the canisters, the three of them dragged the unconscious Jean-Yves through the bushes until they reached Baptiste's car. They hastily bundled him into the back seat and drove away, this time taking a different dirt road. The car careered and bumped its way over the rutted dirt track until it eventually came out in a country lane. Simone sat in the back with the man to make sure he didn't injure himself even more by falling off the seat.

They had almost left the wooded area when a convoy of German armoured vehicles passed by.

Pascal swore loudly. 'That was a near miss. A few seconds later and we would have run into them. I wonder if they spotted the plane.' After a quick discussion they decided to head in the opposite direction.

'Where are we going?' Simone asked.

'There's a farm a few kilometres away. It's a safe house. Let's hope there are no more Germans or we're done for.'

The car pulled up at a farm gate and Pascal jumped out to open it. No sooner had the car passed through the gate when they heard the rumble of army vehicles in the distance and saw lights approaching the brow of a hill – another German convoy. Pascal motioned to Baptiste to back the car behind a thick hedge. They held their breath hoping they wouldn't be spotted and the convoy passed without incident.

'Another near miss; it must be our lucky night,' Pascal said.

Simone sat next to the unconscious man, her heart pounding and her clammy hands stroking his forehead. When they pulled up in the farmyard they were met by the farmer and his wife and daughter.

'What's going on?' the farmer asked.

'The Germans are in the area, Benoît,' Pascal said. 'I'm not sure if they got wind of the drop zone. Fortunately they passed after the drop had taken place or we would have been surrounded.' He showed him the man in the back of the car. 'He veered off course and is badly injured.'

Benoît helped carry Jean-Yves inside the building. Simone could see it wasn't the first time they'd hidden someone, as Benoît's wife and daughter swung into action immediately. They ran into the kitchen, pushed the wooden table away from the centre of the room, and rolled back a strip of rush matting to reveal a trapdoor leading to a cellar below the house.

'Take him down there until we decide what to do with him,' Benoît said. 'Lay him on the bed.'

Benoît's daughter asked if they knew how badly damaged he was.

'He's broken his femur,' Simone answered. Blood was steadily seeping through his trousers. When they cut away the fabric, the full extent of the injury could be seen. The bone was poking through his thigh. 'He needs a doctor straight away. Perhaps I should stay with him.'

Pascal wouldn't hear of it. The daughter told her not to worry; they would take care of Jean-Yves themselves. 'We're used to this sort of thing,' she said, fetching a bowl of water and a cloth to clean him up.

'All the same, I'm a nurse so maybe…'

Pascal cut her short. 'No, Martine, I want you back at the Legrand house straight away. The Germans may start searching the area and you need to be there – as if nothing happened. I'll go back with you.'

There was no time to argue. After Benoît assured them they would get Jean-Yves seen by a doctor in the morning, they said goodbye and headed across the fields until they reached the outskirts of Verzenay. It was about three in the morning. The village was quiet; not a soul stirred.

'Thank God we're home,' Simone whispered. 'Any further and I wouldn't have made it.' Her calf muscles ached so much she thought her legs would give way at any moment.

They approached the Legrand house by the back terrace and Pascal waited until she retrieved a spare key from underneath a potted geranium and unlocked the door. Ulysse had heard them and ran outside, sniffing and wagging his tail in recognition.

'Good boy, Ulysse,' Pascal said, stroking him affectionately. 'It's only us.' He bade her goodnight and turned to leave.

'Where are you going?' Simone asked. 'Aren't you staying here?'

Pascal shook his head. 'No. It's best that I find somewhere else.'

'But where will you go at this hour?'

'Don't worry about me. I'll be fine. Get some sleep. You deserve it – and stay put until I contact you again.'

'What do I tell Madame Legrand?'

'The truth. Better to keep her informed as she can cover for you.' He started down the path towards the outhouses where the wine presses were kept. 'Oh, I meant to say,' he said, glancing back at her. 'Thank you for everything.'

Simone watched him disappear beyond the bushes before she entered the house. He reminded her of Jacques – toughness and bravado masking what was probably a softness he was afraid to admit to. She had come to realise she wouldn't be treated with kid gloves in this job; all the same, his comment heartened her and made her feel appreciated.

CHAPTER 7

SIMONE WAS TAKING a hot bath, soaking her aching legs and thinking about the previous evening's harrowing events at the drop zone, when she heard Ulysse barking loudly on the terrace. A few minutes later there was a soft knock on the bathroom door.

'Mademoiselle Dumont, Madame Marie has asked that you come to the dining room as soon as possible.'

'Is everything all right?' Simone asked, reaching for the towel.

The door opened a little. 'Two Germans are here,' Lucie replied in a low voice.

A myriad of questions raced through Simone's mind. *Did they catch someone last night? Had someone given them away?* She quickly dressed, ran a comb through her towel-dried hair and nervously smoothed away a non-existent crease in her dress. Taking a deep breath, she headed to the dining room where Mme Legrand was sitting at the table chatting with the Germans who had their backs to her.

'Ah there you are, *Chérie*. Do come and join us for breakfast.'

The two men stood up to greet her. When they turned around, Simone fought a rising panic. One of them was the man who had helped her with her suitcase on the train – Bruno Albrecht. He looked as surprised to see her as she him.

'Mademoiselle Dumont, what a pleasure to meet you again.' He bowed graciously and smiled. 'Madame Legrand was just telling me she'd hired a new nurse, but I must say, I wasn't expecting it to be you.'

'Herr Albrecht, good morning,' Simone replied. 'This certainly is a surprise.'

Albrecht introduced his colleague, Herr Mueller, a man in his mid-thirties, who, unlike Albrecht with his impressive field grey

Wehrmacht uniform, was dressed in a dark suit and tie. She glanced at Mme Legrand as she sat down, telling her that Albrecht had helped her with her suitcase on the train.

'That was most kind of you,' Mme Legrand replied. In a calm voice, she informed Simone that the men were here on official business. 'Apparently there was an incident last night and they are looking for traitors against the Reich. I've already told them they certainly wouldn't find them here.'

Simone's heart missed a beat at the mention of the word *traitors*. The word also unnerved Lucie who almost dropped the jug of fresh orange juice she was carrying. Clearly anxious, she fussed about, making sure everyone's plate was replenished which gave Simone a few moments to collect her thoughts. Mme Legrand sensed Lucie's distress and dismissed her from the room. 'Thank you, my dear; that will be all.' When they were alone, she returned to the reason for the men's visit.

'A British plane parachuted containers not far from here last night. It was spotted by a convoy of Germans who happened to be in the vicinity at the time. They drove to the drop zone but were too late to catch those involved.' Simone felt a huge surge of relief on hearing that the men got away, but with all eyes on her, she was careful not to show it.

Mme Legrand continued, 'That's why Herr Albrecht and Herr Mueller are here. Their men are combing the countryside and searching all the villages in the vicinity. That's correct isn't it, Herr Albrecht?'

Bruno Albrecht's pleasant smile faded. 'That's right. Our men our searching every house in Verzenay as we speak. We will leave no stone unturned until we find those involved. As I am already acquainted with this family, I thought it only right that I call here myself.' He paused. 'Sometimes our men can be – well, how can I put it – rather heavy-handed.'

Simone feigned surprise at this news as she helped herself to a slice of bread and plum conserve, and asked how she could be of help. She also wondered how Mme Legrand and Albrecht knew each other, but that was a question that would have to wait.

Mme Legrand put a gentle hand on her arm. 'They would like to ask a few questions, that's all. It's just a formality.'

This time Herr Mueller spoke. 'Mademoiselle, we must account for every person's whereabouts last night.' It was clear he was getting impatient with small talk and came straight to the point. 'Madame Legrand and her maid have already been kind enough to answer our questions, now we would like to know your whereabouts.' He flipped open a small notebook, his pen poised over the page. 'Madame Legrand told us she went to bed at nine o'clock. She said you were still up at this time. What time did you go to bed?'

For the first time, Simone noticed just how cold his pale grey-blue eyes were. 'I stayed up late, reading.'

It seemed inconsequential yet he still wrote it down. 'What time would that be?'

'Maybe around ten-thirty – eleven, I'm not quite sure.'

'I see. Anything else?'

She had the distinct feeling he was trying to catch her out. Why, she wasn't exactly sure. 'After that, I made myself a nightcap of warm milk and honey.'

'And you didn't go outside at all – maybe for a walk in the garden; maybe to drink the milk on the terrace? After all, it was a warm night.'

'I could hardly go out when there's a curfew could I? And no, I didn't drink the milk on the terrace. I drank it in bed.'

He ignored the tinge of sarcasm in her voice. 'Did you hear the sound of an aircraft flying overhead?'

'I've heard the sound of planes flying over many times, Monsieur, but last night I heard nothing. I would certainly have remembered something like that. What time did you say the plane was supposed to have flown over?'

'I didn't, but as you ask, it was sometime during the early hours of the morning.'

Simone noticed he deliberately refrained from being specific. She gave a faint smile. 'I can assure you, I was fast asleep by then.'

'You said you were reading, Mademoiselle, may I ask which book?'

Clearly the man was not going to let up. 'Madame Bovary.'

'Ahhh, Flaubert.' He even noted down the name of the book.

At this point, Albrecht was becoming embarrassed with his colleague and took over. 'I think that we have established you were both safely at home when this incident occurred and we need not bother you any longer.' He turned to Mme Legrand, apologised for their intrusion and thanked her for her hospitality.

She offered to see them out. Albrecht bowed graciously towards Simone saying he hoped he would see her again under more favourable circumstances. She wished him good luck in his endeavours. Mueller on the other hand, did not thank them, and instead asked them if they would report anything that could be deemed suspicious. The women assured them they would. When they'd gone, Simone slumped back in her seat and wiped the sweat from her brow. Outside on the terrace she could hear them talking, but it was too low to discern what they were saying. Minutes later, she heard the sound of a car engine and the men departed. She had a sense of foreboding in the pit of her stomach. These men would stop at nothing to get results.

Mme Legrand returned to the kitchen. 'I think you need a glass of Champagne to steady your nerves,' she said. 'You look quite pale.' She poured them both a glass and at the same time, asked Lucie to clear the table. 'By the way, it's a good job the men were not facing you when you entered the room. You've got quite a few scratches on your legs. I think you'd better tell me what happened last night, don't you?'

After listening to what took place and the problem with the injured man, she though they'd had a lucky near miss and agreed with Pascal and Baptiste's assessment of the situation, that the convoy just happened to be out at that time rather than a situation of someone betraying them.

'It couldn't have been the latter as the drop was only arranged that day.' Simone finished her Champagne. She couldn't help wondering how many others in the Resistance drank Champagne for breakfast. 'I'm worried about the injured man though. He's in a very bad way.'

'There's not much you can do; you can hardly go back to the farm.

Besides, Benoît will have contacted a doctor by now.' She changed the subject. 'I must say, it was quite a surprise to find out you'd already met Bruno Albrecht. Quite a charmer isn't he?'

'I'm not sure I noticed. I was too busy trying to keep my wits about me.'

'A good thing too. I've heard he uses his charms to his advantage – if you know what I mean?'

'Are you saying he sleeps with French women to get information?' At first, Simone thought her reply may have sounded quite crude for a gentile lady such as Mme Legrand and was relieved when she laughed.

'He's quite the Casanova, but underneath that charm he is still loyal to Herr Hitler, so be careful.'

'I noticed he wore a wedding ring,' Simone said.

Mme Legrand laughed again. 'Since when has that stopped some men? I believe his wife is in Berlin.'

'How do you know him?' Simone asked.

'Through the Champagne house and the wine führers. He was posted here about a year ago. Claude told me is with the Abwehr. He moves around, but mostly works in Reims or Épernay. We try to keep in his good books.' She gave a shrug. 'What else can we do?'

Lucie entered the room and asked if she might be allowed to leave earlier as she needed to get back home. She was highly agitated and said her mother would be frightened by the German presence.

'She's quite a nervous girl, isn't she?' Simone said after she'd left. 'She was decidedly jumpy in front of the men.'

'She became worse when her father left to join the Maquis immediately after they brought in the Compulsory Work Service last year. It's believed he went east towards the Jura, but no one has heard from him since. I know that she also had a boyfriend from a nearby village who left the area around the same time. It's said that he went to join a Maquis group in the Morvan. She never speaks of him so I'm not sure what happened to him. Most of our men have left. It's one reason the Germans, especially the Gestapo, have stepped up their surveillance of us. In the past year, they've recruited more collaborators so we have to be ever more vigilant – even amongst friends.'

Their conversation was interrupted by a telephone call from Claude Legrand saying he was back in Épernay. *He* wanted Simone to catch the bus the following day and meet him in town to get her *Ausweis*. She was relieved. Now she could get around a little more.

CHAPTER 8

THERE WERE STILL German soldiers and Feldgendarmerie in the village when Simone caught the bus to Épernay. They were joined by the hated Milice who were easily recognisable in their blue uniform jacket and trousers, brown shirt and a wide blue beret. The miliciens were doing their best to assert their authority, despite occasionally being hurled abuse by one or two villagers. For the villagers' outspokenness, they received a curt warning. Simone witnessed one man – the local baker – being beaten with a baton for calling a milicien a *mouchard*. The hapless man was knocked to the ground and kicked repeatedly until his terrified wife rushed out of the bakery and fell on his body in an effort to try and save him.

'Next time you won't be so lucky,' the milicien bellowed to the bruised and bloodied man. He turned to the horrified villagers and pointed his baton at them. 'That goes for all of you.'

Simone tried to make herself as inconspicuous as possible while waiting in the bus shelter, but that was impossible; everyone boarding the bus was required to show their papers and explain the reason for their journey.

She arrived in Épernay an hour late and was relieved to find Claude Legrand still waiting for her. She told him the Germans were conducting searches and left it at that. He didn't ask why. She found him to be a charming man in his early forties. Like his mother, he had the bearing of an aristocrat – gentile, well-dressed, and, as Simone learnt later, he spoke several languages fluently. Even the German High Command appeared to have respect for him. Threading their way on foot along the prestigious Avenue de Champagne to the German HQ in the centre of town, Simone occasionally stopped to

61

admire some of the most magnificent buildings in Épernay. With their beautiful wrought iron gates, these 19th Century mansions, built in the Neo-classical style inspired by the First Empire, were the homes of some of the world's finest Champagne houses and they quite took her breath away. Claude pointed several out and gave her a short history of the families who owned them. Quite a few had been rebuilt after the devastation which took place during the Great War. Others had operated as temporary hospitals.

This pleasant sight-seeing was fleeting and Simone was quickly brought back down to earth again when they entered the headquarters of the German High Command. Because of Claude Legrand's standing in the community, they were ushered through to the interview room straight away where she was asked a few questions as to why she needed the *Ausweis*. Claude did most of the talking, explaining that his mother was not fit to travel alone since her heart attack, and as her nurse and companion, Mademoiselle Dumont, would be able to take her to doctors' appointments and collect medicines or anything else his mother needed. Getting an *Ausweis* for the car might have seemed a simple task, but at a time when the Germans needed more vehicles, it was anything but simple. Only someone of importance in the community could get away with that. Claude Legrand of the fine Champagne House of Legrand was one of them.

The man in charge entered the details in a ledger and asked to see Simone's papers. She held her breath while he scrutinized them carefully. He noted her Parisian address and there was a tense moment when he said he knew the area because of a previous posting in Paris. She hoped that wouldn't mean he would make further enquiries and was pleased she'd familiarised herself with the place beforehand. He told her they needed another photograph and as she didn't have one, sent her to another room to have her photograph taken. While this was taking place, Claude stayed to chat with the officer and asked why they needed the photograph when previously an *Ausweis* for a vehicle never displayed the driver's photograph.

'Monsieur Claude, I am only doing my job. Since the Resistance has been using stolen vehicles, we need to be sure of the drivers. All new permits now require an authorized photograph.'

There was nothing Claude could say, but he didn't like the fact that they now had "Martine's" photo on file.

Simone's new photograph was checked against the one on her Identity Card, placed into a file, and an *Ausweis* handed over. They were advised to get the car converted as it would be highly unlikely they would receive petrol now, as it was reserved for essential needs, and the officer didn't see driving an elderly woman to and from the doctors or picking up her medicine as essential. In fact he said the car should have been requisitioned long ago.

'Drive carefully, Mademoiselle Dumont. The roads are dangerous these days – even in the countryside.'

Outside the building, Simone let out a big sigh of relief. 'Thank you, Claude. I don't think I would have got this if it hadn't been for you.'

Claude agreed, but said he didn't like her photo being on file, especially when her Identity Card was a forgery.

'You don't have to worry,' she replied. 'I'll be careful. The last thing I want to do is get you or your mother into trouble.'

'Ahhh, my dear Martine, no one knows what we will encounter these days.'

Claude offered to drive her back to Verzenay as it would give them time to get to know each other a little better. He told her his mother had suffered the heart attack when she saw the way the way the Germans were destroying the area, commandeering the fine houses of the Champagne families and rounding up men who had been soldiers in the French army, many of them agricultural workers. It brought back memories of the Great War when the area was decimated. That period still remained etched in the memories of all who lived and fought in the area.

'We were lucky to retain our homes,' he said. 'But as you can imagine, because of this, some have accused us of collaboration and there is always someone ready to sing. You must tread carefully, although from what I've heard, you have already mastered that art. To survive for so long in the Resistance in Paris is no mean feat.'

Nearing Verzenay, they noticed two trucks filled with German soldiers speeding towards them from the same direction. They quickly passed them and were soon out of sight.

'They were certainly in a hurry,' Simone said, looking worried. 'I wonder where they're going.'

Claude frowned. 'I don't know, but something's not right.'

Ten minutes later, their fears were confirmed. The entrance to the village was barricaded and the Feldgendarmerie, aided by the Milice, were ordering the inhabitants into the village square. Claude and Simone were told to leave the car where it was and join the rest of the villagers.

'What's going on?' Claude asked in perfect German.

'You'll find out soon enough,' one of the Feldgendarmerie said.

Claude protested that he must see his mother immediately, but it was no use. The man pointed his gun at them both and indicated that it was in their best interests not to make trouble. At that moment, he saw his mother, escorted by the vineyard manager, Olivier Charpentier, heading towards the square from the opposite direction. They hurried over to them.

'Maman!' Claude gave his mother a kiss on both cheeks and tenderly took her arm as they made their way to join the rest of the villagers. 'What's going on?'

'We have no idea,' she answered. 'We were simply ordered to get to the square straight away.'

The four joined the rest of the villagers, but no-one was able to enlighten them as to the reason they were there. The air around them soon became a stifling, concentrated mixture of fear, curiosity, and excitement, with soldiers standing on guard and barking dogs straining on their leashes. A terrible waiting game began. With each passing minute, Simone feared the worst. Her head felt light, and a dull, throbbing pain in her chest made it hard to breathe. She was sure someone who had been at the drop zone had been caught. She even considered trying to escape but knew she'd never get far, and the repercussions for Mme Legrand and Claude were too dire to contemplate. How long were they going to torture everyone like this? Waiting was even worse than knowing – whatever it was. As a respected member of the community, a shopkeeper brought out a chair for Mme Legrand to sit on, but she stoically refused, insisting she would endure the situation like everyone else.

An hour later, they heard the rumble of two army trucks approaching the square, followed by a sleek black Mercedes, flying the swastika on its bonnet. The villagers peered over each others' shoulders to get a good look as soldiers jumped down from the back and drew back the tarpaulin cover. Other soldiers quickly fanned out around the square, pointing machine guns into the crowd, on the lookout for anyone who might cause trouble. Simone instantly recognized the man in the Mercedes as the man from the Gestapo – Herr Mueller. The look on his face was even harder than she remembered it. Mueller said something to the men standing by a truck and they began to pull two prisoners from the truck – a man and a woman. When she saw the woman, her eyes widened. '*Mon Dieu*! It's Lucie.'

Mme Legrand grabbed Claude's arm to steady herself. 'I can't believe it.'

'*Raus! Raus!*' one of the soldiers called out, pulling them from the truck. Lucie, her hands tied behind her back, fell over and the soldier roughly pulled her back up. Her face was bruised and her eyes red and swollen from tears.

Claude put a protective arm around his mother's shoulder. 'Isn't that Etienne Vernoux?' he asked in a whisper. 'I thought he'd disappeared.'

'Who's Etienne?' Simone asked.

'Her boyfriend – the one who disappeared almost a year ago when they brought in the Compulsory Work Service,' replied Mme Legrand. 'What's he doing back here?'

Simone had a good memory for faces and she didn't recall him being with the maquisards at the drop zone, and if he was there, she was sure Pascal would have mentioned he was Lucie's friend. After the initial gasp of disbelief, a terrified hush descended over the crowd. One look at the villagers' faces told her that this was a shock to everyone. While she feared for Lucie, she was relieved it wasn't Pascal. They didn't have long to find out what was taking place.

The hapless prisoners were forced to stand aside while Herr Mueller delivered a speech to the crowd. The prisoners, he declared, had been found guilty of treason and condemned to death. Their punishment was to take place in full view of everyone as a lesson to all those contemplating disobedience against the Reich. Mueller went on to say that the traitor – Etienne Vernoux – had been found guilty on two counts. The first for having defied an order when he was called up for the Compulsory Work Service, and the second, he was caught hiding out in the nearby vineyards, armed with a gun and attempting to flee when confronted by German soldiers.

'The woman,' Mueller declared, glancing disdainfully at Lucie, 'Lucie Mouran, a resident of this village, was with him. She has confessed to knowingly aiding and abetting his crime by supplying him with food.'

The crowd let out a loud gasp.

'Quiet!' Mueller shouted, angrily. 'Anyone who creates a public disturbance will be shot.' He turned to the soldiers guarding the two prisoners and indicated for them to be lined up against the school wall. The fearful villagers huddled together in small groups.

'My God, they mean to execute them,' Olivier whispered to Claude. 'We can't let this happen. We have to do something.'

He made a move to intervene, but Claude stopped him. 'There's little we can do. We are unarmed and they will kill us too.'

Simone was horrified as she watched the unfortunate couple being taken to the wall and a blindfold placed over their eyes. A woman in the crowd let out a desperate shriek. 'My daughter – no!'

Mueller looked in the direction of the cry and gestured to a soldier to take her away. Everyone looked on as a screaming Mme Mouran, was unceremoniously bundled out of the square. Her screams could be heard for a full minute until finally, a hush descended from the area she had been taken. Simone clasped her hand to her mouth. What had they done to the poor woman?

A group of six soldiers were ordered to take aim and a fearful silence descended over the square. Memories of the day Jacques had taken her to the warehouse in Paris flooded through Simone's brain. It was still as clear and fresh as the moment she had fired the fateful shot. The beads of perspiration mingled with blood on the man's face; the look in his eyes. It was all there, imprinted in her mind forever. Now it was happening again. It didn't matter whether she was firing the shot. One glance at Mme Legrand, fighting back the tears, was enough to fire up her hatred for the Germans even more.

Mueller gave a nod and the soldier directing the firing squad, shouted out – 'Take aim.'

At the moment the men raised their rifles, they heard a car approaching. Another Mercedes drove into the square and the occupant jumped out and angrily stormed over to Herr Mueller, who looked just as surprised to see him as Simone.

'Albrecht!' Claude Legrand said, and started towards them both. His mother caught his arm. 'Please – don't get involved.'

Mueller gestured to halt the execution while he and Albrecht disappeared into the school, leaving the startled villagers questioning what was going on. Ten minutes passed before the two emerged from the building. Mueller gave orders to someone to remove the blindfold from Lucie and take her into the school. At that point, she collapsed on to the pavement in a faint.

'Get her out of here,' Mueller said angrily, 'before I change my mind.'

No sooner had Lucie been taken away than he directed the officer in charge of the firing squad to take aim again. Despite the villager's prayers, this time there would not be another stay of execution.

'Take aim – Fire!'

Etienne Vernoux's bullet riddled body flew back against the wall, and he crumpled in a heap on the cobblestones. Mme Legrand's face was as white as a ghost and Simone worried that she might have another heart attack.

Mueller declared that the body should stay where it was until the morning as a lesson to anyone who tried to deceive them. He turned to

Albrecht, gave the Hitler salute, got back into his car and drove away. After informing the stunned villagers they were free to return to their homes, Albrecht and his men went into the schoolhouse and closed the door behind them.

Claude asked Simone and Olivier to take his mother back home. He would join them later. He turned on his heels and hurried towards the schoolhouse.

CHAPTER 9

ALMOST TWO HOURS had passed by the time Claude returned to the house where he found his mother, Simone, and Olivier shrouded in anguish, sipping cognac in silence to steady their nerves. Even Ulysse, sitting on the rug next to Mme Legrand's feet, sensed something bad had taken place. They looked at Claude expectantly.

'Well?' Mme Legrand said.

Claude helped himself to a large cognac and told them what had transpired. The Germans discovered Etienne sleeping in a barn after one of the villagers mentioned they thought someone was hiding there. The name of the villager was not revealed but Claude had no doubt that the Gestapo were putting pressure on everyone. When they caught Etienne, they realised someone had been supplying him with food. Under interrogation, Etienne refused to name anyone helping him, saying he had stolen the food himself, but it didn't take them long to realise he had a girlfriend – Lucie. Her house was raided and she was taken away for questioning. After being given a beating, she confessed to supplying him with food. When asked how long this had been going on, Etienne said a few days and that he'd only just returned to the area.

'So he took the blame for everything,' Mme Legrand said.

'Yes, and although Mueller realised he had nothing to do with the air-drop – the reason they were in the area in the first place – he wanted a scapegoat. Etienne and Lucie fitted the bill. He would have killed them both had it not been for Bruno Albrecht. He was in Épernay when he heard it was Lucie who was to be executed with Etienne. Knowing who she was, he rushed to intervene.'

'Then we have Albrecht to thank,' Simone said, unsure of how to take this news. 'Why would he save one of our own only to antagonize a man like Mueller?'

'Because he owes me favours,' Claude replied. 'But I'm afraid it's not all good news. He informed me that Lucie may have been saved from the firing squad, but Mueller wants her sent to a camp in Germany in exchange. Albrecht has agreed.'

'Oh no!' Mme Legrand put her hand on her chest. 'What are we to do?'

'What about Pascal?' Simone asked. 'Would he have a solution?'

'Martine's right,' Mme Legrand said. 'Where's Lucie now?'

'They've taken her to Gestapo Headquarters in Reims.'

'How can we get in touch with Pascal?' Simone said. 'We can't wait around for him to reappear. It could be days, especially if he knows the Germans have been here.' She looked at them, waiting for a response.

'He's already here,' Mme Legrand said, and asked Olivier to fetch him from his hiding place.

Simone looked shocked. 'You mean he was here the whole time all this was taking place?'

'He called at the house around lunchtime to assure us none of the Maquis at the drop zone had been caught and that the contents of the canisters were safely hidden away until it was safe to distribute them.'

'Thank God, but how did he manage to get past the Germans; all those checks and roadblocks?'

Claude smiled. 'Pascal is a master of disguises.'

Minutes later, Olivier returned with Pascal.

'Good to see you again, my friend.' Claude shook Pascal's hand.

'Olivier just told me the news,' Pascal said. 'Bastards! Do you have any idea how long Lucie was seeing Etienne?'

Mme Legrand shook her head despondently. 'No. She never said a thing to us. What puzzles me is that she knew we were involved with the Resistance and would have been in a position to help Etienne, so why did she keep it a secret? I wonder how long he'd been back – if indeed he went away at all.'

'Perhaps that's the reason for her nervousness in front of Albrecht and Mueller yesterday,' Simone added. 'She must have feared he'd be caught and left early to warn him. What's happened to her mother? Is she alright?'

'She's fine. I spoke to her at her home,' Claude replied, 'Apparently it was a shock to her too, although she did notice they were unusually low on certain foodstuffs – a few eggs, half a litre of milk, a slice of smoked sausage. When you're on rations, every morsel of food is accounted for. She mentioned something to Lucie but the reply was that she was hungry. Madame Mouran was surprised as she knew she ate here. There was no reason for her to think her daughter would put their lives in danger by helping a fugitive.'

Mme Legrand looked at Pascal. 'Is there anything we can do to save Lucie? She'll never survive a German concentration camp.'

There was a moment of silence while Pascal turned the situation over in his mind.

'What about Fifi?' Claude asked. 'Maybe she can help us.'

'Who's Fifi?' Simone asked.

'She's a friend of mine,' Pascal replied. 'She works at Gestapo HQ in Reims.'

Simone's eyes widened. 'A friend – or a member of the Resistance?'

When Pascal didn't answer, Simone wondered if the woman was more than a friend. She scrutinized everyone's faces and saw they were embarrassed at her question. In an instant, she knew she'd overstepped the mark and apologised.

'She's a secretary,' Pascal said, putting her mind at rest. 'She has access to the deportation files. Occasionally she helps us out.'

'Is she French?'

'She's from Alsace. Because she's fluent in French and German, the Gestapo offered her a job.'

'I see,' Simone replied, not seeing at all. Suddenly she felt vulnerable. Unlike Paris, where she was familiar with the Resistance work and generally worked alone; here she was part of a group and that group depended on each other. It only needed one weak link and everything would come crashing down.

71

Pascal continued. 'I'm seeing her tomorrow evening. I'll see what can be done.' He saw the unease in Simone's eyes and assured her she was trustworthy. 'First we need to know when she'll be sent away. Then we'll work something out.'

Mme Legrand held her chest and took a few deep breaths. 'If you will all excuse me, this sorry episode has made me rather unwell. I will retire to my room. Martine, perhaps you can bring my medicine.'

Simone went to fetch Mme Legrand's medicine and followed her into the bedroom. For the first time, she noticed how frail the elderly woman was. 'Madame Marie, I've prepared a special sleeping draught for you. It will give you a good night's sleep. You'll feel much better in the morning.'

Mme Legrand drank the milky-coloured medicine and handed back the glass. When Simone took the glass from her hand, she clasped her hand around Simone's wrist giving her a fright. 'My dear, I can see you are a good girl, but there is one thing I must say to you. You were out of line this evening. You must learn to trust Pascal and not to ask questions.' She let go of her wrist. 'Thank you for the medicine.'

Simone felt awkward and unsure of what to say. She thanked her for her advice.

When she returned to the sitting room, Claude and Olivier were preparing to leave. 'You and Pascal have things to talk about so I'll take my leave of you,' Claude said. 'Please tell Maman, I'll call her in the morning.'

Olivier said he would go to the Mouran home to offer comfort to Mme Mouran. 'I'll be back in the morning in case you need to ask about the Peugeot. It's been fitted with a wood gasifier but she still drives very well, so I don't anticipate you'll have any problems.'

Simone thanked them both. After they'd gone, she apologised to Pascal again for asking questions out of turn. He smiled. 'I admire your caution, but there are times when you have to trust people.' His words echoed Mme Legrand's. 'Now let's get back to the business in hand shall we? I came here today knowing full well the Germans were in the area, but I needed to speak with you. Jean-Yves, our new radio operator, must be moved to a safer place – somewhere more remote. Now that you have access to the Legrand's car, I want you to take him there yourself. Travelling by cart would be far too painful for him at this moment.'

'Where is this place?'

Pascal pulled out a map and circled a spot. 'It's a deserted farmhouse next to a forest some thirty kilometres to the east of here. It's pretty isolated and will be fine for him to recuperate and send and receive messages at the same time. The Maquis use it for training their men.' He pushed the map towards her and told her to memorize the spot while he poured himself another Cognac. Simone took a good look and handed it back.

'He'll be expecting you at the farm where we left him,' Pascal added, pointing to a spot seven kilometres away.

'When do you want me to go?'

'Tomorrow. I've already discussed it with Madame Legrand.'

'Will you be there?' Simone asked.

'That will depend on what transpires with Fifi. If I'm not, take your orders from Alexandre. He's the chief of the Maquis in the area. He's a good man as you will find out yourself. He's also a very capable chief who has my backing.'

Simone asked if he'd heard from Jacques. He told her the news from Paris was not good. The Gestapo had made a concerted effort to break the various Resistance groups and hundreds of resistants had been shot.

'I haven't heard from him in a while so I am presuming no news is good news and that he's evaded the roundups.' He patted her hand. 'Don't worry. Martine. I'm sure he'll be fine.'

'Is there any more news about the Allied Invasion?' she asked. 'Did Jean-Yves give you news from London?'

'Only that it will be soon. For this reason our work is vital and we still have so much to do. We *must* be ready in time.' He stood up. 'Come on. Enough talk for the moment. It's getting late and it's been a long day. You need your beauty sleep.'

Simone laughed. 'Are you staying the night?'

Pascal shook his head. 'I'm afraid not. The luxury of a soft bed cannot entice me tonight. I have things to do.'

She watched him leave by the back door and head towards his hiding place in the wine shed, wondering what he had to do so late at night. He was such an elusive character – as elusive as Jacques. No sooner had he disappeared than she heard the low droning sound of a squadron of Allied airplanes heading towards Germany. Immediately, the night sky lit up with streaks of bright lights from searchlights and tracer bullets, quickly followed by a series of loud booming noises from German anti-aircraft guns. Simone had lost count of the times she'd seen this spectacle and it always sent chills down her spine. She pulled her cardigan around her and went back inside.

CHAPTER 10

Simone was pleased to see Jean-Yves' leg had been tended to and in a splint. Although he was able to walk with the aid of a walking stick, driving was another matter. Throughout the journey to the farmhouse he winced and grimaced in pain and complained every time Simone took a sharp bend too quickly or drove over a bump in the road. In the end, she pulled up at the side of the road and searched in her bag for a painkiller.

'Here, take one of these,' she said. 'I can't slow down in case a patrol stops us and your constant grimacing is making me nervous.'

Jean-Yves looked surprised. 'You're a feisty one. Do you always carry painkillers in your bag?'

'I'm a nurse. You never know when you'll need them, especially if we're likely to get shot at.'

She started the car again and they drove on in silence until they reached their destination. 'This is the turn-off,' she said. The farmhouse should be just beyond that copse. You'd better grit your teeth, it looks like it's going to be a bumpy ride.'

The car rattled over the narrow, deeply furrowed road at a much slower speed. Huge potholes and large stones made driving difficult and Jean-Yves bit his lip to stop himself crying out, although he did let out a few swearwords under his breath. Simone saw his knuckles were white as he grasped the door handle to steady himself. She laughed and he threw her a dirty look.

Minutes later, the ruins of an old farmhouse came into view. 'It's barely standing,' Simone said. 'The roof has almost collapsed.'

They were met by a group of men carrying Sten guns. Simone recognized a couple of them from the drop zone. A tall man with black hair, a tanned complexion, and sporting a moustache and week-old beard came out of the house and introduced himself as Alexandre. Addressing Jean-Yves, he welcomed him to France.

'And you, Mademoiselle, must be Martine.' He shook Simone's hand. 'Pascal has told me all about you. Good to have you with us. Come on inside and let's get you both something to drink.' He gestured to another man to help Jean-Yves who was grimacing in pain again.

The inside of the building was also in a severe state of ruin except that the area where they were hiding out which had a makeshift roof. 'It may not be the Ritz, but it's more comfortable than it looks. More importantly, it's as safe as can be from prying eyes.'

One of the men boiled up a saucepan of water on a wood fire and made them all a mug of tea and handed round a plate of hard biscuits. Alexandre produced a bottle of whisky and added a decent glug into Jean-Yves's tea. 'Sorry about the leg. How bad is it?' he asked.

'A broken femur. Damned nuisance, but it could have been worse. I just have to take it easy for a while.' He glanced at Simone. 'Nurse Martine will see to that.'

'You'll be quite safe here.' A man with a Spanish accent who was introduced as Enrique entered the room with a brown suitcase and handed it to Jean-Yves. 'Your radio, Señor – safe and sound.'

'Thank goodness for that. Now I need to let London know I'm alright.'

Alexandre asked Enrique to help Jean-Yves prepare the wires for the antennae and the rest of the men left the room giving him some privacy. A few sat around outside in the yard playing cards.

'I heard you are a good shot.' Alexandre said when they were alone. 'Pascal speaks highly of you.'

Simone blushed. 'My handler made sure I knew about small arms. I practiced regularly.'

'You mean Jacques?'

'You know him?'

'Yes. We worked together for a while when we were organizing escape routes. You may even have been involved with that.'

'I wouldn't know. I just followed orders. Jacques told us only what we needed to know. He said it was the safest way to operate.'

'I agree, but I think you will find here is a little different. We work as a group. Our lives depend on one another – especially as the Allies are about to invade.' He swung his arm out, emptying the dregs of tea from his mug. Simone noticed a few streaks of grey in his dark hair. She thought it suited him.

'Are you from around here?' she asked. 'I can't pinpoint your accent.'

'I was born near the Swiss border but moved around quite a bit. I lived in Paris for a while before coming here. I suppose I'm a bit of a nomad.'

'What brought you here – the Resistance?'

'You're partly correct. Actually it was a woman.' He laughed. 'I followed her here and then we parted company. *C'est la vie.* By then I'd become accustomed to the area and decided to stay.' Alexandre changed the subject. He told her they'd heard about what took place in the village.

'Did you know Etienne?' she asked.

'I knew of him, but he wasn't one of us. He was a loner. Everyone thought he'd left the area. Maybe now we'll never know what brought him back.'

The conversation was interrupted when one of the lookouts whistled that a car was approaching. Alexandre stood up and hurried to a lookout between the trees from where they had a wide vista across the undulating fields. Baptiste's car was snaking its way at a snail's pace along the rocky road and, as it neared, Simone saw that Pascal was with him.

Pascal, smartly attired in a fresh pair of light grey trousers and a dark blue ribbed pullover, called a couple of men to help remove a cache of rifles stored under rush matting in the boot.

'How is he?' Pascal asked, referring to Jean-Yves.

'He's fine,' she replied. 'I gave him a strong painkiller.'

Pascal didn't waste time as to the reason they were there. The containers from the last drop had been collected and hidden around the farmhouse. Now, Pascal and Alexandre needed to distribute the contents as soon as possible. They went inside the farmhouse while the men collected everything from a safe hiding place and brought them inside. Both Pascal and Jean-Yves checked the contents carefully to be sure everything was accounted for.

'Good old Buckmaster,' Pascal said. 'There's even more here than I asked for.'

The men cast their eyes over a mound of Bren guns, Sten guns, small arms and rifles, silencers, ammunition, and an assortment of explosive devices, including grenades, fuses and chargers, all of which needed to be checked. Added to this were knives, wire-cutters, short spades, ropes, and rations of biscuits, dried fruit, chocolates and whisky to lift the men's spirits. There were even two field Medical and First Aid kits. The first one contained surgical instruments and drugs, including vaccines, syringes, intravenous anaesthetic suitable for use by qualified medical persons such as Simone, and the second included bandages, cotton wool, adhesive plasters, antiseptic ointments and bandages. Someone asked if any of this could be used to help Jean-Yves, but after a lengthy discussion, it was deemed better to leave them for emergencies and try and obtain whatever they needed from a local pharmacist for him. In no time at all, the contents were distributed to everyone. Pascal gave Jean-Yves co-ordinates for a new drop zone and told him to arrange for more supplies to be sent out as soon as possible.

He turned to Alexandre. 'Did you mention our last conversation with Martine?'

Alexandre shook his head. 'No time. She only arrived a short time ago.'

Simone's eyes widened. 'What's all this about?'

Pascal said, 'I didn't mention anything earlier as I wanted to give you time to settle in. I was going to tell you, but when the situation deteriorated in the village, I didn't think it the right time. One of the reasons Jacques suggested you was because you are a quick learner and know how to keep your cool. I wanted someone who could learn about explosives and sabotage – as good as those in SOE. Are you up for it?'

'Do I have a choice?' Simone answered, her words tinged with sarcasm. She looked at their faces. 'I thought not.'

Pascal grinned and Simone couldn't help thinking how handsome he looked in his smart clothes. He'd even got rid of the five o'clock shadow she'd become accustomed to. 'It won't be long now before the Allies land – maybe even a couple of weeks and we need everyone trained and ready to go. What we are asking of you is no more than is asked of other female agents in the field.' He paused to judge her response. 'It's dangerous work, Martine.'

She realised her comfortable days looking after Mme Legrand were all an illusion. Sipping Champagne on the terrace with the matriarch of a great Champagne family was going to be a rarity. From a slow start, things were starting to move at an alarming pace and she had no idea where it would end.

'When do I start this training?'

'Tomorrow,' Alexandre replied. 'I want you back here as early as possible. Expect to be here all day. Another thing – Have you ever handled a sniper's rifle?'

'Only small arms. I've never had a need for anything else.'

Alexander went outside and returned with a large sack. He took out a rifle and fixed the telescopic sight into place. 'Do you know what this is?'

'A Mosin Nogent PV. The Russians use it.'

He took out another from the sack, this time without a telescopic sight. 'And this one?'

'A Karabiner 98k. It was not designed to accept telescopic sights, but modification has made it possible.'

He took out the last.

'That's an American – the M1903A4.'

'Are you quite sure you've never used a sniper's rifle?' he asked. 'You identified these in a flash.'

'I told you, I've never used one, but I did learn about them from others in the Parisian network.'

'Well Martine, I must say, that's remarkable. You obviously have a good memory. Which one would you like?'

Images of the man she'd shot in Paris flooded back. 'Are you seriously going to give me one of those?'

'We need to be prepared for any situation, and a good sniper can make our life a lot easier, so I am offering you a rifle to practice with. Which is it to be?'

She pointed to the Mosin Nogent. 'Given that most sniper rifles have some sort of problem, I'll take this. I've heard it's the one most favoured by snipers. Besides, if the female Russian snipers use it, so can I.'

This time Pascal laughed. 'You've heard about those women then?'

'Jacques told me. He has a lot of admiration for them.'

Pascal looked at his watch and said he'd better be getting a move on as he had a rendezvous. 'Would you give me a lift back?' he said to Simone. 'Baptiste has things to do here.'

Simone looked at Jean-Yves who had fallen asleep on a makeshift bed. 'Make sure he rests,' she said to Alexandre.

'Don't worry. He'll be fine. We've dealt with worse.' He walked them outside and held open the car door for her. 'Wear something comfortable next time,' he said. 'The blouse you're wearing is far too pretty and delicate for the sort of exercises you'll be doing.'

The car wound its way back down through the fields, ablaze with colourful spring flowers. 'Where would you like me to drop you off?' Simone asked.

'Reims.'

Simone suddenly remembered he was trying to arrange a meeting with Fifi and wondered if that was the reason he was so smartly dressed. They drove for several kilometres in silence, both lost in their thoughts. 'Can I ask you something?' she said after a while.

'Fire away.'

'Why couldn't I have been told in Paris that this work entailed more training – explosives, and now training as a sniper?'

Pascal turned away to look out of the window for a few seconds. 'How could we have told you that? We had to rely on you accepting to undertake this mission.' He turned back to look at her. 'I would never purposely put you in danger, Martine, but the Germans have stepped up their activities and we need all the good people we can get.' He paused to light a cigarette. 'One day when this damn war has ended, and you are sitting at home, surrounded by your children and grandchildren, you will be glad you played a vital role in freeing your country from Nazi tyranny.'

There was little Simone could say to that. When they entered the outskirts of Reims, Pascal told her where to drop him off. 'There's a black-market restaurant near here that I frequent,' he said. 'Drop me off at the end of the road. I'll walk the rest of the way.'

'Is there a pharmacy nearby?' she asked. 'I'd like to pick up more bandages, ointments, and painkillers for Jean-Yves.'

'There's one two streets away. The owner helps the Resistance.' He gave her a coded sentence to use. 'If you don't use it, you'll get nothing. Things like that are hard to come by these days and the Gestapo make regular checks on pharmacists.'

Pascal turned to walk away and she called out after him. 'Any idea when I'll see you again?'

'Soon. Let's hope we have some good news by then.'

Simone knew by this comment he meant after his meeting with Fifi. She waited a few seconds before driving away. At that moment, she noticed a slim platinum-blonde woman, her hair swept back in an immaculate neat French roll, turn the corner and head in the same direction. She quickly scanned the street and saw Pascal enter a bistro with a red awning. The woman was impeccably dressed in a pale pink floral dress with matching deep pink gloves and handbag. Could that be Fifi? she asked herself. As the woman approached the bistro, she looked around to see if she was being followed before entering,

The blonde woman had only just entered when a small man wearing a grey suit, appeared from the opposite direction. Simone thought his face seemed familiar. Then she remembered – the bald-headed man in the breakfast room at the Hôtel De La Cathédrale. She felt a shiver run down her spine. *What was going on? Was Pascal walking into a trap?*

It crossed her mind to go after him, but she knew that was unwise. When the man came to the bistro, rather than enter, he turned his head to glance through the window, and walked on. It was too much of a coincidence.

The man stopped at the far corner of the street, lit a cigarette and stood for a while looking back down the street. Simone realised she had to leave straight away before she attracted unwanted attention. She drove to the pharmacy.

The pharmacy was closed but she could see the pharmacist behind the counter. She tapped on the window and beckoned for him to open up.

'What a beautiful day; not a cloud in the sky,' she said in a low voice.

The man replied with a similar coded phrase and ushered her inside. 'What can I do for you?'

'I'd like several rolls of bandages, ointment, and a bottle of painkillers, please.' The man fixed his eyes on her for a few seconds before fulfilling her order. She also asked for an assortment of herbs: lemon balm, catnip, passionflower, hop flowers, valerian root, and chamomile. 'Anything that will give a restful sleep.'

The pharmacist also gave her a small bag of St. John's wort, nettle leaf, and lavender. 'On the house,' he said. 'Do you know how to mix the right quantities?'

'I'm a nurse,' she replied. 'I've had lots of experience making tisanes.'

The man was curious. 'I haven't seen you around here before. He glanced towards the car outside. 'But I recognize that car — even though it's been converted. It belongs to Madame Legrand, doesn't it?'

'Yes. I'm her companion.'

'I haven't seen her for a while. A wonderful lady. Give her my regards.'

On hearing that Simone was Mme Legrand's companion, the pharmacist refused to let her pay, even though she insisted. She put the items in her bag and thanked him. 'By the way, can you recommend a good bistro near here?'

'Let me see. There's Bistro Chez Nous, but that doesn't do such good business since the Gestapo raided it a while ago. There's also Bistro Thierry. That's run by our friends – if you get what I mean.'

Simone nodded. 'Where's that?'

'Two streets away – but you might find it rather full at this time of night.'

Simone got in the car, put the herbs on the passenger's seat and everything else under the seat in case she was stopped and searched, and drove in the direction of Bistro Thierry. It was almost six o'clock and the sun was setting. Thankfully, the bald-headed man had disappeared. She drove down the street slowly in order to get a good look inside the place. The tables were decked out in chequered tablecloths with a lighted candle on each one. Any later and the blackout curtains would have been drawn. She strained to catch a glimpse of Pascal and had almost passed when she spotted him sitting with the blonde lady. With their heads slightly bent towards each other, they appeared deep in conversation. Then she noticed something else. They were holding hands across the table.

'*Merde*, Pascal,' Simone uttered under her breath. 'What's going on?'

CHAPTER 11

CROUCHED BEHIND A stone wall, Simone fixed the telescopic sight on her rifle and peered through a small hole with her 8x magnification binoculars to survey the field below. Her senses heightened, she was conscious of the serenity of her surroundings. The dampness of the early morning dew had dissipated, leaving behind a fragrant scent of earth and grass in the warm spring air, and from somewhere close by, a song thrush sang a beautiful mating tune.

'Can you see it?' Alexandre asked. 'Have you spotted anything unusual yet?'

Her gaze concentrated on one particular spot; an unusual clump of grass almost 300 metres away. The earth around it looked to have been disturbed. 'I think so.'

She carefully placed the rifle on a piece of wood and took aim. A split second later, the gun fired. Alexandre jumped up and gestured to one of his men further down the hillside, to check the target. The man ran over to the spot Simone had identified, pulled out a piece of cardboard hidden behind the tufts of grass, and waved it in the air. He gave the thumbs up.

Alexandre looked pleased. 'Excellent. You have a good eye. If that had been the enemy, you would have shot him clean through the head.' Simone looked towards the target without uttering a word. 'Now, we'll move to another spot and try it again,' he said.

She followed him through the woods until they reached a few large rocks. 'Here. This will do.' They sat down on the soft ground and this time he gave her a Mauser K98. She noticed it had the Nazi eagle and a number on it. Clearly it had once belonged to the SS and she wondered how he got it.

'It's one of the best bolt action rifles ever made,' Alexandre said. 'Safe and robust.' He handed her a five-round clip. 'When you've finished your training with me you'll be accustomed to several rifles.' He watched while she checked it out. 'There's something I must point out. Your aim is superb, but I noticed on your last shot, you hesitated. It was only a fraction of a second, but in the field, that would be enough to get you killed.' Simone had not even realised.

One of the men whistled, and she settled into position again, resting the rifle on a rock jutting out of a narrow crevice. Moments later there was another whistle.

'No. Your position has been identified.' Alexandre said. 'What do you think you did wrong?'

She pulled the rifle back. 'I'm not sure. I was careful when I placed the rifle there to steady it.'

Alexandre tutted. 'He must have seen the glint of your rifle. In the field, that too would get you killed.' She looked around, noticed several nearby bushes and began to crawl towards them. 'Keep your head down!' Alexandre called out.

She reached out and broke off several low-lying branches, taking care not to shake the bush. Then she slithered back to her hiding place and assembled them in such a way that the rifle would remain camouflaged.

'Good. Now let's try again.'

Slowly she moved the rifle into position on the rock and carefully looked through the telescopic sight. This time she had to find the target without looking through the binoculars first. It was her tenth practice that day and already she was drained. Alexandre was proving to be a demanding teacher.

'Do you see it?' he asked. 'If you think that's it – fire.'

The wood had undulating slopes filled with the roots of trees, ferns and a variety of moss-covered rocks. Their composition appeared normal, except for one area where there was a gap between a gnarled tree and a bush. If the enemy was hiding in such a place, he would be well-covered, but the more she looked, the more her eye settled on that spot, and like the previous spot, the earth looked to have been disturbed. Alexandre waited patiently. Then she fired. Moments later there was a whistle and both sat up looking in the direction of where she'd fired. A man appeared out of nowhere and ran to the spot, picked up the cardboard, camouflaged in leaves, and held it up.

They moved to another area of the wood and repeated the exercise. After that, Alexandre suggested they return to the farmhouse for lunch. When they arrived, the men were gathered around a fire outside eating stew. A large pot simmered away on the fire. One of the men scooped out two more bowlfuls for them. Simone was hungrier than she thought. It had been a tense morning and she'd been eager to please Alexandre.

After they'd finished, the men settled down for a quick nap, leaving Alexandre and Simone alone to talk. He continued to lecture her, and then asked questions to make sure she understood it all. She wondered where he'd gained all this knowledge. He reminded her of Jacques. There was a mysterious quality to them both.

Simone excused herself to check on Jean-Yves. He was lying on a make-shift bed in the house, working on his coding.

'How are you feeling?' she asked.

'It's still painful, if that's what you mean.'

'Let me take a look.' She sat down on the bed and untied the bandages. He grimaced when she tried to take them off. *'Putain!'*

The bandages were stuck to the wound with congealed blood and she went to get a bowl of warm water to wash them. Gently, she applied a wet cloth until they came away. Jean-Yves relaxed. 'How is it?' he asked.

'It's only been a couple of days, but already I can see you're healing well. No redness or unusual swelling, so that's a good sign. The doctor did a good job.' She took out the ointment and after thoroughly dressing the wound, applied fresh bandages. 'I've also brought you more painkillers. Try to make them last, I'm not sure when I can get more.'

Jean-Yves thanked her. 'I appreciate it. You have a soft touch. After the way you took those bends yesterday, I didn't know what to expect.'

Simone smiled. 'How many times have you been to France?' she asked, as she emptied the bloodied water and prepared a saucepan of water to boil the used bandages.

'Three. Like Pascal, I was born here.'

'Really, where?'

'Paris. We moved to Dijon before the war broke out. My father was French. He died not long after the armistice – a car accident. So my mother and I escaped to England. About a year later I joined SOE.'

She stirred the bandages in the boiling water while, at the same time, watching the men outside. Some of them were heading back into the woods. When she'd finished, she strung the bandages over a makeshift line to dry. Alexandre came into check on Jean-Yves and was pleased to see a little colour back in his cheeks.

'Come on,' he said to Simone. 'We'd better get a move on. No time to waste. I want to go through explosives with you now.'

After a long and exhausting day, Simone returned to Verzenay where she found Olivier in the driveway, preparing wood for her car. He told her that Mme Legrand had spent the day comforting Lucie's mother. The whole village was still in shock and no-one could understand what had taken place. Even Etienne's family had not known he'd returned to the area. He added that they had now moved Etienne's body to his family home where it would stay until the day of the burial. He could see that Simone was tired and changed the subject.

'How did you find the car?' he asked, referring to its conversion. 'Not as good as it could be, is it, but at least it will get you around.'

'We're lucky to have it. I don't think I could have cycled long distances day after day.'

'Well, I'd best be getting back home now. If you need anything, let Madame Marie know.'

After he'd gone, she made herself a drink and sat outside on the terrace with Ulysse by her side. He looked up at her with his large dark eyes and gave a soulful whine. Simone stroked his head. She was glad of his company.

It was dark when Mme Legrand returned and like Simone, she

appeared drained and exhausted. 'What a terrible day. I don't know how the poor woman will cope,' she said, referring to Mme Mouran. 'She simply had no idea what Lucie was doing. It's a tragedy. I do hope Claude or Pascal can do something to free her.'

'Have you heard anything from either of them?'

Mme Legrand shook her head. 'Nothing. We must pray for a miracle.'

Simone noticed her breathing was laboured. 'Let me take your pulse, Madame Marie. You don't look at all well.' It didn't take long for her to realise she was more ill than she let on. 'Your blood pressure is sky-high. You must not exert yourself – physically *or* mentally.' She went to get her tablets and prepared a tisane with the herbs she'd purchased the day before. When she returned, Mme Legrand was fanning herself and her face looked flushed.

'This damn war!' she said under her breath.

Simone handed her the mug of deep yellow and fragrant warm tea. 'It won't be long now. Soon the Allies will be here and life will be back to normal again.'

Mme Legrand closed her eyes for a few seconds and inhaled the aroma. 'Nothing will be the same again, you know. It wasn't after The Great War, and it won't be again.' She took a few sips. 'This is wonderful. I can feel it doing me good already.'

'I got it from the pharmacist in Reims. Pascal recommended him. I didn't want to tell him who I was, but he recognised your car. He sends his regards.'

'I've known him since I was a young girl. A good man; one you can trust.'

'I was thinking that I might go there again tomorrow, maybe on my way back from the farmhouse. I'll get you something for your blood pressure. I might even treat myself to an aperitif in one of those cafés near the cathedral.'

'Good idea. Be careful though, there are frequent raids.'

Simone laughed. 'Don't worry; I'm used to that sort of thing.'

Mme Legrand reminded her that Sylvie was also used to raids. It was a sobering thought. Not even a good fake Identification could fool a determined Gestapo agent.

The next day was the same as the last. More exercises at the farm in the use of various guns and how to prepare explosives. This time there were a few new faces, including several women. During this time Simone learned more about Alexandre's maquisards. They were a diverse mix of people from all background. Some were staunch communists; others had an allegiance to de Gaulle, there were quite a few Poles who'd escaped the Polish mines, and a large number of Spanish Republicans. Because of their differing ideologies, Alexandre strictly forbade any discussion about politics, putting group loyalty before any ideology. They could argue about politics once the Germans had gone. Simone had learnt early in the Occupation that a strong leader was everything. Jacques, Pascal, and now Alexandre, were all natural leaders.

Simone was a quick learner and Alexandre was happy with her progress. It was exhausting work, yet at the same time, exciting. In Paris, she'd mostly worked alone. Here she was part of a wider team and she felt honoured to be working alongside such determined men and women.

Returning from the farm, she drove into Reims to get Mme Legrand's medicine and afterwards parked the car near the cathedral where she ordered a *Lillet Blanc* at an outdoor café in the Square des Jacobins, a couple of streets away. It was a beautiful evening. People were out and about; the French refused to let the German presence ruin their evening. It was as if they deliberately flaunted themselves by having a good time. Women dressed up in their best clothes, paraded arm-in-arm along the streets, and sat in groups laughing and smiling. Simone was sure it was all an act; after all, she'd frequently done it herself in Paris, listening in to conversations which might prove useful for the Resistance. Underneath, she knew they were just as fearful of the Germans as she was. They were unpredictable. It was noticeable there were few Frenchmen between the ages of eighteen and sixty, except for those who were probably lucky enough to have found themselves a good doctor willing to stick their neck out to diagnose a severe illness. It was also highly likely that only a few would have genuine exemption cards because of their work or position.

She had almost finished her drink when she noticed the same platinum-haired lady she'd seen with Pascal arrive. She headed in the direction of the café and joined a group of men at a nearby table – plainclothes Germans. Simone was conscious of being seen and turned her chair slightly. From where she sat, she could see their reflection in the café window, but was not close enough to overhear their conversation, although she was aware they were speaking German. She caught the attention of two German soldiers at the next table who gave her a friendly smile and offered to buy her a drink.

The fair-haired one of the two called the waiter over and told him to bring her another of whatever it was she was drinking. Simone told them she was fine, but the waiter, fearing trouble if he didn't do as asked, brought her another *Lillet Blanc*.

'Sorry, Mademoiselle,' he said in a whisper. 'I don't want any problems.'

She smiled. 'That's fine. I can handle myself.'

Simone turned her attention back to the blonde woman who appeared to lap up the men's attentions. It wasn't difficult to see why. She was easily the most attractive woman there. At that moment, she noticed a familiar figure enter the street and walk towards the café – Pascal. He was carrying a rolled-up newspaper under his arm. A surge of conflicting emotions raced through her mind. What would he think if he saw her? Was his appearance something to do with the blonde woman? She felt a sudden urge to get up and move to a table inside the cafe, but that would only make her more noticeable.

The closer he got, the more she realised his gaze was focused on the blonde, and she hoped he hadn't noticed her. Yet the more she thought about it, the more she knew that was highly unlikely. Pascal was the sort of person who noticed everything; he just didn't let on. Moments later, he passed the café, dropped the newspaper in a rubbish bin before crossing the road again, eventually stopping for a few seconds to look back before disappearing down a side-street. A few minutes later, the blonde woman stood up, said goodbye to the men, and walked in the same direction.

It all took place so quickly but it was enough to pique her curiosity and she decided to follow them. She called the waiter over, paid for her first drink and nodded a polite thank you in the direction of the two men. One of them asked her to join them.

'I'm sorry, I really must get home.' Simone didn't give them time to argue. She walked away as quickly as she could without attracting undue attention.

Nearing the corner of the side-street, something made her look back. One of the young Germans was following her. 'Oh no!' she said, under her breath, picked up her pace and turned into the side-street. There was no sign of Pascal or the blonde woman. In fact, the street was empty. It crossed her mind to turn back but she knew the German was catching up on her. Instead, she chose to continue down the narrow street with its closed shutters and darkened doorways, hoping to find another café in which to take refuge. There weren't any. As she picked up her pace, so did the man. Worse still, he was gaining ground. The street curved sharply, narrowing and becoming darker and more sinister, and the man's footsteps grew closer, echoing on the cobblestones. Her mind raced. Should she run – not having the faintest idea where to and attracting attention – or should she stay and confront him. She chose the latter.

At a point where the door to an apartment block was set back in a darkened recess, Simone stood and waited. Moments later, the man reappeared.

Her heart beat wildly as he neared her. 'Mademoiselle, it's getting dark and you are far too lovely to be walking the streets alone.' He came closer and grabbed her wrist, pulling her towards him. 'What about a little kiss?'

'Not here,' replied Simone, in a whisper. 'We could be seen.' She stepped into the recess, pulling him into the shadows.

The man made lewd comments and lurched forward to kiss her.

His breath stank of beer and sausage, causing Simone to jerk her head back in disgust. He became aggressive. 'What's the matter, little French girl? Do you want to play games?'

With one hand, he roughly grabbed her chin and covered her lips with his mouth, slamming her body into the wall with such force that she momentarily felt light-headed, and with the other hand, he clawed at her breasts like a wild animal. As he kissed her, she looked into his cold brown eyes with horror realising he was going to rape her. All of a sudden his eyes widened, he loosened his grip, and jerked his head backwards. The lips that had only seconds before, repulsed her, tried to speak, but the words would not come. With his wide eyes still staring at her, he slowly slithered to the ground crumpling in a heap at her feet.

In his haste to take her, he was unaware of Simone's right hand reaching into her belt. In one swift move she had pulled out a concealed switchblade and thrust it into his throat. She stared at the bloodied knife in her hand and was so startled and frightened at what she'd done that it took her a few seconds to stop shaking. She folded the knife blade back into the handle, slipped it back into the concealed compartment in her belt and peered into the street to make sure no-one had seen her. It was empty but she heard a voice call out, 'Günter! Where are you?' The man's friend was looking for him.

Simone ran away as fast as she could and somehow managed to find herself back in the Square des Jacobins. Glancing back to check that she wasn't being followed, she hurriedly walked in the direction of the car, turned a corner and bumped into someone with such force, she almost fell over.

The man put his hand out to catch her and apologised. 'Well, well, if it isn't Mademoiselle Martine. You certainly are in a hurry.'

CHAPTER 12

To Simone's horror, she was face to face with Bruno Albrecht.

'Herr Albrecht, I'm so sorry. It was my fault. I wasn't looking where I was going.' She gave him one of her innocent looks. 'I was taking a walk and suddenly realised it was getting late. I must get back to Verzenay or Madame Marie will be worried about me.'

'Not before you join me for a drink.' Albrecht gave her one of charming smiles.

'But, sir, I'm afraid…'

'I won't take no for an answer. You can tell Madame Marie that it was me who was personally responsible for keeping you out late.'

Albrecht put a gentle hand on the small of her back and guided her back in the direction of the Square des Jacobins. Still traumatised after what had just taken place, she reasoned that it was better to go with him than make a scene.

'Just a quick drink, then I really must be on my way,' she replied.

There were several cafés in the square and Simone desperately hoped he would choose a different one to the one she'd sat in earlier. Unfortunately, he directed her straight to the same café. With a pounding heart, and fearful someone would recognise her, she suggested they sit inside where there was a radio playing popular French songs. Thankfully, the plainclothes Germans who'd been with the blonde woman had left, as had the second soldier, but the waiter recognised her. With a flourish, he flipped his white cloth over his left arm and with his right, pulled out a chair for her. Their eyes locked and in an instant, he understood she was not there of her own choosing.

He directed his attention to Albrecht. 'Good evening, sir. What can I get you?'

'A fine cognac for me, and Mademoiselle will have…'

'A glass of Champagne,' Simone replied, her cheeks reddening.

'Certainly.' He turned on his heels and walked to the bar to place their order. As he did, he looked back towards her and winked, as if to say, it was alright; he understood.

'What did you do to your hand?' Albrecht asked.

His words brought her crashing back down to earth. She had been so caught up in trying to get away, that she failed to notice there was blood on her hand. Immediately, she withdrew it and put it on her lap.

'Oh, that. It's nothing. I caught it on something earlier.'

'It doesn't seem like nothing to me. That's quite a bit of blood you've lost. I'm surprised you didn't notice. Let me take a look.'

Simone gave a nervous laugh and insisted she was fine. 'It looks worse than it is. If you'll excuse me, I'll just go to the Ladies Room and wash it.'

She hurried past the waiter, aware that his eyes were following her. Once there, she locked the door and leaned on the sink for a moment to catch her breath. In her haste to leave the scene of the crime, she'd put the knife away and not bothered to check if there was any blood on her hands. With a sickening feeling in the pit of her stomach, she washed the German's blood off her hand, took the knife out again and cleaned it, and checked her clothes for any spots of blood. When she'd finished, she realised there was no wound on her hand. How would she explain that to Albrecht?

'*Merde!*' she said to herself. There was only one thing to do. Using her knife, she bit her lip as she cut her hand to make a genuine wound some three inches long. The blood started to ooze, and it took several minutes for it to stop. She took her handkerchief from her bag, wrapped it around her hand, and headed back to the table.

'I'm sorry about that,' she replied. 'It happened this morning when we were loading wood for the car.'

Albrecht apologised for what had taken place in Verzenay the other evening. 'There's little I can do when there are Gestapo raids. It was unfortunate about the maid.'

'Unfortunate! It was a tragedy,' she said, her voice tinged with anger. 'The poor girl did nothing wrong.'

'You don't know that – or do you?'

She shook her head. 'You're right. I don't. It's just that she's such a sweet, timid girl and the whole affair has upset everyone, Madame Marie, in particular.'

'Martine. I am afraid that when it comes to the Gestapo, they are not to be taken lightly, and Herr Mueller in particular, is not someone to cross. He answers to Berlin and must produce results. Himmler himself demands it of him, and in turn, he demands it of his subordinates. When I discovered what was taking place, I did what I could because of her relationship with Madame Marie. I could do nothing for the boy. I am sorry.'

'Do you have any idea what will happen to Lucie?' Simone asked.

'All I know is that she's being held at Gestapo HQ here in Reims. I cannot say any more. Mueller keeps things close to his chest. He trusts no-one; not even me.' He changed the subject. 'Tell me about yourself. How are you finding your position with Madame Marie?'

This was something Simone had dreaded – questions. She had to think fast.

'There's not much to say. I've only been here a few days.'

'What were you doing in Paris?'

'I was a nurse there too.'

'Which hospital?'

Simone felt her throat go dry and took a sip of Champagne. 'At Lariboisière.'

'Do you live nearby?'

There was no doubt about him. He was smooth and charming, even with his questions. 'Not too far away - Clichy.'

'What made you leave?'

'I saw the advertisement in the newspaper and applied. I am sure you appreciate that Paris is a dangerous place at the moment. I needed a change.'

She could tell from his eyes that he was taking a strong interest in her and she had to play it cool.

'Is there a love interest?' Albrecht asked. As soon as he said it, the gentlemen in him realised it was an inappropriate question. 'I'm sorry. I didn't mean to pry. It's just that a pretty girl like you… Well, you know what I mean.'

'It's all right. There was someone, but he was sent to work in Germany. I have no idea where he is or even if he's alive.' It crossed her mind to ask if he could help locate him, but then she realised, she was there under an alias.

'Then perhaps you would do me the honour of allowing me to show you some of the sights of Reims. Do you like opera? I believe Wagner's *Die Meistersinger von Nürnberg* is being performed at the moment.'

The cut in Simone's hand was beginning to throb and spots of blood were seeping through the handkerchief, reminding her that she had just killed someone. 'That is most kind of you, Herr Albrecht, but…'

'Please, Martine. Call me Bruno.'

She shifted a little in her seat. 'Thank you – Bruno – but forgive me if I'm mistaken, isn't that a wedding ring you're wearing?'

He looked bemused. 'You are quite right. I have a wife who is very dear to me, and two children. That does not mean that I cannot escort you out for an evening – as a friend.'

Simone wanted to tell him they were anything but friends, but she held her tongue. At that moment, there was a commotion in the square. Cars appeared and the police started to block off the street. A voice called out over a loudspeaker for everyone to stay where they were.

'What's going on?' Albrecht said. He told her to wait while he stepped outside to confer with one of the policemen.

Simone watched through the window as he flashed his Identification. They entered into a short conversation as the man appeared to explain what was happening. The blood drained from her face and she felt a terrible sense of foreboding. The waiter came over and stood by her side to take a look. 'Trouble again,' he said. 'Probably some drunken German got killed.' She shot him a concerned look, which didn't go unnoticed.

Albrecht returned. 'Apparently there's been a murder. A German soldier was stabbed in a nearby street.' Simone clenched her fist causing the cut to bleed more and the waiter detected a look of panic on her face.

'I must get back,' she said to Albrecht. 'I've stayed far too long as it is.'

'I'm afraid the police want to question everyone first. It shouldn't take long.'

'My hand,' she exclaimed. 'The wound seems to have opened up again. Will you excuse me if I go and bathe it again. I won't be a minute.'

The waiter offered to bring them both another drink on the house, while they waited. When Albrecht wasn't looking, he followed Simone to the Ladies Room and knocked on the door.

'Mademoiselle, are you alright?'

His presence startled her. 'I'm fine, really I am. I have a minor cut that's all. Do you have a plaster?'

He told her to wait while he went to find one. When he returned to the bar, the police entered the premises and wasted no time asking about everyone's movements over the past hour. They informed the waiter that one of two men who had frequented his café was found dead. The waiter looked shocked.

'If I could help you, I would, but the last I saw of them, they were fine. They paid their bill and left. I don't know what else to tell you.'

The policeman noted the approximate time in his book, ignored Albrecht, and moved to question someone at an outside table.

The waiter found a plaster and returned to the bathroom. 'Mademoiselle, I have your plaster. I want to warn you that the police are here.'

Simone opened the door a little and peered out at him. 'Please; I can't go out there right this moment.' He handed her the plaster and nodded. 'Whatever it is that took place, I want you to know your secret is safe with me.'

She took the plaster and thanked him. 'Can you let me know when they've gone?'

She applied the plaster to the clean wound and took deep breaths to compose herself. Five minutes later, there was a knock on the door and the waiter told her the police had moved to the next café.

'Ah, there you are,' Albrecht said. 'I was beginning to worry about you.'

Simone apologised. 'I really must get going.' She looked out of the window. There were still lots of police around and now they were joined by the Milice. 'How long do you think they will keep us here? If it gets any later, I won't get back before curfew.'

Albrecht offered to escort her to the car. 'If you're with me, you'll be fine. Come on.'

On the way out, Simone thanked the waiter for the plaster. 'You were most kind. I appreciate it.'

He gave her a reassuring half-smile. 'I was only too happy to help, Mademoiselle.'

Outside, Albrecht flashed his Identity Card again and they were let through the barricade. 'Where is your car?' he asked.

'Not far – two streets away.' She told him he didn't have to escort her; that she would be fine, but he wouldn't hear of it.

'The streets are not safe at night,' he said. When they reached the car, Simone thanked him for the drink. 'And the Opera? Will you accompany me one evening?' His voice was as smooth as velvet. The perfect gentlemen.

'We'll see.'

He reached into his pocket and handed her a card. 'You can reach me on this number.'

As she drove away, she noticed he stood there watching her. Rounding the corner, she gave a friendly wave. He waved back.

Simone barely remembered the drive back to Verzenay. It was all a blur and by the time she arrived at the villa, she was in quite a bad state. The delayed reaction of what had taken place surfaced; her hands shook and she felt quite nauseous.

CHAPTER 13

Mme Legrand was extremely concerned when she saw the state Simone was in. 'What on earth's happened? You look terrible.' She saw her hand, the blood now leaking through the plaster, and quickly fetched a bowl of water and a towel.

'I killed someone, Madame Marie,' Simone blurted out. 'I killed a man – someone's son – someone's brother – someone's…'

'Pull yourself together and tell me what happened.'

Simone ripped the plaster off her hand and plunged it into the warm water. Mme Legrand gasped when she saw the cut. It was red and swollen. 'I was having a drink in a café in Reims and when I got up to leave, a German soldier followed me. I lured him into a doorway. He became violent and I knew he would rape me if I didn't…'

'Didn't what?' Mme Legrand said. 'Kill him?'

'I had no choice. It all happened so quickly.'

Mme Legrand sighed heavily. 'Oh, my dear girl, please stop torturing yourself.' She put an arm around her to comfort her. 'I hate to say it, but these days people are murdered all the time. Did you get that cut when you… killed him?'

Simone shook her head. 'There's more to this story. As I was heading back to the car, I bumped into Bruno Albrecht. He insisted I go for a drink with him. Unfortunately, he took me to the same café in the Square des Jacobins. The waiter recognized me, but I could see he was sympathetic to my situation.'

'This waiter, does he know what you've done?'

'No, but he saw the men in the café earlier. They bought me a drink. He must have seen one of them follow me and the other one follow his friend. I went to the Ladies Room when Albrecht noticed blood on my hand. In my haste to leave the scene of my – crime,' Simone could hardly believe she was using those words, 'I hadn't noticed. It was the German's blood. When I washed it off, I did this to myself – to make it look as if I had cut myself. I stayed in the Ladies Room until the police left. It's highly likely I would still be there if it hadn't been for Albrecht. Now I'm afraid there will be reprisals and I couldn't bear that.'

'We will have to wait and see. It certainly is the last thing we needed after what happened to Etienne and Lucie.'

Simone went to bed early that evening, but sleep did not come easily. When she closed her eyes, the swollen face of the man in Paris, together with the young German soldier in Reims, surfaced like a grotesque scene from a Gothic novel. Before she accepted this job, she had never killed anyone. In the space of a couple of weeks, she had now killed two. She had blood on her hands and it could never be washed away!

The next day, she found Pascal in the sitting room with Mme Legrand. The look on his face told her he knew what had taken place. Mme Legrand left the room to give them time to talk alone.

Pascal did not look at all pleased. 'Madame Marie told me what happened. The thing is, when I heard what took place, I knew it was you.'

Simone was still feeling light-headed from lack of sleep, but his sharp words brought her back to earth with a thud. 'How?'

'Do you think I didn't see you in the café? Of course I did. I saw everyone. It's my job. What's more, something inside me told me you'd follow me.'

'You've got it all wrong,' she said. 'I never meant to follow anyone. I was just relaxing.'

Pascal laughed. 'You saw the woman too, and decided to follow us. Isn't that true?'

'It wasn't intended to be as you seem to be portraying it. I didn't exactly spy on you, I was just curious, that's all. But you disappeared. I was going to turn back…'

'When the German started following you. Yes, I saw him. We were in an apartment on the first floor. I watched you both go down the street.'

Simone's eyes widened. 'You *what*? You *saw* me?'

'As soon as I realised he was following you, I knew there would be trouble, but you turned the corner out of sight. I was about to step outside to help you when his friend appeared. Five minutes later, there was a commotion. When I learned the man had been murdered – and more importantly how he'd been killed – I knew it was you. Only someone with knowledge of silent killing would do that.'

'I don't believe it! I could have died. The man was going to rape me and you didn't come to my aid?' Simone grew angry. 'I could have *died*,' she said again, this time emphasizing the word, died.

Pascal's eyes were like steel. 'But you didn't, did you? You rose to the occasion. I'm proud of you – even if you are a snoop.'

Simone was indignant, but he was right. She was a snoop and if she hadn't followed him, none of this would have happened.

'I suppose you want to know who the woman is?' Pascal said with a half-smile.

'Fifi?'

'That's right. She happens to live in that street. We were meeting up again because she had news for us. Lucie's name is on a list of people to be deported to Germany in three days' time.'

'How does she know?'

'She saw the list at their headquarters at 18, rue Jeanne d'Arc. That's what she wanted to tell me.'

'Is there any way we can save her?' Simone had been instrumental in rescuing people from the hands of the Gestapo in Paris, and she knew it didn't always work out as planned.

'There is a way. I'll discuss it later when we see the others.'

At that point Mme Legrand entered the room with a tray of coffee, rolls and conserves. 'I know you've got a lot to discuss, but you must both be starving. Please eat.'

The aroma of real coffee was a luxury Simone wasn't going to forego. As soon as she'd finished her breakfast, she excused herself and went to her room to change into something more suitable for another day at the farm. When she returned, Mme Legrand and Pascal were outside deep in conversation with Olivier. She went to join them. Their conversation stopped when they saw her.

'Come on,' Pascal said, cheerily. 'We'd better get a move on. Half the day's gone already.'

At the farm, Pascal wasted no time in gathering Alexandre and several other resistants to discuss an important mission which, he hastened to say, would involve quite a few of his men.

'It's about the girl who was taken away after her boyfriend was shot – Lucie Mouran, Madame Legrand's maid,' he said. 'I've just learned that her name is on a deportation list. She's being sent to Ravensbrück and the train leaves in three days' time.'

The men looked at each other. 'What has this got to do with us?' one of them said.

'I want to get her off that train.'

Alexandre lit up a cigarette and took a deep breath. 'You mean you want us to help you rescue her? Are you willing to risk the lives of our men at this very moment when the Allied invasion might take place any day now and we are needed for other work?'

The men agreed with him. They argued that while they sympathised, she was not a member of the Resistance and they thought the risk was too great. Pascal was quick to point out that whilst she wasn't actually involved in resistance work, she *was* aware that Claude and Marie Legrand were, not to mention himself, Baptiste, and now Martine, and she also knew about the secret tunnel in the sheds, even though she'd never been in them.

'She could easily have saved herself by collaborating and turning us in,' Pascal said. He paused while they considered his words. 'So, what is to be? Will we leave her to die a miserable death in a notorious German concentration camp – or will we act like decent men...' He glanced at Simone, 'and women.'

His speech had the desired effect and the men agreed. 'What do you have in mind?' Alexandre asked.

'I have it on good authority that Lucie, along with several other prisoners, will not leave by train from Reims direct to Germany. Instead, they are being transported by truck to a small town halfway between here and Metz where the Germans are collecting prisoners destined for Germany. From there they'll be put on the train bound for Germany. It's all part of the deception plan to fool the population about what is taking place.'

'If the girl is among this crowd, how will you locate her? Or are you intending to save more prisoners?' Alexandre looked at the faces of his men and could see they were worried too. Their immediate thought was that with so many prisoners, there was bound to be a large group of German soldiers on watch.

Pascal agreed. 'It's the only thing we can do. We cannot rescue her in Reims as the outcome would not be in our favour. Neither can we leave it until later. No, this is the best option.'

'What is the plan?' Alexandre asked.

Pascal put a map out on the table and showed him. 'As you see, the station itself is small. There are coupling yards and several sheds. The other prisoners will be held in those sheds until the train arrives. I will be in touch with our men who are working for the railroads. We need their help for this. The people involved will be shown a picture of Lucie and make sure she's put onto the last carriage. That is the one we will target. When the train moves out of the station that's when we act. I cannot say any more at the moment.' He paused to light a cigarette and answer a barrage of questions.

After a lengthy discussion, it was agreed the plan would go ahead. Alexandre would draw up a list of experienced maquisards he wanted with him, and Pascal would give him more details sometime before the rescue was to take place. The meeting concluded and the men returned to their exercises, while Simone checked on Jean-Yves' leg.

'It's much better,' he said to her. 'Hardly any pain today. Under your care, I'll be back playing football in no time at all.'

Pascal was pleased with his progress and asked him to send another message to London. He handed him a list of things he needed. 'Can't be long now, my friend, and we must be ready.'

Later that evening, Olivier and Mme Legrand told Simone that Pascal had requested they show her the secret tunnel, just in case anything "unforeseen" happened when they rescued Lucie. Their words worried her. It meant the rescue mission was going to be far more dangerous than he let on. She followed them down the garden path to the wine shed, where Olivier deftly moved away the statue of the Virgin, exposing the stone steps of the hide-out. Using his torch to guide them, he asked her to follow him. Mme Legrand chose to stay behind with Ulysse and keep a lookout.

Descending the steps, the air became noticeably cold and damp and the smell of earth filled her nostrils. The tunnel narrowed for a few metres before opening up into an underground chamber stacked with wine casks containing weapons and ammunition for the Resistance.

'It's for use when the Allies land,' Olivier told her.

'Let's hope a bomb doesn't drop on us,' she replied. 'There's enough here to blow up the whole village.'

'Pascal wanted you to know what was here. He expressly said that should anything happen to him, you were to see that they were distributed to Alexandre's maquisards.' They walked on further and entered another small room with several mattresses, blankets, and cooking implements. 'I've lost count of the people we've hidden here,' Olivier said. 'Allied airmen and refugees from Occupied Europe; in fact, Pascal himself stayed here for a while before he was taken to Paris. I believe that's when you first met.'

Simone told him she never got to know how he came to be in Paris. He never volunteered to tell her. After the room, the tunnel narrowed again, until eventually they came out inside an old, vaulted tomb in the village churchyard. It was a morbid place that sent shivers down her spine. A large statue of an angel stood against the back wall of the tomb, its wings open and its eyes looking down mournfully at two stone sarcophagi. Olivier pushed open the iron gate and they exited into the churchyard. Simone felt relieved; it was as if she'd exited from the bowels of the earth. She sucked in the fresh night air to rid herself of the unpleasant, musty smell that clung to her like a shroud.

'The priest – does he know about this?' Simone asked.

'Of course Father Thomas knows,' Olivier replied. 'It was his idea to use this tomb as an exit. There are no longer any members of the deceased's family living here, so no-one to offend.'

CHAPTER 14

PASCAL HAD ONE more meeting with his closest friends before asking them to make their own way to the small town where the rescue of Lucie Mouran was to take place. The train was due to depart just after midnight. This was a blessing, as it gave the men more time to move about in the darkness.

Simone was advised not to take Mme Legrand's car. Instead, she was to cycle to a hamlet ten kilometres away where she would meet up with Baptiste and Alexandre. From there, the three drove in Baptiste's car to a wooded spot three kilometres away from the railway station where they were to join other maquisards. Alexandre distributed extra weapons and ammunition to his men before they moved on. Simone was given a Liberator pistol and a sniper's rifle with two loaded magazines.

'You're not seriously asking me to use this,' she said to Alexandre. 'My first time in the field.'

'You've passed your test with flying colours, Martine. That doesn't mean you get a medal – you just get to use it instead.' He thrust the rifle towards her. 'Now let's get going.'

With barely any moonlight and no path to guide them, they clambered through the woods trying their best not to get their clothes snagged in bushes or low-hanging branches. They didn't have far to go, but with Alexandre forbidding the use of a flashlight, the walk took twice as long as expected. Eventually, they reached the brow of a small hill. Alexandre gestured for them to keep still while he went ahead to survey the area. He returned ten minutes later to report that the railway station was at the bottom of the hill and from what he could see, the surrounding area looked quiet.

He directed them to a certain point and gave them their orders. 'Martine, I want you to stay here – behind this log. Focus your rifle on the railway station itself. It's less than 300 metres which means any shot you fire has more chance of a hit. She took the rifle off her back, lay down in the soft earth, loaded the magazine and steadied the barrel on the moss-covered log. When she looked through the sight, she had great difficulty seeing anything at all.

'Don't worry,' Alexandre said. 'Your eyes will soon become accustomed to it.'

Baptiste was directed to another spot several metres away and told to do the same thing. 'Now, here's what will happen. As soon as the prisoners arrive, they will join the others in the holding yard. The train should arrive shortly after. At that point the floodlights will go on and the prisoners will board the train. The railway workers working with us have been shown a photograph of Lucie and will make sure she is on the last carriage.' Alexandre stopped for a moment to prepare his own pistol and Sten gun. 'Under no circumstances are you to do anything until the train begins to move out of the station and you hear an explosion.'

This was a rescue operation unlike any Simone had taken part in before. 'What explosion?' she asked, growing more nervous by the minute.

'About 500 metres from the station, the rail tracks curve.' He pointed to their right. 'Just over there. That's where Pascal intends to blow up a section of the railway – just before the train gets there. It will alert the guards. That's when I and some of my men will make our way towards the last carriage. You two are to cover us. The lights will still be on so you shouldn't have any difficulty spotting us.' He checked the time. 'I have to go now. I know I can trust you both. The only thing you have to worry about is that you don't shoot the wrong people.'

With those last words still ringing in her ears, Simone watched him disappear down the hillside and out of sight. Hiding behind the log, she glanced towards Baptiste, and even though she couldn't see him, his closeness was reassuring. She levelled her rifle, looked through the sight and settled down to watch the station. The time ticked by. Ten minutes, fifteen, thirty, and still nothing happened. She began to wonder if something had gone wrong. At one point, a railway worker stepped outside the building for a cigarette, momentarily lighting up the platform.

'That's our signal,' she heard Baptiste say in a low voice. 'Something is about to happen.'

Simone was relieved. She was beginning to get cramp. Minutes later, a light went on and three tarpaulin-covered trucks drove up outside the station. German soldiers, accompanied by dogs, ordered their prisoners to get out and directed them to the platform. Simone tried to count how many there were – probably twenty. It was hard to tell. They waited in line for some fifteen minutes until eventually the sound of a locomotive in the distance told them the train was here. Adrenaline raced through Simone's body and all her senses tensed, resembling a predator searching for its prey. Alexandre's words during her training flooded her mind. *The first rule of a sniper, never shoot at a target you haven't identified. Shoot only once, then become invisible or immediately move away.* And most of all, *compassion for your enemy is suicide.*

She heard Baptiste ask if she was alright. 'Keep your nerve, Martine and you'll be fine.' She counted eight railway workers, all moving about amongst the Germans. All of a sudden, she saw another group of people heading across the railway tracks from a shed in a siding: the other prisoners. They were in the shadows and it made them hard to count, but she estimated about another thirty at least. There were also several children. Within minutes, the Germans started to direct the prisoners onto the train. The railway workers helped, and for a minute, Simone wondered if they weren't working for the Germans. In the seething mass of pushing and shoving, she spotted Lucie. She was wearing a light brown coat and was being escorted onto the last carriage along with a few other women.

It took less than ten minutes to transfer the prisoners to the train. A whistle sounded and the locomotive started to chug out of the station towards Metz. Peering through her lens, she prepared to take aim. The train had just started to round the bend when there was a loud explosion. Floodlights lit up the area and from her hiding place Simone saw the locomotive veer off the tracks and topple on its side, pulling the second carriage with it.

All hell broke loose and the Germans started running towards the front of the train where a gun battle immediately began to take place. At the same time, Alexandre and his men ran towards the last carriage and opened the doors while a railway guard rushed to their aid pointing to the section of the carriage where Lucie was. The sound of machinegun fire from the front section of the train told Simone this was not going as well as they'd imagined. With the Germans occupied at the front of the train, the prisoners in the last carriage took the opportunity to jump off and run into the woods. Shots rang out, this time closer, and more German soldiers now appeared coming from the holding yard and spotted the prisoners escaping. In the midst of this mayhem, the railway guard found Lucie and pushed her off the train into the arms of one of the maquisards. A shot rang out and the guard fell to the ground. Through her telescopic sight, Simone saw a German guard on top of the railway carriage aiming at the people below and she pulled the trigger. The man rolled off the roof, landing at the feet of prisoners scrambling away. The Germans arrived and she noticed one aim his gun at Alexandre who was directing the prisoners towards the woods and at the same time firing back at the Germans. Alexandre was a good shot, but the Germans were arriving thick and fast.

'Oh, God, Alexandre!' she mumbled to herself. 'Get out of there.'

Almost immediately, she noticed another German take aim towards him and fire. The bullet missed. Simone levelled her rifle at him and shot him before he had time to fire again. He too, crumpled to the ground. Within minutes, the Maquis melted away into the woods and fields, taking as many of the prisoners with them as they could. The Germans were in hot pursuit, some of them heading her way. Others stopped to round up the less fortunate prisoners unable to make a getaway.

Baptiste called out. 'Okay, Martine, this is it. Empty your magazine while you can.'

As soon as more shots were fired, the Germans realised where they were and fired back. 'Come on, let's get out of here,' Baptiste shouted. 'We've been spotted.'

Simone rolled away from her hiding place and got up to run away just as a hail of bullets from a volley of automatic-weapons fire whistled past her. She ran in the direction she had come from, crashing through bushes and cutting herself in an effort to get away. The sound of barking dogs grew nearer and she feared they'd catch up with her before she could get away. At one point she lost Baptiste and wondered if she was going the right way. Gradually the sound of the Germans and their dogs faded and she realised they must have gone in a different direction. She soon caught up with Baptiste, and together they raced the last fifty metres to the car and drove back to the hamlet. Hearts pounding, they were both so filled with adrenaline that neither spoke until they got there. The houses were in darkness. Baptiste swerved into the yard and parked the car behind a cowshed. The owner came running towards them from the house.

'It's us – Baptiste and Martine,' he said. 'Anyone else back yet?'

The man shook his head. 'Not yet.' He directed them to a hiding place in a loft and told them to stay there for a while.

Throughout the early morning, several maquisards filtered back to the farm and each one faced a barrage of questions: Were you injured? Was anyone killed? Most of all, they wanted to know if the mission had been a success. Had Lucie, Alexandre and Pascal made it? It was a long night.

Sometime before dawn, Alexandre arrived. Simone was so relieved she wanted to throw her arms around him. He told them that not only had they rescued Lucie, but eight other prisoners including two children. All were being transferred to another Maquis group where they would spend the rest of the war in hiding. He was sorry they weren't able to rescue more and hoped some had made their own getaway.

'And Pascal?' Simone asked.

Alexandre looked at her, his eyes filled with sadness. He shook his head. She let out a gasp and covered her mouth with her hand. 'Oh, God! No.'

Everyone looked upset and no words could ease their pain. Simone slumped down on a wooden crate and covered her face with her hands. 'What happened?'

Alexandre put a comforting hand on her shoulder. 'After the locomotive derailed, there were German soldiers in the first carriage and they immediately started firing. Our men put up a good fight before getting away, but Pascal was shot while attempting to help a maquisard who'd been hit in the leg.'

'Was he killed instantly?' Baptiste asked.

'No. He was badly injured and couldn't get up. Rather than face the wrath of the Germans, he shot himself. The Germans shot our other man in cold blood. A couple of our men who'd been with him witnessed it. They fired at the Germans but were outnumbered and had to make a getaway or risk being killed themselves.'

The room went quiet and Simone felt the blood drain from her face. 'It was as if he had a premonition,' she whispered.

'Pascal was not the superstitious type,' Baptiste said. 'I've known him for a long time.'

'Well something made him make a strange comment to Olivier.'

Alexandre asked what it was, but with others there, she decided not to tell him about the cellar. The group spent the next few hours in hiding until eventually, everyone went their separate ways. At that point, it was still unclear how many maquisards had got away unscathed. It was to be several days before the full cost of the rescue operation was known.

Simone cycled back to Verzenay in the afternoon. She was stopped twice at checkpoints but managed to continue unhindered. When she arrived at the Legrand house, the pent-up emotions erupted and in an outpouring of grief, she burst into tears in Mme Legrand's arms. The news of Pascal's death plunged them both into despair. He had been tireless in his effort to help the Resistance, and now he was gone – trying to do what he always did, help others. For two days, Simone sat on the terrace staring out towards the garden. Pascal was the reason she was here and now she had no reason to stay. She told Mme Legrand she would be returning to Paris at the end of the week. Unbeknown to her, Mme Legrand made a call to Claude and begged him to intercede.

Claude came to the house to speak with her. While he sympathized with her loss, his tone was tough. 'Think what you're doing, Martine. We've all been affected by Pascal's death, but that doesn't mean we give up.'

'I'm not giving up. I'm just going back to Paris.' She looked at him with her large dark eyes, wet with tears. 'You have all been so kind, but I am not needed here anymore. You can manage without me.'

'Martine, snap out of this pitiful state. It's unbecoming. Is this what Pascal would have wanted? Is it what Jacques would want? No. You *are* needed here. The Allies will land at any moment now – maybe in less than a week and we still have much to do.'

'You don't know that,' she replied miserably. 'They've been saying that for months. Anyway, I don't even know why Pascal brought me here in the first place. It's better if I go back to Paris.'

Claude was becoming impatient. 'None of us has a clear role. We are just trying to survive until the time is right and we can act to rid France of this oppression – all of us – together. Remember de Gaulle's words – *Whatever happens, the flame of French resistance must not and shall not die.* So please snap out of it and stop this self-pity. Pascal wanted you to train with the maquisards to help them. Have you forgotten it was you who fired the shot that saved Alexandre's life?'

'Who told you that?'

'Baptiste. He told us how accurate your shots were. Your part in the escape saved lives – maybe not Pascal's, but others. And Lucie is free.'

Simone thought about Alexandre's words when he questioned if the escape was a wise move. 'Was it worth it to save the life of one young woman when other lives were lost?' she asked.

'That is what we do. We try our best to save people being incarcerated by the Germans. Unfortunately, it doesn't always work out the way we planned. Pascal was right, Lucie was not an active member of the Resistance, but she did not give anyone away. That alone meant we had an obligation to her.' He paused to let his words sink in. 'Look, Martine, this is not the first time we've lost good men and it won't be the last, but I can tell you one thing, Alexandre needs you. The Maquis need you.'

Mme Legrand looked on while her son pleaded his case. 'I believe Pascal asked you to distribute the weapons to the Maquis, is that right?' Simone nodded. 'He did that because he trusted you.' He sat back in the chair and patiently waited for a response.

'Alright, you win,' she said after a while.

Claude looked pleased with himself. 'Now that answer was worth fighting for. Can I tell Alexandre he can expect you back at the farm?'

'You have my word.'

Mme Legrand smiled. 'And now, I think we all deserve to open a bottle of grand cru, don't you.' She pulled out one of their old vintages, one that had been hidden away from the Germans, and raised a toast. 'To Pascal.'

Claude and Simone raised their glasses towards her. 'To Pascal,' they said in unison.

CHAPTER 15

SIMONE APPROACHED THE farmhouse to find it unusually quiet except for one maquisard keeping watch.

'Where is everyone?' she asked.

'They're inside. No-one is in the mood for work today.'

She pushed open the farm door to find the men gathered around the table finishing off the whisky SOE had sent over.

'Well, if it isn't our little Parisian girl,' one of them said, slurring his words. 'Come and have a drink with us.' He roughly pushed another maquisard off a wooden crate which passed for a makeshift chair. 'Give the little lady a seat,' He waved her over.

One glance at the almost empty bottles, told her they'd drunk far too much.

'Where's Alexandre?' she asked.

A man indicated towards the back door. 'He's outside – told us he needed to clear his head and think straight.'

She headed outside where she found him sitting in the grass with Jean-Yves.

'I wondered when you'd be back,' Alexandre said, his voice tinged with sarcasm. 'We thought you might have deserted us and gone back to Paris.'

Jean-Yves tried to break the tension. 'Martine, you'll be happy to know that there's an unusually large amount of traffic on the airwaves. The BBC is broadcasting almost twice as many coded messages as normal. That's a good sign something's about to happen.' Simone asked if he'd informed London of Pascal's death. 'I did, and I also took the liberty to tell them you were staying and carrying on Pascal's work with the Maquis. They were pleased. Buckmaster and Vera said, "hope to meet you one day when this dreadful war is over" – their exact words.'

Alexandre updated her on the rescue operation. Although most prisoners had been rounded up, others had managed to successfully flee the area and made it to safety. They were now under the protection of the Maquis. The bad news was that five other maquisards had been killed during the rescue attempt, including the one Pascal attempted to save. From what they could ascertain from the railway guards, at least thirty-five Germans died. They were surprised there had been no reprisals.

Simone discussed the weapons Pascal had hidden in the Legrand cellars and told him he had expressly asked her to make sure they were distributed to the Maquis for when the Allies attacked. Alexandre felt now was the time to do it. The problem was how to get them from the cellar to the farmhouse. It wouldn't be easy. He wanted to call a meeting with his most trusted men first.

'There's one other thing, I wanted to ask you,' Simone said. 'It's about Fifi. What do you know about her?'

'I only know that she works as a secretary for the Gestapo and occasionally passes on information,' Alexandre replied. 'Why do you ask?'

'Do you trust her?

Alexandre looked surprised. 'What's going through that pretty head of yours?'

'I find it odd that there was no mention of the Germans already on the train. Surely she must have known. Was it a trap? And then there's Sylvie. How come she was picked up and sent to Paris when others were set free?'

'Pascal trusted her.' He narrowed his eyes. 'And so does Claude for that matter. He knows her too. In fact, it was he who brought her to Pascal's attention.'

Simone thought about it. That made sense. Claude had connections to Bruno Albrecht and the Gestapo. 'I wonder if she's heard about Pascal's death?'

'His body was taken to Gestapo HQ so it's highly likely she would know. Pascal told me what happened the other evening in Reims. He admired your quick thinking, but he wasn't very happy you followed him. The situation could have had dire consequences for us.' He could tell it still bothered her and warned her not to put them all at risk by doing something stupid.

Alexandre allowed his men a couple of days to mourn the loss of Pascal and their other comrades and then it was back to business. Jean-Yves received messages from London about two more airdrops in the following week and a plan was put into effect to transfer the weapons in the Legrand cellar to the Maquis. It was a test of their unity that Pascal had worked so hard to implement.

Simone was astonished at the way everyone came out to help. Even Sonia arrived from as far away as Charmont-sous-Barbuise. She conveyed condolences from the Troyes Resistance at the loss of Pascal and the other maquisards, saying how much he would be missed. He was much loved and respected.

Over the next few days, under the pretence of afternoon get-togethers, Mme Legrand invited her trusted women friends into her home during the day, where they would partake in *petit fours, biscuits roses de Reims,* and Champagne, and, aided by Simone and Olivier, disguised and concealed small arms and equipment for them to carry away to the Maquis. Objects were hidden in cakes and loaves of bread, in biscuit tins, and secreted away in the ladies' baskets, and about their person, in the most ingenious ways. Several demure, middle-aged ladies even wrapped knives, switches and fuses, and other small items in a cloth and hid them in their French rolls, while others concealed them on their person, stitching pockets onto their underwear or creating false hems in their clothes.

Along with agricultural carts used for transporting everything from hay, vines, and logs, which were frequently stopped and searched, larger items were also hidden in bundles of faggots and carried away by both men and women on their backs. This type of concealment was ideal for those riding bicycles or walking through the fields and vineyards. During the early hours of the morning, Alexandre ventured into the village with some of his men. Rather than bother Mme Legrand, Olivier and the village priest, Father Thomas, met them in the churchyard where Father Thomas would keep watch while Olivier disappeared into the tunnel with the men. There, Simone handed out more weapons, carefully making a note of everything that went out and who took it. It was imperative that everything was accounted for, down to the last wire-cutter and grenade.

There were also days when, under the guise of taking Mme Legrand to see the doctor, she and Simone would hide Lee Enfield rifles and Sten guns in a hidden compartment under the seat of the car, and drive to the farm themselves. On those particular days, it was noticeable that the maquisards were on their best behaviour in front of Mme Legrand. She would always leave a few bottles of Champagne for them too, for which they were always grateful. One of the maquisards, Enrique, even went as far as presenting Mme Legrand with a large bunch of wildflowers which she put in a Meissen vase in her drawing room, saying that such a gift by such brave men had more worth than a pearl necklace.

Within less than a week, the Legrand cellars had been emptied, London had sent out more parachute drops, and the Maquis' stock of weapons had multiplied. They were extremely happy. Simone continued with her training at the farm, and where once the use of explosives would have scared her, she soon found that she was as efficient in saboteur work as she was a good shot.

When things had settled down, Simone took another trip to Reims on the pretext of obtaining medicine for Mme Legrand. It was late afternoon and she decided to take a stroll past the café in the Square des Jacobins, where she'd had a drink on the fateful night she'd killed the German soldier. She purposely walked by on the opposite side of the road just in case anyone recognised her, but was pleased to find there was hardly anyone there. She'd almost passed by when she glimpsed the waiter through the open door wiping glasses at the bar. At that moment, he happened to look up and a flash of recognition crossed his face. She picked up her step. Seconds later, she heard him call her.

'Mademoiselle!' She turned around and he waved to her. 'Mademoiselle, wait.' He ran after her and caught her arm. 'Please. I mean you no harm.'

'Let me go.' Simone shook herself free. 'Or I will call the police.'

The waiter smiled. 'I don't think you will do that, especially after what happened.'

Simone's face reddened. 'I have no idea what you're talking about.'

'I can assure you, I'm a friend.' When she didn't reply, he told her he was just about to finish his shift and invited her to have a drink at another café.

There was something about him that made Simone think he was genuine and she accepted. 'All right, but if you're not back in three minutes, I will leave.' She waited anxiously while hoping he wouldn't alert the police.

Within minutes, he was back. 'There's a little place a few streets away from here,' he said. 'It's run by a good friend. It's safe to talk there.'

Simone gave him a sharp look. 'Talk about what?'

He ignored her. The café was tiny; two small rooms with rudimentary wooden tables and chairs, the walls covered in aged posters of French singers and actresses. Two elderly men sat in one room playing cards at a table by the window. The man acknowledged the elderly man behind the bar and asked him to bring them two beers.

'We'll sit in the back room. No one will see us there.'

The owner promptly brought the drinks and left them alone.

'What's all this about?' Simone asked.

'The night you were here, I knew it was you who killed that German soldier. It didn't take much to put two and two together. I watched you cross the road and saw the first German follow you. The two of them were always flirting with young women. The more they drank, the more their behaviour became threatening.' Simone wondered where all this was leading.

'Of course, at the time, I didn't fully know what had taken place, only that there had been a murder and the second soldier told the police it was his comrade. Your behaviour was also telling. You were agitated and seemed to want to get away – even from the man you were with when you came back to the café. And then there was the blood on your hand.' He took out a packet of cigarettes from his jacket pocket and offered her one. 'I just knew you had something to do with it.'

It worried her that she had appeared nervous in front of him that night. What if Albrecht had noticed that too? She needed to be more careful and hide her emotions better.

'I want you to know that I am a friend. I don't know you, but I hate the Germans as much as you appear to.' He introduced himself as Serge.

'Martine,' Simone replied. She digested his words carefully. He could have alerted the police or the Gestapo, but chose not to, so maybe he was what he said. 'Why are you doing this?' she asked.

'I don't really know. I suppose I took a liking to you – plus the fact that I hate the Nazis.'

Simone seized this chance to ask a few more questions.

'Tell me,' she said, taking a long draw on her cigarette. 'Do you happen to know the blonde lady who was sitting with the group of Germans that evening?'

'All I know is that she works for them. Many think her a collaborator.'

'Why's that; just because she works for them?'

Serge lifted his shoulders in a nonchalant shrug. 'Maybe.'

'Do you know her name?'

'I believe its Ella. At least that's what I heard them her. Why do you ask?'

Simone realised that like herself, Fifi must be a code name and Ella might be her real name, but then some people had several code-names. Perhaps she would never know.

'It's just that I thought I recognized her from somewhere; an old school friend, but as she was with the Germans, I didn't want to ask.' She hated lying to him.

'As I said, I don't know much about her, but I do know where she lives.'

Simone pricked her ears. This was exactly what she wanted to know. 'Where is that?'

'It's in the street opposite the café – Rue Saint Julien – the street where the German was killed. I can't recall the number, but I can show you if you like.'

Not wanting to seem overly anxious, she suggested they have another drink first. Serge proved to be a very kind, somewhat reserved man who told her of his plans to travel overseas when the war ended. She told him she wanted to study and become a teacher. It was all pleasant small talk – a façade – and she felt a twinge of sadness that life had become so complicated that she must constantly live a lie. It dawned on her that for the past four years that was all she'd done. They finished their drink and left.

Turning into the street where the German had followed her, Simone felt a cold chill run down her spine. She recalled the man's eyes staring at her as he slid to the ground. It was like a reoccurring nightmare. Serge stopped outside the doorway of a three-storied, cream-coloured building. 'This is where she lives; in one of these apartments, but I can't tell you which one.' Simone checked the names on the wall, but without knowing Fifi's surname, she was stumped. 'What was your friend's name?' Serge asked.

Simone carried on with the lie. 'I think it was Trochon – yes that's right,' she replied and looked at the names again. 'There's no Trochon here so perhaps I made a mistake and it wasn't her at all.'

'Is there an E for Ella?' Serge asked.

'No. Only surnames.' She looked at her watch and rather than risk more awkward questions, thanked him for his concern about her welfare, and said she really had to be getting along. Thankfully, he never asked where she lived. He told her he hoped to see her in the café again and that next time the drink was on him.

During the drive back to Verzenay, Simone thought about Serge. She considered herself a good judge of character and liked him. She'd make a few enquiries with Mme Legrand, who seemed to know most people in Reims. Then there was Fifi, or Ella, as Serge thought she was called. She had so much to think about with the Maquis and the last thing she needed was something else to occupy her mind. Yet the woman intrigued her. She was becoming obsessed. Pascal wouldn't have liked it, and neither would Alexandre for that matter. She resolved to go back again and try and find her.

If Simone had any thoughts about a little chat with Mme Legrand about Serge that evening, she was mistaken. There was a heavy bombing raid that night. Three waves of B-17s targeted the railway station in Reims and quite a few surrounding neighbourhoods were hit. Mme Legrand was anxiously waiting for her with Baptiste and Olivier.

'Thank goodness you're safe,' she said. 'We need your help.'

It turned out that a British bomber had been shot down in the suburbs of Épernay, and out of a crew of nine, five surviving airmen had bailed out, landing in the grounds of a large vineyard in the area. The owners were friends of the Legrand Family and sympathetic to the Resistance. Knowing the Germans would conduct a thorough search the property, the Resistance was contacted and the men were transferred to the hideout in the cellars where they would be well cared for until they could be transferred to an escape line. Olivier had found them civilian clothes, but two of them were suffering from fractures and cuts.

Olivier took her into the tunnel to tend to their wounds while Mme Legrand prepared the men a pot of stew. The small room in the hideout was barely big enough to accommodate a handful of people, but despite their injuries and bad luck at being shot down, the men were in good spirits. Simone tended their wounds and dispensed painkillers, while one of the men told her in broken French, that the RAF had bombed major installations and cities in Germany, making it impossible for Hitler to carry on much longer.

During the last few months, Simone has been heartened by wave after wave of bombers heading towards Germany, and although not religious, prayed they would return safely. During her time with the Resistance she'd lost count of the downed airmen she'd helped. German and Vichy propaganda would never tell them the full truth of the devastation they caused, but she knew from other sources that it was bad. A war was being fought and there was little to be gained lamenting the deaths of innocent Germans too. By the time she'd finished attending the men's wounds, Mme Legrand arrived with steaming hot food and two bottles of fine Champagne. They couldn't believe their luck.

Early the next morning, Simone checked on them before leaving for the farm. They were all fast asleep on their mattresses. Mme Legrand left a tray of bread, boiled eggs, and dried sausage on the floor for them, and the two women retreated quietly. Heading back through the garden, Simone brought up the subject of Serge. Thankfully, Mme Legrand put Simone's mind at rest. She knew his family and said the café had been used as a letter-drop on several occasions. When asked why Serge was not more forthcoming, she laughed, saying he was probably as wary of her as she was of him. Besides, for all he knew, she could be a German spy. Simone agreed but was appalled that her fellow Frenchmen might view her in that light.

CHAPTER 16

June 2, 1944

DURING A LONGER than usual meeting with Alexandre and a group of his men, he told them it was estimated that almost sixty people had been killed in the Allied bombing that night. He also informed them that the night before, *Radio Londres* had signalled the opening lines of the 1866 Verlain poem, "Chansons d'Autumne" – Long sobs of autumn violins. This was the signal that the invasion was due to start in a few days and all sabotage plans were to be in place ready to be carried out as soon as the order came through. Alexandre requested that Simone be with him during these operations.

'I need everyone,' he said. 'This is the time to put your training into action again.' After what she'd gone through during the last few weeks, she readily agreed. 'You can leave earlier today,' he added. 'No exercises. I have some urgent tasks for you. I want you to drop off two pistols to a house in Reims. After that, you are to leave a coded message somewhere else. The message will be in a rolled-up newspaper.'

Simone immediately thought of Pascal and the newspaper he'd dropped into the bin; seemingly a signal to Fifi to follow him. These tasks suited her perfectly as it gave her a chance to check out Fifi's apartment again.

She arrived in Reims around lunchtime, completed her tasks for Alexandre without incident and then headed to Rue Saint Julien. The problem was, there was nowhere to sit and watch the apartment block without attracting attention so she decided to walk up and down the street in an effort to look less conspicuous. About ten minutes later, her

123

luck changed. She was close to the building as a man entered, leaving the door ajar. Without even as much as a second thought, she slipped inside and found herself in a hallway with a staircase and an elevator. The man was nowhere in sight but she could hear his footsteps as he walked up the stairs. A few seconds later, the footsteps stopped and she heard the sound of a door close.

Looking around, Simone noticed a small table with a few letters on it. She quickly scanned through them looking for anything that could point to Fifi. Only one had an E – E. Rozier. *Did E. stand for Ella?* The woman lived in apartment 3. Looking around, there were two on the ground floor so she deduced apartment 3 must be on the first floor. Whoever it was must still be out, otherwise she would have picked up her post. If she was going to act, she had to do it now. She silently mounted the stairs. There were another two apartments on the first floor. Outside number 3 was a doorbell over which was the name E. Rozier. Simone knocked softly. There was no answer. Remembering the times she had been in this situation in Paris, she took out a hairpin from her bag, picked the lock as soundlessly as possible, and pushed the door open.

The shutters were closed, but streaks of afternoon sunshine through the slats were enough to lighten the room and allow her to see. The room was luxuriously decorated with silken drapes and fine paintings. A tiger skin covered the floor in front of an ornate fireplace. On the mantelpiece were framed photographs and porcelain ornaments. The largest of the photographs contained a picture of Fifi. Serge was right: her name must be Ella and this was her apartment.

What Simone had expected to find, she wasn't sure, but she started to look around. The items in her wardrobe revealed her taste for beautiful clothes – labels by famous Parisian couturiers, a fur coat, silk underwear. All expensive clothes for a secretary. An array of books by renowned literary authors in French, German, and English in her bookshelf told her that Ella was also a linguist and well-educated. One of them – the Brothers Karamazov, was lying on a small coffee table next to a lamp in the art nouveau style. Simone picked it up and flicked through the pages. Inside was a short love-letter.

My dearest darling,
There is a pain in my heart which I cannot quiet. Something tells
me that after tonight, our paths will not cross again. If that is so, I
urge you to take care.
I will always love you.
Forever yours,
P.

Simone was intrigued. Was "P" Pascal? Did he suspect something was amiss? If so, why didn't he abort the raid at the railway station? Next to the book was what appeared to be a small jewellery box. She opened it and was astonished to find a loaded pistol, which she immediately pocketed.

All of a sudden she heard the sound of footsteps coming up the stairs. In a panic, she thrust the letter into her pocket. Faced with confronting Fifi – if indeed it was her – or remaining hidden, she chose the latter and squeezed herself into a gap between the heavy drapes and the shuttered bedroom window. There she waited, the gun cocked and ready to fire.

The door opened and closed, and from the sound of the footsteps on the wooden floor in the living room, she could tell it was a woman. The radio was switched on and she heard the beautiful voice of Lucienne Boyer singing *Parlez-Moi d'Amour*. The woman starting humming to the music. Simone's heart thudded loudly in her chest as she listened to her move around the apartment, half expecting her to walk into the bedroom and open the shutters at any moment.

Several minutes passed and Simone heard two cars pull up in front of the apartment. Peering through the slats, she saw four men get out. The doorbell rang. The woman asked who it was through the intercom.

A man's voice replied. 'Fräulein Rozier, we would like a word with you.'

Simone heard the outside door open and while the men hurried up the stairs, she could hear the woman running around the apartment opening and shutting drawers. '*Merde*,' she muttered to herself. 'Where did I put my pistol?'

The men entered the apartment and in a stern voice, addressed her in German, 'You are under arrest. Please accompany us to Gestapo Headquarters.'

'What's all this about?' she replied. 'There must be some mistake. I work there. In fact I've only just returned from there.'

The man told her to do as he asked and not to make a fuss, but she ignored him and picked up the telephone. He took it from her hand. 'I'm sorry. No telephone calls.'

'How dare you.' The woman's voice rose in anger tinged with fear. 'I want to speak with Herr Mueller. He will sort this out.'

The men were in no mood to argue. One of them grabbed her arm, escorted her down the stairs, and roughly bundled her into one of the waiting cars while another quickly searched the drawers and cupboards. At one point he came into the bedroom and started searching the drawers of her bedside table. Simone aimed her gun carefully in case they came to the window.

'There's nothing here,' another man shouted from the other room. 'Let's go.'

They left, slamming the door behind them. Simone peered through the slats in the shutters. Except for the two cars, the street was deserted. If there had been any passers-by in the street, the sight of two Gestapo cars would have been a signal to vacate the area immediately. The cars drove away and there in the back of one of the cars, Simone recognised Fifi's platinum blonde hair.

Simone moved away from her hiding place and listened for a few moments behind the door for a while in case anyone from the other apartments had come out to see what was going on. After five minutes of silence, she slipped out of the building.

Mme Legrand was on the telephone when Simone entered the house and the look on her face told her that something was wrong.

'That was Claude,' she said. 'He's just received bad news and is on his way here.'

Simone could guess what it was. She was in two minds whether to say what she'd done for fear of being chastised, but there was too much at stake not to say anything. The news was as expected; Fifi had been arrested by the Gestapo and was undergoing interrogation.

When she told them she'd witnessed the arrest, Claude's face reddened with anger. 'What are you trying to do, get us all killed?' He threw his hands in the air in sheer desperation. 'Pascal told me you were a sensible woman, but with the death of the German soldier and now this, I'm beginning to wonder.' Mme Legrand tried to calm him down. 'Why did you go there in the first place? Tell me,' he continued, his voice filled with anger. Simone wasn't sure what to say, but Claude persisted. 'Tell me, Martine.'

'I felt something was wrong. When we executed Lucie's escape, why did we not know there were German soldiers on that train? We could all have been killed. Surely Fifi must have known they were being sent away on a troop transport train?' She extracted the note from her pocket. 'I found this in her apartment – along with a gun.'

Claude read the note.

'If "P" is Pascal, not only was he in love with her, but he felt something was wrong.'

Claude looked surprised. 'He certainly kept this to himself. I would have cautioned him against it if I'd known.' He shook his head. 'It was me who introduced Fifi to our network. I knew her before the war. She's Jewish. Her parents went into hiding after the war began and we gave her a new identity – Ella Rozier – and the apartment. She's provided us with valuable information before. I don't believe she's a traitor. It's highly likely she didn't know the train was carrying soldiers. We can't know everything, you know.'

'Whatever's happened, she must have been under suspicion and was being watched. Maybe they saw her with Pascal too,' Simone said. 'What about Bruno Albrecht? Does he know her?'

'It's possible. Bruno knows everyone – especially pretty women.'

Simone told him she bumped into him in Reims. 'He pestered me to have a drink. I was with him when they found the German soldier's body.'

'Be careful. He's an acquaintance, but he's with the Abwehr and that makes him dangerous.'

'I didn't exactly want to be in his company.' Simone grew indignant. 'He was persistent.'

She asked if Albrecht could help, but Claude seemed reluctant to ask him. 'He certainly doesn't know about our involvement with the Resistance, or that we planted Fifi there. We would be exposing our hand. No, it's impossible.'

Deep in thought and still in shock, they considered their options, all of which were limited. Claude was right. To make enquiries would attract suspicion and knowing that the Allies would land at any moment had put the Gestapo on high alert.

'Alexandre will have to be told,' Claude said, 'although Fifi had no way of knowing exactly what the Maquis were doing or where they operated from – unless of course Pascal told her – but I doubt it. He was her only contact and as head of the network, he wanted it kept that way. Even I didn't see her.'

'I have her gun. Maybe she could have saved herself if I hadn't taken it.'

Claude didn't agree. 'She might have shot one or two, but she would certainly have been outnumbered.'

'There *is* one other thing. Bruno Albrecht asked if I wanted to go to the opera with him. At the time I said no, but after this... well, it's possible I could go and see what he knows.'

Mme Legrand gave her a stern look. 'It's too risky.'

Claude intervened. 'She has a point, Maman. Maybe she can find out something. It's worth a try, but on one condition, that a couple of our men tail you in case you get yourself into trouble again.'

She went to her room to get the telephone number. Claude and his mother watched on while she made the call.

'Herr Albrecht, this is Martine... I'm fine, thank you... It's about your kind offer to take me to the opera. I've decided to accept if that's still alright by you?'

Albrecht was delighted. There followed a few brief sentences in which she arranged to meet him at a café opposite the Opera House – La Fontaine. That would give them time to talk.

CHAPTER 17

ALEXANDRE WAS CONCERNED and disheartened to hear of Fifi's arrest, but as he didn't know her, he judged it to be out of his hands. He had more immediate issues which took priority. The sabotage plans could not be put back and the last thing he wanted was to get involved with problems concerning the Gestapo. He didn't share Simone's anxiety about the German troops on the train that night. Like Claude, he thought it was a coincidence. He also advised her against going to the opera with a German Abwehr officer, telling her that she would end up dead. Simone argued her point and in the end, Alexandre said he could spare her for one day only. After that she was needed for the sabotage operations. She gave him a peck on the cheek and thanked him. Jean-Yves, who happened to be in the room at the time preparing for a radio transmission, laughed out loud, saying that the little Parisian girl had him wrapped around her little finger.

Alexandre smiled and privately confessed to Jean-Yves that he did find her somewhat of an enigma. He also realised it was a while since he'd felt so concerned about another woman and it was not something he wanted. Life in the Resistance was too uncertain.

Dressed in her smart grey suit with a soft, low-cut lace blouse, Simone arrived at La Fontaine seven o'clock sharp. To complement her outfit and add a touch of luxury, Mme Legrand lent her a beautiful art nouveau brooch in the shape of a butterfly, designed by Lalique. She wore her dark hair loose around her shoulders in the style of a film star; feminine and glamorous. After days of gruelling exercises scrambling around the countryside with the Maquis, it felt good to dress up for a change.

130

Albrecht greeted her warmly. 'I am honoured you could make it after all.'

The waiter pulled out a chair for her and at the same time, his eyes momentarily indicated to a man on the next table. Albrecht had already ordered a bottle of their finest Champagne, and the waiter poured her a glass. Simone commented on the café's elegant interior and while looking around, admiring the large gilt mirrors and vases of fresh flowers, she caught the eye of the man on the next table as he glanced over his French newspaper drinking a glass of beer. It was a pre-arranged signal from Alexandre and Claude that someone was covering her. Patrons, many of them men in German uniform and accompanied by attractive women, soon started to fill the place and were immediately served by waiters with false smiles, discretely listening to conversations and remembering faces for the day of reckoning.

While surreptitiously checking out the patrons, Simone asked Albrecht about the opera – Richard Wagner's *Die Meistersinger von Nürnberg*. She knew little about opera, but did know that it was a four-and-a-half hour operatic odyssey and National Socialist favourite that had been performed at the Berlin State Opera to mark the founding of the Third Reich in March 1933, and she wasn't particularly looking forward to it.

Albrecht complimented her, telling her how attractive she looked. Simone pretended to be flattered and apologised for not having any evening clothes suitable for the opera. As she was talking, she noticed a black car pull up outside. A chauffeur got out and held open the passenger door. Simone's heart missed a beat. It was Herr Mueller. She glanced across at the man with the newspaper who immediately got up, whispered something to another man sitting at the bar, and left the building via a side entrance. The second man took his seat, and from the way he looked at her, she knew he was another member of the Resistance. If it hadn't been for the company, being tailed like this would have struck her as funny. As it was, there was nothing funny about it.

'Isn't that Herr Mueller?' Simone said.

Albrecht turned around to look. By now Mueller was half-way

through the door. He had a young red-haired woman with him who appeared to be not much older than twenty. 'He didn't strike me as a man who had much time for women,' Simone added. 'He seemed far too pre-occupied with his work.'

Albrecht laughed. 'She's his mistress. Anyway, he's probably celebrating.'

Simone pricked up her ears. 'Why is that?'

'You could say he's caught a fish.'

She gave a naïve smile. 'What on earth does that mean?'

'He caught a traitor.'

Simone felt the hair on the back of her neck rise. 'That's terrible. Do you know who it was?'

Albrecht leaned closer. 'I shouldn't be telling you this, but it was one of his secretaries. Someone he thought he could trust.'

Simone feigned shock. She glanced at the man on the next table to make sure he'd heard. He gave her the faintest nod.

'What on earth did the woman do – what did you say her name was?'

'I didn't! Why do you ask?' His response was sharp and his smile faded.

She flashed him one of her engaging smiles. 'I was merely interested to know if she was French or German, that's all. I apologise for being rude, and I apologise on behalf of my countrymen if she was French.' She pulled out a cigarette from her bag, placed it between her red lips, and leaned forward for him to light it. In doing so, she exposed a hint of cleavage; enough for him to soften his sharp look. She took a sip of Champagne, pretending not to care about the woman.

'She was French,' he said. 'In fact, she lived not far from where we had a drink the other evening.' It was hard for Simone to act indifferent, but it was something she had to do. Considering her to be an innocent young woman, Albrecht continued. 'She passed information on to the Resistance.'

'How on earth did they find out? I mean the Gestapo are clever, they're hard to fool.'

'Mueller had her followed. It appears she had a lover. We tailed him, but he was clever and always gave us the slip. I think he knew the Gestapo was on to him.'

'We,' Simone said. 'I thought you said Herr Mueller caught the girl?'

'He confided in me a few weeks ago and I said I would see if I could find out anything about them. The man proved to be elusive, but after I managed to intervene over the regrettable incident with the maid on behalf of my good friend, Claude Legrand, something happened. Mueller noticed a file missing. That file contained information on deportees to Germany and the young woman's name was in that file.'

'I don't understand. What did she do – this secretary –whatever her name is?'

'Ella Rozier.' Finally hearing confirmation of the truth gave Simone a sickening feeling in the pit of her stomach. She wanted to leave immediately, but she gritted her teeth; she had come this far and she had to persevere for the sake of the Resistance. 'We had people watch her and Mueller decided to set a trap. The only reason a file would go missing was is if someone there worked for the Resistance. They have ambushed convoys and trains before to rescue prisoners. This time we decided to put them on a train with German troops heading to fight the Soviets. That way if there was an ambush, they would be outnumbered. It was not mentioned in the report. Only Mueller and myself were aware of it.' Albrecht looked pleased with himself. 'The file was mysteriously returned to the office, and the Resistance, not realising there were soldiers already on the train, fell for it.'

'How… How many were killed – or did you capture anyone?' Simone tried to sound calm. 'Did you find the man you were looking for – the secretary's lover, I mean?'

'Six terrorists were killed during the operation. The rest got away. We didn't even know if the lover was one of the dead until Mueller had the idea to bring the secretary in and identify the bodies before they were disposed of. She said she'd never seen them before, but there was one in particular that she appeared to be particularly distressed about. When we *pressed* her about this man, she denied she'd ever seen him before. I must say, she resisted well, despite almost being beaten to a pulp. She was taken back to her cell unconscious, and when she came to, an informer told us she couldn't stop crying.'

With a constricted throat and a sinking feeling, Simone asked what happened to her.

Albrecht shook his head. 'She hanged herself.'

Simone let out a gasp and knocked her Champagne glass off the table. The man on the next table quickly reached over and picked it up. 'Let me help you, Mademoiselle.' He put it back on the table, before walking away.

'Oh dear, I'm terribly sorry. What you've just told me is so distressing.'

The waiter came over, mopped up the spilt Champagne and refilled a new glass. Albrecht reached across the table for her hand and squeezed it with a gentleness that belied the cold, indifferent way he'd told Fifi's story.

'I really didn't want to talk about it, but as you asked… Now look, I've ruined our evening, haven't I?'

'No, no. I'll be fine in a moment.' She took a few deep breaths and smiled. 'We can't let this ruin the opera can we?'

She had been so absorbed by his words that she failed to see Mueller approach from behind her.

'Well, well,' he said, with a cruel smile on his face. 'I do believe this is the charming Mademoiselle Martine. What a surprise.' He turned to Albrecht. 'Bruno, you *are* a dark horse. Where have you been hiding this lovely lady?' His insincere words and cold eyes gave Simone goosebumps.

'Mademoiselle Martine kindly agreed to accompany me to the opera this evening,' Albrecht replied. He checked the time and said it was time they made a move or they'd be late.

Both men gave the Hitler salute and Mueller bade them a good evening. 'Enjoy yourselves.' He bowed slightly towards Simone and then turned to Albrecht, thanked him for his help, and brusquely walked away.

Exiting La Fontaine, Simone observed the two men who had been watching her standing by a lamppost chatting casually. When they exited the opera house, four hours later, only one of them was still there, sitting on a bench reading his newspaper. Albrecht offered to drive her back to Verzenay. Wanting to appear grateful for the evening, she accepted. Throughout the drive, Simone appeared cheerful, talking about the opera, Reims, and other light-hearted subjects. As the car pulled up outside the Legrand residence, she thanked him for a lovely evening.

'Oh, by the way,' she said in an innocent voice, 'you didn't tell me if Lucie was in that group of prisoners. What happened to her?'

'Yes, she was with them.' His eyes looked deeply into hers for a few seconds. 'She managed to escape.'

For a split second, Simone didn't know what to say. 'Oh! Well I am sure Madame Marie would be interested to know that. She was a good girl.'

Albrecht smiled. 'You *will* tell Madame Legrand to advise us if she knows of her whereabouts, won't you? After all, I helped her once – because of my friendship with Claude – but I cannot help her a second time.'

Watching the car disappear out of the driveway, she let out a deep sigh. The Resistance was not going to take this lightly.

CHAPTER 18

It was Claude's idea that Fifi infiltrate the Gestapo and her death hit him hard. In the space of a week, he had lost two of his closest friends. Their loss was a tragedy for everyone in the Resistance. While he had never admitted to Resistance work or showed anti-German feelings towards Albrecht, Claude had always assumed their long-standing friendship was genuine, but this latest revelation left them in no doubt that no-one was safe. Even his mother would be under suspicion. Over the past six months, the Gestapo had recruited thousands of collaborators. The net was closing in and it was no longer wise to trust everyone.

Alexandre already knew most of what had taken place, thanks to the men he'd sent to shadow her. His only comment was that Pascal knew the risks associated with affairs of the heart in the Resistance, especially with someone working for the Gestapo. After spending so much time with him over the past few weeks, Simone understood that he was not being callous; it was a survival mechanism. Being too sentimental in war was dangerous. Jacques used to tell her that. There was no time to dwell on Fifi's and Pascal's deaths, but Alexandre assured her that, at some time in the not too distant future, they would seek retribution.

For the moment they had to get on with the job in hand. At 23:15 on 5 June, *Radio Londres* sent out the next set of lines from Verlaine's poem, *"Blessent mon coeur / d'une langueur / monotone"* – Wound my heart with a monotonous languor. It meant the invasion would start within 48 hours and that the Resistance should begin their sabotage operations, especially on the French railroad system. It was their first call to action, and Alexandre informed Simone she was to be involved. He gathered his men, divided them into groups, each one under the leadership of an experienced maquisard, and distributed the array of weapons SOE had sent over during the past few months. The groups were to fan out in a radius of forty to fifty kilometres and each was allocated different tasks, from cutting telegraph wires and chopping down trees to block roads, to setting explosives on railway tracks and at signals, with the aid of railway workers in the Resistance. Ambushes of German patrols were given to specific groups of highly trained maquisards.

Alexandre's group, which Simone was to work with, set off in the direction of a large forest some thirty kilometres away and through which ran a main road from Metz to Reims. Earlier in the day, they were informed by local intelligence that a convoy of armoured vehicles was on its way towards Reims and the object of the mission was to blow it up. That night there was a massive air raid, scoring hits on factories, airfields and ammunition dumps, all coordinated to keep the Germans busy while the sabotage acts were in progress. The group reached a particular stretch of road in the forest just before midnight and set about preparing it with explosives. Their only source of light was provided by a tiny flashlight. Everyone knew their job and worked quickly and in silence. Alexander himself would be the one to press the detonator.

When the explosives were in place, he directed everyone to hide in the forest at certain points along the length of a particular stretch of road. Simone and several other maquisards, including Enrique and Carlos the Spaniards, were to cover the last section of the road. Their job was to allow the convoy to pass and the moment they heard the first explosion, to fire on the last trucks, preventing them from turning around. 'Kill and cause chaos,' Alexandre said.

Simone hurried along the road, armed with her knife, pistol and Sten gun. She also had her sniper rifle slung over her shoulder. Hidden in the oppressive silence behind trees in the thick, leafy forest, they waited. After a while, a pre-arranged whistle warned them the convoy had been spotted and everyone took up their positions. Within minutes they heard the rumble of vehicles approaching and, as the convoy rounded the bend, the headlights lit up the road. Simone flattened herself behind a tree trunk and aimed her sniper rifle towards the convoy. She counted eight trucks. As the last passed by, she heard a loud explosion further along the line. The first truck had burst into flames, setting off a chain reaction. A third truck, filled with ammunition caught fire and exploded in an immense fireworks display sending chunks of metal and body parts into the woods. As predicted, the last two trucks stopped and then tried to turn around while German soldiers jumped out of the back of the vehicles. Simone looked through her sight and fired, killing the driver of the last truck. The other maquisards immediately started firing.

All around her, explosions and gunshots rang in her ears. The Germans were no match for the Maquis lying in wait in the darkness of the forest and as they scattered for cover, they were mown down in a hail of gunfire. When they thought it safe, Alexandre and his men moved out of the trees towards the burning vehicles, finishing off the injured Germans. This macabre scene of shooting the wounded and taking their guns was one of those things Simone could not afford to be sentimental about. After fifteen minutes it was all over. The night air was thick with the smell of gasoline and burning metal, and sections of the forest had caught fire. The group had lost two men and one was injured. Not a single German survived.

Alexandre signalled for them all to get away, and by the first light of day they were back at the farm. Simone collapsed on a mattress inside the farm house and within minutes was fast asleep. When she woke up a few hours later, the sun was streaming through the window, the terrifying sounds of the dying replaced by shrill bird-calls. Alexandre was sitting by her mattress with a bowl of hot soup.

'We did it,' he said happily, handing her the soup. 'Our operations were a success. We caused enough damage to throw the Germans into chaos. Mission accomplished.'

Just as she finished the soup, Jean-Yves appeared in the doorway, a beaming smile on his face. 'Good news from London. It's just come over the BBC. The Allies have landed on the beaches in Normandy. The invasion has begun.'

Alexandre pulled off his beret and threw it in the air with a loud yelp. 'Dieu merci! Call the men.'

He snatched the empty soup bowl from Simone and pulled her up. 'Come on, little Parisian girl. This deserves a real celebration.'

Within a matter of minutes, word had reached the maquisards in the fields and woods around the farm and they rushed inside, cheering with joy, and pulling the last few bottles of drink from their hiding places. Their elation was palpable; glasses were filled and refilled, and everyone congratulated their comrades. By the time Carlos the Spaniard had started to sing songs from the Spanish Civil War to Enrique's guitar playing, Simone had become quite tipsy.

'How Pascal would have loved to see this day,' Alexandre said.

'And Fifi,' Simone replied. She noticed his eyes were moist with tears. He turned away, too embarrassed to look at her. She put a hand on his arm. 'It's all right, you know. To feel sadness, I mean.'

He nodded. 'The price of freedom is costly. We pay with our lives so that others may live.'

'Pascal knew the risks. All of them did; no-one died in vain. I am not particularly religious but after what I've witnessed, I *would* like to think they are looking down on us and celebrating in our joy. We can't change anything, so let's move forward.'

Soon the Spanish songs were replaced with The Partisans' Song. Everyone stood up and sang in unison. There was not a dry eye in the room.

When someone fired a rifle shot in a drunken stupor, Alexandre could see some of the men were getting out of hand and put an end to the celebrations.

'This is only the beginning,' he said. 'We still have much to do.' The smiles vanished and the atmosphere became sombre and tense. 'We cannot let our guard down. The Germans will retaliate. Mark my words; they will make us pay before they leave French soil.'

CHAPTER 19

THE LANDINGS IN Normandy combined with the co-ordinated sabotage acts threw the Germans into a state of anger and disarray. The Wehrmacht's commanders had insisted the Atlantic Wall was impregnable; a great fortress of concrete and steel that would repel any Allied landing and slaughter the invaders. Now all those carefully laid plans had fallen apart

At first, German propaganda downplayed the landings, fearing French uprisings, but it was too late. Word swept through the population like wildfire and, taking advantage of the continuous Allied bombings and fighting in the vicinity of the Normandy beaches, sabotage groups continued their harassment. Knowing that supplies would be sent from Germany, Alexandre's maquisards, aided by the railway workers in the Resistance, created havoc. Train lines and bridges were blown up in towns and throughout the countryside.

For the next two nights, Simone was a part of these operations. Each day she reported the Maquis' excellent work to Mme Legrand and to the airmen hiding out in the tunnel. Those fit enough wanted to help, but as their French was practically non-existent, Alexandre deemed it too much of a risk, particularly in light of more roadblocks and Gestapo raids on towns and villages with the aid of collaborators.

Throughout the last few weeks, working with the Maquis, Simone realised she had developed a strong affection for Alexandre. She tried to fight it because it bothered her for two reasons. The first was that she'd already promised her heart to Pierre, who was now in forced labour in Germany. She'd always clung to the thought that he was still alive and that they'd be reunited after the war, but as time went on and the horrors of the fate of many French in Germany filtered back, she no longer believed it. Second, there was the warning about getting too close to members of the Resistance whose lives hung in the balance. Would Pascal have survived if he hadn't spent time with Fifi? she asked herself. Knowing all this did not help. She found herself wanting to be by Alexandre's side whenever she could, regardless of the danger they were in.

As predicted, the situation was extremely dangerous and each day they survived was a day they rejoiced. Over the past few days, the Maquis and Resistance had lost many men and women, either in combat or through collaborators; prayers for the dead were turning their joy into despair and hatred. After a raid on a bridge one night, Simone returned to the Legrand villa to find Olivier trying to console a tearful Mme Legrand. Claude had been put under house arrest by none other than his friend, Bruno Albrecht. His mother wanted Simone to take her to Épernay to see him, but since the invasion, more cars were requisitioned and the majority of French were banned from driving. They discussed travelling by bus, but even the buses were erratic through lack of petrol. In the end, Simone decided it was best if Mme Legrand stayed and she went to see him herself. She would make the journey by bicycle.

Mme Legrand pleaded with her to be careful.

'Don't worry. I'll be back before sunset. If I'm not, please contact Alexandre and tell him where I am.'

She took the longer route through the wine villages, a distance of thirty kilometres, and was stopped twice but was waved on after saying she was a nurse and was going to pick up medicines in Épernay. When she reached Claude's villa, the beautiful ornate gates were padlocked and two armed guards stood outside smoking. Simone was told Claude was not permitted to receive visitors – on orders of the German High Command. As she argued with them, she glanced towards one of the windows and saw him looking at her. She was close enough to see that his face looked drawn.

The guards would not budge until finally she said she was a friend of Bruno Albrecht and gave them his number to check. One of the guards went over to a guard post and telephoned. When he came back he unlocked the gate to let her pass. 'You have one hour,' he said.

A curved set of marble steps topped with a balustrade of terracotta urns, led to the grand entrance of the Legrand villa. Two more soldiers stood on guard and one opened the door to let her enter. Claude was standing in the hallway to greet her. In the space of a few days, he seemed older, less debonair, less sure of himself.

'Hello, Martine. Thank you for coming.' He shook her hand. 'How is Maman?'

'Distressed as you can imagine. Olivier and I thought it best she stayed at home. To see you like this would only make things worse.'

'Let's go to the sitting room and I'll tell you what happened.' He led her through his elegant home, telling her all the servants had been taken away for questioning. She noticed he stooped slightly as he walked; a man with the weight of the world on his shoulders.

Claude made her a cup of tea, apologizing that he could not serve Champagne. 'Albrecht's men raided my cellars and took it away.' He winked. 'Naturally there are some hidden – thankfully not in the house.'

'Tea will be fine, thank you.' She waited until he sat down and then asked him why he was under house arrest.

'Albrecht came to see me. At first I thought it was just the usual friendly visit, but when I saw he was not alone, I realised something was amiss. After what you'd told me. I couldn't help thinking he'd been digging around and found out my involvement with the Resistance, but as always, Albrecht is clever. He keeps his cards close to his chest. He told me about the invasion in Normandy and said those armies would soon be wiped out, so it was unwise for the French to get their hopes up. I could tell he didn't really believe it. Then he came to why he was here – Mueller wanted me to collaborate.'

Simone listened carefully. Albrecht did not seem to be the sort of man Mueller could order around.

'Naturally, I told him there was nothing to say, that I wasn't involved with the Resistance, so why would I collaborate,' Claude continued.

'I was told that as a prominent and widely respected man in the Champagne industry, I *had* to know of people who were against the Germans. The men responsible for so many successful acts of sabotage against the Reich needed to be brought to justice, and Gestapo HQ wanted results. If not, they would round up innocent people and make examples of them. "Think of your Mother," Albrecht said. "She could be rounded up too. Everyone is under suspicion." Naturally that filled me with dread. He has given me twenty-four hours to think about it or I will be taken to Gestapo HQ at Rue Jeanne d'Arc.'

Claude put his head in his hands in despair. 'I always thought he was different from the other Nazis, but I was mistaken. Underneath that gentlemanly and aristocratic exterior, he is no better than Mueller and his cronies.'

'Have you given him any reason to suspect you?' Simone asked.

'Of course not.'

'And you're sure you haven't been seen with any of the Resistance?'

Claude shook his head. 'I've always been careful – even with Pascal and Alexandre. The thing is, he led me to think he was sympathetic to the French – and he was good at it.' He paused for a moment. 'Maybe I let my guard down and he suspected something. I'm not sure of anything any longer.'

Simone felt powerless to help him. 'What are you going to do? Can you escape?' It seemed a silly question and she already knew the answer.

'If I do, he will think me guilty and target not only my mother, but all those in the village, especially Olivier and anyone else she has close contact with. It would kill her. You would also be under suspicion.'

'He already knows I'm here.' Simone replied. 'I had to get a guard to telephone him in order to be allowed to see you.' There was a few minutes silence while they considered their options, but other than making an escape, they were limited. 'It's only a matter of weeks before the Allies move out of Normandy and join up with those coming from the south. Let's hope you can hang on until then. If not Alexandre will...'

Claude could tell what she was thinking. 'I don't want any of you involved. You've risked enough as it is. The Resistance needs people like you and him. I am nothing to the Gestapo, so let's not give them a reason to cast their net wider. I will go with them when they come for me, but I will not co-operate.' A clock on the mantelpiece chimed 3:00. 'It's time you made a move. Go back and assure my mother I am fine.'

She understood there was no more to be gained by arguing, and agreed. When she got up to leave, he told her he had other news to impart. 'Just before this happened, I received a message from Jacques.'

'Jacques! How is he?'

'He's just learned that his son is with the Free French Forces who landed in Normandy with the Allies. After receiving word that the Germans are sending in more armoured divisions from other parts of France, he decided to leave Paris and work with the Resistance there.' He gave a little half-smile. 'A father's love for his son is just as potent as a mother's.'

'It's already bad enough in Paris: it will be even worse in Normandy. Do you know whereabouts he's gone?'

'I have no idea, but I believe he has a sister somewhere near Caen. I would suspect he might use that as a base.' Claude could see she was worried and apologised for mentioning it. 'He'll be fine. Don't worry.'

Simone bade him farewell with an affectionate hug and kiss on the cheek, wondering if she would ever see him again. Enveloped in a cloud of apprehension and doom, she cycled back to Verzenay, thinking about his predicament.

In Verzenay, Olivier awaited her return with the dire news that the Gestapo had been to the house and arrested Mme Legrand. All he could tell her was that it was in connection with her son. 'The Germans are recruiting collaborators and they're paying well. They've even been pressurizing people in the villages round here and are offering enormous sums of money and anonymity if they "sing". Two men from the next village were seen driving away in a car with the Milice and it's likely it was one of them.'

The news sickened Simone. 'Madame Marie will never survive a Gestapo interrogation. We have to do something.'

'They have doubled the guards around their headquarters. It will be impossible to mount an attack now.'

'*Mon Dieu*! When will this end?' Simone paced the room.

'Alexandre was here just after you left,' Olivier said. 'He arrived about an hour before the Gestapo and stayed for five minutes. He asked me to give you this. He said it was urgent.' He handed her a cigarette packet. Inside was a short message scribbled on a note. He wanted her to meet him at a safe house in Reims the next morning. After reading it, she set it alight and watched it burn in an ashtray, wondering what was so important that he would risk coming to the Legrand house himself rather than send Baptiste or another trusted friend.

'We have to get those airmen away from here as soon as possible. It's not safe,' she said. 'The Gestapo could come back at any moment.'

Olivier agreed, but with two of them barely able to walk, it wasn't going to be easy. They decided to go to the escape tunnel and give them the news straight away.

'Prepare yourselves,' Olivier said to the men. 'The Gestapo were here today. They're targeting the family so it's best if we move you out of here tomorrow. I can't tell you where you'll be going, but rest assured it will be somewhere safe.'

Simone checked the two men's wounds and gave them painkillers for the journey before returning to the house. 'I think its best I leave here too,' she said to Olivier.

'Where will you go? We need you – and what about Madame Marie? What shall I tell her?'

'At the moment, I don't know what I'll do, or where I'll go. Maybe I'll hide out with the Maquis until the Allies come. It depends on my meeting with Alexandre. Madame Marie will understand. In the meantime, I'll leave it to you to contact Father Thomas and others in the Maquis about moving the men.'

He told her not to worry, that it would all be taken care of and he looked forward to her return.

'There's something else you can do,' Simone said. 'Take care of

Ulysse. He cannot stay in this house alone.'

Olivier laughed. 'Of course, we will be delighted to have him.' He called the dog over and playfully rubbed his head. .

Simone gave Ulysse one last hug and told him she would miss him. He licked her face affectionately.

'Take care of yourself, Mademoiselle Martine.' Olivier said. He turned to Ulysse, 'Come on, boy, let's go.'

Simone packed her suitcase and shortly before dawn, tied it securely onto the bicycle. She took one last look around the beautiful villa which at first she'd found overwhelming, but which now felt more like home, and cycled away towards Reims. The euphoria of the Allied landing and the recent successful sabotage acts were dissipating fast. They'd entered a new phase – a game of cat and mouse with the Gestapo wanting to round up as many people as possible, regardless of whether they were innocent or not, and she was well and truly engulfed in it.

The house in Reims where she was to meet Alexandre was not far from the Hôtel De La Cathédrale. She checked the window on the first floor and saw a blue pot of bright red-geraniums on the window sill, a sign telling her it was safe to enter. She rang the doorbell and a middle-aged woman wearing an apron and carrying a mop, opened the door. After giving the codeword, the woman peered out into the street to check Simone wasn't being followed before ushering her inside.

'Second door on the first floor,' she said, 'You can put your bicycle over there. It will be quite safe.' She indicated an alcove filled with an array of boxes and wooden trunks.

Simone took her suitcase, walked up the narrow staircase and knocked softly on the second door. Alexandre opened it slightly to double-check it was her, and asked her in.

'Were you followed?' he asked.

'I'm fine, but I've got bad news.'

'If it's about Claude and his mother, I already know. I was told in the early hours of the morning.' He indicated for her to take a seat at the table where he was in the process of cleaning two pistols.

'What's going on?' Simone asked. 'Does this have anything to do with Fifi – or Pascal?'

'It could be more to do with Mueller pulling rank over Albrecht – the Gestapo pulling rank over the Abwehr, so to speak. He's the one behind it and Albrecht is going along with it.' He wiped the grease from one of the guns and started polishing it. 'You should count yourself lucky you didn't get hauled in yourself.'

Simone was rather taken aback at the matter-of-fact way he spoke. 'Olivier didn't mention they were looking for me – only Mme Legrand. Besides, if they wanted me, they could have taken me in when I went to see Claude. I had to get one of the guards to phone Albrecht.'

Alexandre laughed. 'He has a soft spot for you, Martine. Surely you can see that.' Her face reddened and she looked away. 'It's easy to see why,' he added.

His remark made her blush even more. 'What is that supposed to mean? He has a wife.'

Alexandre smiled even more. 'Maybe, maybe not. I wonder if she's still alive? All those German cities the Allies have bombed...'

'That's a rather callous remark,' Simone replied.

'He's a man who happens to like pretty young French women, and you, my dear Martine, fit that bill perfectly, which is probably why you are sitting here now and not in a cell in Rue Jeanne d'Arc.' He pushed a cigarette packet towards her. She took one and lit it nervously.

'Olivier said you wanted to see me urgently. Why here, and not at the farm? I didn't think you came into the city.'

'I've been working closely with the Resistance here, particularly after Pascal's death. This is one of several safe houses I use. The other reason I didn't want to meet at the farm is because I don't want the maquisards to know what we're discussing in case they're picked up. There are ambushes and round-ups everywhere at the moment, especially since the bombing of the main railway.' He slipped one of the guns into his belt and took a good long look at her. It unnerved her and she took a long drag on her cigarette.

'What is it?' she asked.

'Martine, I confess to feeling a little uncomfortable about what I am about to ask of you, but I want you to do something for us.'

She looked at his face, trying to read the expression in his eyes. 'I think I know what it is.' She turned away, unable to face him. 'You want me to see Albrecht again – to get information. That's it, isn't it?'

This time it was Alexandre's face which reddened. 'It's not quite as simple as that.'

She exhaled the cigarette smoke. 'Don't beat about the bush, it doesn't suit you.'

He put his hand out to take hers and she instinctively pulled it away. 'Believe me, if there was anyone else I could get to do this – little job – I would.'

'There are other pretty women in the Resistance, you know.'

'Not like you.'

'You sound like Jacques and Pascal. Let me remind you that I am just like all those other women who put their lives in danger for France.'

'Not quite. Jacques saw potential in you – so did Pascal. Jacques trained you, but I was the one who polished you like a diamond. I am the one who taught you the art of being a first-rate sniper and an expert in sabotage.'

Simone burst out laughing. 'You make it sound like a finishing school.'

'That's exactly what it was. A finishing school on the art of survival and you passed with flying colours. There's something else – something you haven't put into use yet. You speak fluent German. Now, do you want to hear what it is I want you to do or not? If the answer is no, you can pick up that suitcase and walk out of that door right this minute, and catch the next train to Paris.'

His tone told her he'd had enough of the small talk and she knew he was not to be messed about with any longer.

She gave a deep sigh. 'Alright, you win. What do you want me to do?'

In an instance his face relaxed. He pushed the second gun towards her: a High Standard HDM.22 calibre semi-automatic pistol, equipped with an integral suppressor. 'I want you to eliminate Albrecht.'

Simone raised her eyebrows. 'What! Can't we just ambush him and finish him off?'

'And risk hundreds being killed in reprisals. Haven't you heard what happened on 10 June?' He proceeded to tell her about Oradour-sur-Glane, a commune in the Haute-Vienne department in west-central France, where over six hundred of its inhabitants, including women and children, were massacred by a company of troops belonging to the 2nd SS Panzer Division *Das Reich*, a Waffen-SS unit. 'This was a reprisal because they suspected there were resistants there. We can't risk such a massacre here. No, it must be more subtle than that. I want you to try and get a job at Gestapo Headquarters.' He paused for a few minutes while she digested his words. 'There's something else. Albrecht is not the only one I want you to kill. I want you to eliminate Mueller too.'

'You've got to be joking,' she replied, angrily stubbing the cigarette out in the ashtray. 'Why don't I take out a couple of Panzer divisions as well?'

'This is no joke, Martine.'

'You're out of your mind. Look what happened to Fifi. Do you want me to end up like her? Anyway, why would they trust me when they know I'm a friend of Claude's and came here to work for his mother? It doesn't make sense.'

Alexandre stood up and walked over to the window. 'The last thing I want is for anything to happen to you.' He stared into the street below for a minute or so and then turned around to face her. 'When you took this job – working with the Resistance here, I mean –Jacques told you he picked you because you were special. That's right isn't it?'

Simone clearly recalled Jacques words the night he told her he'd picked her out. *"I cannot give you precise details, but it's highly likely you will be asked to do things you've not done before. I think you know what that means – possibly eliminate someone – it will depend on the circumstances."*

'What he didn't say was that this assignment came from higher up.' Alexandre sat back down again, leaned back in his chair and clasped his hands together, circling his thumbs around each other as he watched her face.

'He told me SOE wanted a woman to work with Pascal. That's all.'

'It's more than that. What I'm about to say, I do so to put your mind at rest – because I trust you – and because… because, I have become fond of you.'

She noted the way he used the word *fond*, as if it embarrassed him to reveal his feelings. 'Go on,' she said.

'This is classified information. It's a directive from British intelligence. I understand that de Gaulle approves, as does SOE, and in this case, possibly MI6.' Simone was too stunned to reply. Alexandre took a deep breath. 'So, what is it to be?'

'Thank you for being honest with me,' she said after awhile. 'I will give it my best shot. Let's hope it doesn't backfire.' She slipped the gun in her bag. 'I already have a Ballester-Molino, you know.'

'These guns are hard to come by. This one belonged to Pascal. Now, let's get down to business, shall we. Regarding your accommodation, you can't stay here. I'll get you a room at the Hôtel De La Cathédrale, but be careful, there are more Germans staying there at the moment. I want you to meet me later this evening at Bistro Thierry – 7:00 p.m. sharp. I'll explain the rest to you then.'

CHAPTER 20

At the Hôtel De La Cathédrale, Simone walked confidently past a group of Germans to the reception desk and asked to see the manager. The receptionist on duty disappeared into a nearby office. She noticed a slight movement in the closed blinds covering the window and recognized the manager peering at her. He came out immediately and greeted her.

'Mademoiselle Dumont, how lovely to see you again. As you can see,' he said, indicating the Germans, 'we are fully booked, but a room has been reserved for you. He picked up her suitcase and showed her to the same room she'd been given when she first arrived in Reims. In a low voice, he told her he was very sorry to hear about Pascal.

'If there's anything I can do, please don't hesitate to ask,' he said.

She asked why there were so many more Germans here and was told all the hotels in Reims were full at the moment with officials from Germany coordinating troop movements being sent to Normandy. 'They've even confiscated more villas.'

After the manager left the room, Simone took off her shoes and lay down on the bed. She needed to think. The more she thought about the events of the past few weeks, and now Alexandre's life and death request, the more she realised she'd lost sight of the real world. Life in the shadows of the Resistance was taking its toll on everyone. Fatigue was catching up on her and she needed to sleep for a long time, yet sleep eluded her. She only had a few hours to go before she met up with Alexandre again and she couldn't afford to be late. She took a pick-me-up pill and went to freshen up.

Simone arrived at Bistro Thierry at one minute to seven. The place was pleasantly homely, with an assortment of family photographs lining the walls, and soft French music playing from a radio on a rustic sideboard filled with plates and glassware. Alexandre was there and waved her over. A tiny white candle flickered on the table, casting a warm glow on their faces. Without asking, he ordered her a beer, saying that Champagne was off the menu – courtesy of a raid by the Germans who stole their last stock. The evening was warm, a glorious French summer of the type she'd enjoyed before war ruined everything. She wore her delicate, cream silk blouse with the deep V-line lace inset and a pencil-slim light brown skirt.

Alexandre took a sip of his beer and watched her. His eyes told her that he approved. 'I believe you've lost weight.'

'Is it any wonder,' Simone replied. 'All those kilometres I've cycled: all the sleepless nights.'

His eyes flashed. 'You are still beautiful though. In fact being here tonight may have its disadvantages,' he said, referring to the lack of Champagne and basic menu, 'but seeing you like this, and catching the scent of your perfume, reminds me that the war has not killed *all* of my senses – at least not yet.'

'So the whole time I was using a sniper's rifle and risking my life with explosives, you never noticed I was a woman?' She grinned, but her reply was tinged with sarcasm.

'I noticed you from the moment Pascal brought you to the farmhouse.'

Embarrassed, Simone cast her eyes over the menu. 'I see. Well, you kept your thoughts to yourself,' she replied. 'I am beginning to think all you men are the same.'

'What's that supposed to mean?'

'Oh nothing; forget it. Can we order? I'm famished.'

After recommendations by the manager, they both ordered rabbit stew. Alexandre's flattery quickly dissipated and he was back to his old self – guarded and cool. 'Let me fill you in on the situation,' he said. 'The Allies thought they would have got further than they have by now, and at the very least, they should have taken Caen, but things have not quite gone according to plan.'

'Please don't tell me the Germans are gaining the upper hand as their radio broadcasts state.'

'No. They can't win. The Allies have superior airfire and the Resistance is causing havoc, but there are still three strong Panzer units in the area and they will fight to the last man. Caen is a ruined city, but as we speak, the Germans are holding out. Our intelligence tells us that Hitler is expected to arrive any day now to confer with Field Marshalls Rommel and Rundstedt.'

'What exactly do you want me to do?' Simone asked. 'I thought the plan was to kill Albrecht.'

'It is, but first I want you to get close to him; win his confidence.'

Simone reminded him that he had just taken into custody the family she worked for.

'Use your imagination and spin him a story. As I said before, he likes you so he will want to believe you. Your assignment is to get close to him and the Gestapo, and then report back to me. When the time is right, I will tell you when to act.'

The waiter brought out their bowls of rabbit stew and they ate in silence. After their plates were taken away, Simone leaned forward and in barely a whisper, told him that she wouldn't sleep with Albrecht. 'That is out of the question,' she said.

Alexandre flashed a smile. 'I will not ask what you do to gain his trust; that is your business.' He leaned forward too. 'Although I confess, I *am* happy to hear that.'

'Are you?' Simone saw a glimmer of feeling for her in his eyes, but just like previous times, it was gone in a flash and she realised it was wrong to bring feelings up at a time like this.

'Do you want me to stay in the hotel? Won't they think it odd?'

'They won't ask questions.' He handed her a folded note. 'These are the places Albrecht hangs out. Find him and act quickly. Time is of the essence.'

She took a quick glance and saw that two of them were ones she was familiar with: Café Fontaine opposite the Opera House, and the one where Serge worked. 'You already know the waiters in those two places,' Alexandre said. 'They're with us so will keep an eye on you. If you get into any difficulty, don't hesitate to let them know.'

'Where can I contact you – at the apartment?'

'Only as a last resort – in case you are being followed. The manager here or at your hotel can be trusted; otherwise there are certain letter-drop points. I marked them on the note with an X. These letter-boxes are monitored and we will get back to you within a few hours.' Simone cast her eyes over the note. 'I wouldn't worry too much about Claude or Mme Legrand. I don't think Albrecht will do anything untoward to them. They are too well known. I think it's either a bluff to keep Mueller off his back, or he will use them as a bargaining chip to try and save himself.'

'Let's hope you're right.'

Alexandre checked his watch. 'Time to go. You need your beauty sleep before you start work tomorrow.' He went over to the manager to pay the bill and Simone noticed them deep in conversation for a few minutes. All of a sudden there was a commotion outside and armoured vehicles entered the street. A voice called out over the loudspeaker for everyone to stay put.

'Another raid,' the manager said. 'Get away while you can.'

Alexandre hurried back to Simone. 'Quickly, let's get out of here.' He led her down a narrow corridor and out through a back door into a pitch black cobblestone alley. Several other patrons were also making a hasty retreat. He heard her swear when the heel of her shoe became caught in the stones.

'*Merde!*' I think I've broken a heel.'

'Take them off. Hurry! No time to dawdle.'

She slipped her shoes off and he took her hand as they ran down the alley. They had only just turned a corner when two Germans came out of the back entrance and shone a flashlight up and down the alley. Seeing it was deserted, they went back inside.

'That was a close call,' Alexandre said. A few turns later, they came out into a back street leading to the side entrance of the Hôtel De La Cathédrale.

Simone put her shoes back on. 'Damn! I twisted my ankle,' she said, grimacing.

Alexandre knelt down and rubbed it for her for a minute or two. 'Is that better?' He stood up to face her and kissed her full on the mouth.

'Much better,' a startled Simone replied.

He tenderly stroked her cheek with his right hand, letting it linger on her soft skin, and with his left hand, he pushed open the hotel door. A blast of piano music and someone singing in German drifted into the street.

'Take care, Martine.'

This fleeting moment of tenderness had caught her off guard, but before she'd had time to register what had happened, he was halfway down the road. Still feeling the touch of his hand, she stepped inside. She was on her own now.

*

In the morning, Simone gave her shoe to the concierge and asked him if he could find someone to repair it for her. After breakfast, she decided to go shopping for a new dress. The manager told her where the best dress shop was. 'It's where the German wives and mistresses go,' he said, 'but I'm afraid it's about the only place you'll find something decent, these days.'

Maison de Paris, run by a Parisian couturier, was in the main street near the Opera House and it was one of the few shops still doing a brusque business. Simone entered the premises just as a pretty young woman wearing a fox fur and holding a small dog, was leaving. A slender, middle-aged woman bade her a pleasant good morning and asked what she could do for her. Simone told her she was looking for a pretty summer dress; something to liven up her wardrobe.

The woman introduced herself as Madame Blanche, looked her over, noting the brown skirt and silk shirt she was wearing, and with barely an audible tutting sound, went over to a rack and pulled out a forget-me-not blue silk dress with a fitted waist. 'What about something like this?' she said. 'A most flattering style.' She draped the dress over one arm in order to show it in its best light, and smoothed down the fabric. Simone couldn't help noticing the expensive rings and bracelet she wore. They glinted like treasures from Aladdin's cave. 'Such beautiful fabric too,' Madame Blanche added.

'A little too formal,' Simone replied.

'May I ask if it's for a special occasion?'

'I just want something that I can wear during the day; maybe for cocktails too. Not evening wear.'

'Is there a gentleman involved?' the woman asked with a knowing smile.

'Excuse me!' The remark took Simone by surprise.

'What I meant to say was, is this for someone special – a gentleman maybe. There may be a war on, but most of my clients still like to charm their menfolk. After all, my clothes are not cheap, and it's often their menfolk who pick up the bill.'

Simone thought about it. 'Well, I suppose it is for a man, but I'm afraid he will not be paying. What else can you show me?'

Madame Blanche pulled out another half a dozen and Simone picked out one in particular, a plum-coloured wrap-dress with a V-shaped neckline with a shadow-like allover leaf pattern in a paler shade. She tried it on. It fitted perfectly and Madame Blanche complimented her.

'I'll take it,' Simone said.

By the time she came to pay, the business-like Madame Blanche had also persuaded her to take a matching belt and gloves in a lighter shade of plum.

'How much do I owe you?' Simone asked, as she reached into her purse and pulled out a handful of ration cards.

When she saw the shocked look on Madame Blanche's face, she felt embarrassed.

'I am afraid we don't usually take ration cards,' Madame Blanche said, haughtily. 'You see, it's not easy for me to get my hands on good fabrics these days and…'

'That's quite all right,' Simone replied. 'What is the cost?' When she was told the exorbitant price, it took her all her determination not to walk out. It had been a silly idea in the first place. She did not belong in such an establishment. She took out the wad of money that Jacques had given her, and counted it out on the counter.

There was a moment of awkwardness, but both women rose to the occasion. Madame Blanche took the money, wrapped the goods in tissue paper and placed them in a large black bag with the name *Maison de Paris* emblazoned on one side in gold embossed lettering. She bade her a good day and said she hoped to see her again.

'Thank you,' Simone said.

As she walked out of the shop, the telephone rang and she heard Madame Blanche speak in German. '*Guten tag*, Herr Winkler. Yes, Madame's gift is ready. I shall have someone deliver it to your hotel immediately.'

Simone returned to her hotel. Clearly Madame Blanche's customers were all connected to the Reich and by the look of her jewellery, she had profited well by them. She wondered what would happen to her when the day of reckoning came.

At the reception desk, the manager of the Hôtel De La Cathédrale handed her back her repaired shoe along with her key. His eyes glimpsed the bag she was carrying, but tactfully, he said nothing. Back in her room, Simone refreshed herself, styled her hair in the soft, feminine style of a film star, sweeping it back at the sides and letting it tumble loosely onto her shoulders, and slipped into her new dress. She wondered what Jacques would make of her spending so much of the money he gave her on a dress. Even more, she wondered what Alexandre would say if he saw her now. His fleeting moment of affection and caring words had given her the added impetus she needed to carry out her assignment. It occurred to her that when she first joined the Paris Resistance, she was just an ordinary person, a nurse with dreams of a home and family. How the war had changed her. Never in her wildest dreams did she think such respected resistants like Jacques, Pascal, and now Alexandre, would put such faith in her.

She desperately hoped she would not fail them.

After applying lipstick and a light brushing of face powder, she double-checked her two guns before leaving the room. Her Ballester-Molino remained hidden in the false compartment of her suitcase, and Pascal's she wrapped in a face towel and placed in a drawer. Finally, she dabbed a little Chanel No 5 on her wrist and behind her ears, and left the hotel.

CHAPTER 21

IT WAS FOUR-THIRTY in the afternoon when she arrived at Café Fontaine. At that time of day, most German officers were busy at work and the place was half empty. She took a seat at the bar and ordered a drink. The waiter who had served her the night she was there with Albrecht recognized her.

'Good afternoon, Mademoiselle,' he said, as he waited for the bartender to fill his order for two women on another table. Their acknowledgement of each other was just enough to put her at ease.

After more than an hour, the café began to fill, but there was still no sign of Albrecht. Simone had taken a chance to go there first, but it looked like she'd made the wrong choice. People were starting to notice her sitting alone, so she decided to wait another half an hour before trying a different café. At six-thirty, she paid her bill and left the premises. She'd only gone a short distance when a car passed – Albrecht's car. He saw her, pulled up and got out.

'Mademoiselle Martine, what a pleasure it is to see you again.'

Simone wanted to play it cool yet at the same time she needed to keep his attention. She acknowledged him with a pleasant smile. 'I was just having a drink in Café Fontaine before going back to pack. I leave Reims in the morning.'

'You are leaving?' He seemed surprised.

'Well, I have no reason to stay here now, Herr Albrecht. As you may be aware, Madame Legrand was taken into custody, so I have no job.' She desperately hoped he would show concern and not bid her farewell.

'If you will allow me to explain.'

Simone looked over his shoulder and saw he had someone with

159

him. 'There is no need to explain anything – neither do I want to detain you as I see you have company. You mustn't keep him waiting.'

He moved closer and looked almost embarrassed. 'Why don't you join us? Herr Klaebisch will only be staying a short while. He has other things to do.'

Simone looked away, as if pondering the invitation. So he was with Otto Klaebisch, the notorious *Weinführer* for the region of Champagne. It would be interesting to meet him. What would he have to say about the arrest of Claude and Mme Legrand? As she knew she would, she agreed. Albrecht was more than delighted and Simone returned to Café Fontaine with them.

When Albrecht introduced Simone as the companion of Mme Legrand, he took a long look at her and sighed. 'A messy affair. I wish I could have done more for them.'

'I'm not sure what you mean, but what I do know is that both Madame Marie and her son have been very good to me and now I'm without a job.' She was careful not to press the point of whether they were innocent or not.

Albrecht interjected. 'What Herr Klaebisch is trying to say, Martine, is that we were ordered to bring them in. Since the bombing of the railway, the Resistance has been extremely active and Berlin demands action. We know that the heads of the Champagne houses have been doing their best to make things difficult for us, despite maintaining their friendliness.'

'I am sure I would have known if there was anything untoward going on. Madame Marie rarely saw anyone and she was too ill to leave the village.'

'There is also the matter of supplying us with inferior Champagne,' Klaebisch added. 'That is an act of sabotage.'

Simone wanted to laugh. 'Do you call supplying inferior Champagne an act of sabotage? I can't imagine Madame Marie or Monsieur Legrand stooping to such a level.'

'Maybe you do not know these people as you think,' Klaebisch replied.

'All I know is that I now have to find another job.'

Klaebisch finished his drink, saying that he had to leave. 'It was a pleasure to meet you, Mademoiselle.' He turned to Albrecht. 'Enjoy your evening, Bruno. Heil Hitler!'

'So that's the famous *Weinführer* I've heard so much about.' Simone said. 'How could he say such a thing about Monsieur Legrand? It's preposterous.'

'Never mind him,' Albrecht said. 'I'm sorry you've been affected by recent events. Where are you going and what will you do?'

Simone was amused that someone like Albrecht could be so concerned about her. In his world, she was nothing. 'I'm not sure. I could go back to Paris – back to my old nursing job, but I had thought about a change – maybe secretarial work. With the war on, I can put my German to good use.'

Albrecht looked surprised and addressed her in German. 'So you speak German? Why didn't you say? You *are* a dark horse.'

'You have always addressed me in French, Herr Albrecht.'

'Tell me, how good is your German?' Simone decided to impress him and suggested they continue the conversation in German and he could see for himself. He laughed. 'Well, well, I *am* impressed. Your German is excellent.'

When she'd finished her drink, Simone said she'd better get a move on as she had things to do before she left in the morning. He asked where she was staying and she told him the Hôtel De La Cathédrale.

'Allow me to drive you there.'

'Really, that's not necessary. You've been too kind as it is.'

Albrecht wouldn't hear of it and during the drive back he broached the subject of offering to get her another job in Reims.

'You mean in the same capacity as a companion and nurse?' she asked innocently.

'No, I mean as a secretary. You said you wanted a change didn't you?'

Simone couldn't believe her luck. 'I did, but this is quite unexpected. What do you have in mind?'

'The secretary we lost a few weeks ago – the French woman – I don't believe her position has been filled. I could put a word in for you.'

Until this moment, Simone had gone along with this act, half thinking that nothing would come of it and she would be on the next train to Paris, but his words sent a searing pain through her chest, leaving her in no doubt as to who and what he was referring to. He wanted her to step into Fifi's job. It was a sobering thought.

'That is most kind of you,' she replied. 'But I would need to know as soon as possible as I'd planned on leaving in the next day or two.'

'You will have a reply by nine o'clock tomorrow morning.'

'Just one more thing, I recall you said the French secretary worked at Gestapo Headquarters. Is that where you are offering me the job?'

'Yes – at 18, rue Jeanne d'Arc.' He paused for a moment. 'Do you have a problem with that?'

Simone pretended to be shocked. 'I'm not sure...'

'Martine, you would be well paid. There is also another point which you would do well to reflect on.'

'What is that?'

'The Allies may have landed in Normandy, but the war is not over yet – by a long way. Herr Hitler has taken this badly and is sending his best divisions to fight them.'

'May I remind you that I am French. What you say offends me.'

'Don't be so sensitive. Times are hard for the French, but if you do your work well, that's all that matters to us.' His words were cold and detached. 'We aim to win this fight, and when we do, you will be on the winning side – with us.'

She pretended to consider his words and as daunting as the situation was, accepted his proposal with an air of graciousness.

He looked pleased with himself. 'Excellent. Oh, and one more thing, no more Herr Albrecht. I told you that last time. It's Bruno from now on.'

'Goodnight – Bruno.' Simone gave him one of her pretty smiles before going inside the hotel.

The manager was sitting behind the desk sorting through a mound of paperwork. 'Is everything alright? You look rather pale.'

'I'm fine, thank you, but I wouldn't mind a nightcap – something strong. I'll have it in my room.'

She sat by the window in her room watching the people in the square below and mulling over what had just transpired while drinking Calvados. The manager had told her it had been recovered from the retreating Germans in Normandy. It had taken a lot for her to accept Alexandre's proposal. 'One day, I will wake up and all this will seem like a dream,' she said to herself.

The next morning, she was finishing breakfast in the dining room when Albrecht entered the hotel, walked straight into the breakfast room, pulled out a chair and sat down next to her. Several Germans having their breakfast recognized him and stood to attention, saluting him with a Heil Hitler.

'The job is yours,' he declared, looking pleased with himself. 'When can you start – today?' He snapped his fingers and called the waiter over. 'Bring me a roll, sausage, and cheese.'

A few minutes later, the waiter returned with his order and started to pour out ersatz coffee for him. Albrecht gave him a dirty look.

'Don't insult me by giving me this,' he snapped. The waiter looked embarrassed and apologised, saying they had no real coffee. 'What sort of a place is this? There are fellow Germans here,' he looked around the room as he said it. 'Don't tell me you force them to drink this.' The room fell silent.

'Please, Herr Albrecht – Bruno,' Simone said, laying her hand on his. 'I beg you. Leave it alone. They are doing their best under the circumstances.'

Her soft words worked and he calmed down, but did not apologise. 'At least you won't have to drink this dishwater in your new job. I can see that we will have to find you somewhere better to live.'

'I am fine here,' she replied. 'It's central and they have looked after me well.'

Albrecht let out a deep sigh. 'As you wish. Now, tell me, can you start today? There's much to do.'

Simone needed to let Alexandre know what was happening as soon as possible, but not wanting to lose the chance of the job, she said yes. Albrecht told her to present herself at 18, rue Jeanne d'Arc in two hours' time and to mention his name. She asked if he would also be there.

'I have to go to Épernay now, but I'll be back later this afternoon. Perhaps you will do me the honour of letting me take you out for a celebratory meal this evening.' Simone said she would look forward to it. 'Excellent. I will pick you up here at seven o'clock sharp.'

After he'd gone, Simone looked around the room at the other guests. All were staring at her. She quickly finished her roll and left. At the reception desk, the nervous waiter was deep in conversation with the manager. He hastily moved away when he saw her.

'I apologise for his behaviour,' Simone said to the manager. 'He had no right to speak to him like that.'

The manager gave her a look as if to say he understood what was going on and she mustn't feel bad. 'You are among friends here. We do what we have to. Let's leave it that.'

CHAPTER 22

SIMONE SHOWED HER Identification to the guards at 18, rue Jeanne d'Arc. At first they were reluctant to let her in but, after informing them she was starting a new job, her bag was searched and she was asked to take a seat in the reception area along with a dozen or so other men and women. While she waited, she flicked through a German magazine, occasionally looking around to see what was taking place. As with every other Reich establishment, large portraits of Hitler and Petain dominated the room. There was also a stand filled the faces of at least fifty men and women; *Wanted for Sabotage, 500 Francs for the Whereabouts of this Person*, etc. A few people ran their eyes over the images. As they did so, an official appeared, took down two notices and added another three. Elsewhere, smartly-dressed men went about their business carrying folders or escorting some forlorn looking soul to another part of the building. Every now and again she heard someone sobbing or begging for clemency. A beautiful vase of red lilies had been placed on the receptionist's desk, and two potted plants stood on either side of the entrance doorway, yet despite this touch of elegance, it was a desolate place, devoid of a soul. At one point, a door burst open and a woman was led outside. She was told not to return or she too would face the same consequences as her daughter.

After some time, a blonde-haired woman came down the stairs and called out Simone's name. 'Fräulein Dumont, please follow me.'

She was taken to a large room on the first floor where six other women sat busily typing away at their desks. Another portrait of the Führer hung on the wall, and a small flag with the swastika was placed on every desk. The woman introduced herself as Fräulein Olga Bauer, the person in charge of the secretarial section. She asked Simone to empty the contents of her bag on to a table and each item was inspected before being put back.

'You will sit here,' she said, directing her to a desk by the window not far from where a dark-haired young woman worked. 'Talking is forbidden. We are here to work and not pass the time in idle chatter, so if you have any questions, please address them to me.'

Seeing everyone at their typewriters, Simone felt a sudden pang of anxiety. In her eagerness to accept the job, she'd forgotten one very important thing – she couldn't type. Fräulein Bauer saw her hesitate and asked if she had a problem.

'I was informed that I would be doing secretarial work, but I am afraid that didn't include typing.' Simone saw the look of contempt on the woman's face.

'Wait here.' She stormed out of the room. None of the other typists lifted their heads to look at her, leaving her in no doubt as to their fear of offending the officious Fräulein Olga. A few minutes later, she reappeared with her superior, Obersturmbannführer Hermann, an unremarkable man about forty-five years of age, short, stout, and balding. He was unsmiling and arrogant, like so many civil servants of his ilk in the service of the Reich. Simone was told later that he was merciless in pursuing and punishing Jews because, as he once said to someone, he couldn't bear the sight of them. This morning however, he was in a good mood.

'Fräulein Dumont. I see you have been sent here by Herr Albrecht. It would have been wise of him to have checked if you could type before he sent you here. However, what is done is done, and we will have to give you other work.' He placed a large folder marked Top Secret in front of her together with a brown ledger. 'You can start by entering the details of these papers into this book.' He opened the file and removed the top sheet of paper. It was headed "Executions". Simone took a deep breath as he explained more.

'Transfer these names to this ledger – here, and then fill in the other columns – age, address, etc. Where there is a tick, mark the death as one of these.' He pointed to four other reasons which included suicide, illness, etc. 'It doesn't matter which.'

With that, he bade her good day and left the room. Fräulein Olga organized a photograph Identity Card for her, which Simone was to wear at all times. She checked that she had enough pens and ink and returned to her desk. Simone spent the next two hours on the gruesome task of transferring names from one place to another. The work was sickening, but at least it gave her a chance to see if she recognized anyone from Alexandre's group. She didn't, but she did try to memorize the names of the victims and their addresses. Under the watchful eye of Fräulein Olga, it was impossible for her to write anything down and slip it in her bag. She would have to bide her time for now.

A bell rang and the girls were told they could go to the canteen for a half-hour break. One by one, they silently filed out of the room. In the canteen, they lined up for coffee and a slice of cake or a bowl of vegetable soup, cheese and smoked sausage. Most girls chose everything. Simone asked if she could join them at the table. Away from Fräulein Olga, the girls were much friendlier. She learned that they were French and that most of them had only been there for about six months.

'The German secretaries were called back to Germany,' one of them said. 'So we took their places. And now the Allies have landed, our work has intensified. Even coming here every day is fraught with danger as this building is one of the first the Resistance will attack. The Germans don't care; we French secretaries are dispensable. Did you know the place was almost bombed a week ago, and a low-flying plane fired shots through the window? Thankfully it was on the other side of the building or we could have been killed.'

Simone pretended not to know about it, but she was aware of the incident. Apparently it was an Allied pilot acting alone. Alexandre's men had praised his daring.

'We heard it was Herr Albrecht who got you the job,' another said.

'Yes, that's right. Although I barely know him, so it was very kind of him. He told me that you were short-staffed. Apparently I am taking someone else's place. I believe she left suddenly.' Simone hoped that by playing innocent, the women might open up.

They looked at each other. 'You mean Ella.'

'He didn't tell me her name. Why did she leave?'

There was a moment of silence until one of them opened up. 'She didn't exactly leave. Something happened and she was...' The woman was unsure of what to say. 'We heard she was tortured and died soon after. Fräulein Olga said she was a traitor.'

Simone feigned shock. 'That's terrible.'

When the same woman told her she had been given her desk, Simone felt a lump rise in her throat. It would be a constant reminder of the danger she was in.

'Do you know what she did?' Simone asked.

The first woman told her they'd overheard a conversation that she'd given information to the Resistance. 'Fräulein Olga got into trouble for not watching her. It accounts for her being such a tyrant to work for. Be careful of that one.'

Another woman laughed. 'To her we are French scum.'

On the way back to the room, the woman who sat next to Simone introduced herself as Mimi. She told her that although all the secretaries were French, that didn't mean they were sympathetic to the Germans. 'I took this job because I needed the money and they feed us well. I have invalid parents to look after. Some of the others took the job for the same reason. All the same, just be careful who you speak to. This is a place seething with collaborators and one or two would love to get into Fräulein Olga's good books.'

Later that day in the privacy of her hotel room, Simone scribbled down a coded message, sealed it in an envelope and handed it to the hotel manager just as Albrecht arrived to pick her up for their dinner date.

'It's urgent,' she whispered to him.

'Leave it with me. I'll see that he gets it straight away.' He placed it in his inside jacket pocket and called his wife out of the office, telling her that he was slipping out for half an hour. His wife seemed unsurprised, leaving Simone in no doubt that she was used to his secretive comings and goings.

168

Albrecht's face beamed with delight when he laid eyes on her. She wore her new plum-coloured dress and he commented on how it suited her and that he'd noticed it the day before. She wanted to tell him that it cost a small fortune but thought better of it.

'How was your first day?' he asked, as they drove away.

She told him it was fine but that Fräulein Olga seemed to take an instant dislike to her. He laughed. 'Take no notice. She got into trouble over the last secretary, so she's wary of everyone now.'

Simone remembered her first impression of Albrecht, and Mme Legrand's remark; that he was a charmer. In the few times she'd been in his company, he certainly lived up to his reputation.

The restaurant was in a small chateau set within extensive grounds a few kilometres outside of Reims. She gasped when she saw it. Such elegance was not what she was used to, especially since the German Occupation. Albrecht parked his car next to others, each one bearing a flag with the swastika. When they entered the chateau, the maître d' greeted Albrecht as someone of great importance – someone who obviously dined there on a regular basis. Other patrons also acknowledged him. They were shown to a table near a window with a glorious view across the lawns, and presented with the menu.

'What do you suggest?' Albrecht asked the maître d'.

'For starters, *Mein Herr*, perhaps the foie gras. We received it today. Then there's fish in aspic – your favourite, and of course the venison.'

'If you will allow me to choose for you, Martine,' Albrecht said. Simone was so shocked at the array of fine foods that she wouldn't have known what to choose anyway. This way, she wasn't going to make a fool of herself.

The sommelier came over and opened a bottle of Dom Pérignon, poured a little into the glass, and waited for Albrecht's approval. 'Excellent,' he said. The waiter filled their glasses and placed the bottle in the ice bucket. A few minutes later, another waiter arrived with an *amuse-bouche* of Beluga caviar on triangles of rye bread. Simone took a bite as she watched the well-dressed waiters circulate through the elegant room like robots, carrying trays of delicacies and fine wines,

169

the like of which few Frenchmen had laid eyes on in years. In the corner of the room, a pianist played popular German music.

Albrecht noticed the stunned look on her face. 'I wanted to surprise you,' he said.

'You certainly did.' She glanced at some of the women wearing stylish evening dresses and glittering jewellery and told him she felt rather plain surrounded by such sophistication. 'This is where we celebrated the Führer's birthday. Both Field Marshalls Rommel and Rundstedt have dined here too.'

'I'm flattered, although I wish I'd known; I'd have worn something more elegant.' She had nothing more elegant to wear anyway, and the remark was meant more as a statement to cover a moment of awkwardness.

'Don't compare yourself to these women,' Albrecht said. 'You have a natural beauty. That's what attracted me to you in the first place. In fact, you may not know this, but you are exactly the sort of woman the Führer would like.'

'Oh really – except that I am French.'

Albrecht laughed. 'The Führer has nothing against French women; only those who do not respect Germans.'

Half way through the meal, Simone broached the subject of Fifi. 'I have been told that I am sitting at the desk of the woman who was tortured for being a traitor. It wasn't exactly what I wanted to hear on my first day.'

Albrecht was dismissive. 'There are certain things I cannot discuss, Martine. You must respect that.'

She apologised. Getting information wasn't going to be easy as he appeared to be so guarded. 'But you *can* tell me what's happening with Claude Legrand and his mother, can't you? I'm still worried about Madame Marie's health. It's important she takes her medicine.'

Albrecht put his knife and fork down and took a sip of Champagne. 'If you must know, they are being sent to Germany.' On hearing this news, Simone suddenly lost her appetite and reached for a glass of water. 'I was hoping you wouldn't bring this up. Now, I see it's ruined your evening – again.'

'Why are you sending them to Germany? On what charges?' She stared at her plate for a while. The rich food that she'd enjoyed up until that moment made her feel nauseous. 'You know full well Madame Marie will never survive one of your infamous camps.' The disdain in Simone's voice was evident.

Albrecht gave a deep sigh. 'There is still a great deal of doubt as to their role in the Resistance, but as yet we have found no evidence against them. Since the invasion of Normandy and the acts of sabotage carried out over the past few weeks by the Resistance, Mueller has Himmler on his back and he is not in the mood to give people a second chance these days. The Legrands are nothing to him. He doesn't care whether they own a Champagne house.' He gave a little half-smile. 'He doesn't even like Champagne. He wanted them executed as an example to the Resistance. I, on the other hand, who have known the family since before the war, especially Claude, persuaded him to spare them saying that by executing them, the Resistance would retaliate even more. He thought about it and agreed. It was then that he decided to send them to a camp; Madame Legrand to Ravensbrück and Claude elsewhere, but I came up with a better idea.'

Simone could not imagine what *a better idea* might be. The Legrands seemed doomed. 'Which was?'

'They are being sent to a safe place in Bavaria where they will be guarded around the clock, but treated with dignity. It's a place for VIP prisoners and as the owners of one of the most renowned Champagne houses, I want to use them as bargaining chips if we do fall into the hands of the Allies – God forbid.'

'Isn't that rather callous?' Simone said. 'You're really saying they haven't done anything wrong at all…'

Albrecht put his hand on hers. She was trembling. 'Enough. Stop this talk immediately. You're spoiling the evening.'

The conversation was interrupted when the other patrons began to clap. A woman in a long gold dress joined the pianist on the stage, took the microphone and in a sultry, flirtatious voice, said what a pleasure it was to be with them.

Albrecht leaned closer to Simone and in a whisper said she was a very famous singer from Berlin – a favourite of Dr Goebbels. 'She's on her way to entertain the troops in Normandy. We are lucky to have her here tonight.' The woman threw a kiss to everyone and began to sing *Schön ist die Welt*. It was obvious everyone adored her.

Despite being in the company of such a star, Simone couldn't concentrate. Her mind was in turmoil. She was there to find a way to assassinate Albrecht and Mueller. Mueller, she could understand, but Albrecht? Did he deserve to die that way when he had intervened on behalf of Lucie and was now trying to save the Legrands?

Throughout the rest of the evening, she tried to put her concerned thoughts behind her and looked for something less depressing to talk about. It was vital she kept up his interest in her, otherwise he might not ask her out again and that would make her assignment virtually impossible. Knowing that he didn't want to talk about his marriage or his life back in Germany, she asked about his love of art, literature, and films. At least there they found common ground.

During the drive back to Reims, Albrecht stopped the car by the side of the road. Simone felt a surge of fear and it crossed her mind that he was so unpredictable, he might even kill her. Holding her handbag with her right hand, she carefully opened the secret compartment underneath the bottom, and using the thumb and index finger of her left hand, edged out a small knife ready to use it. To her relief, Albrecht had no intentions of killing her. Instead, he told her that he'd fallen in love with her.

The relief at not having to fight for her life was so great she almost burst out laughing. She let go of her knife, and took his hand, carefully playing him. 'Bruno, this is most unexpected. I don't know what to say, except that…'

He leaned over, wrapped her in his arms, and kissed her. It was not what she wanted but she reciprocated. His kisses soon moved from her mouth to her neck. With her eyes wide open, she could see his smooth blonde hair glistening in the soft moonlight. His hair gel bore a strange musky fragrance, manly and sensual. Frighteningly, she felt herself becoming aroused. She pushed him away.

'Bruno! Please stop!'

He pulled back and looked at her. 'Surely you must know how I feel?'

'Take me back,' she said, smoothing her hair and dress.

'Let me explain.' He moved closer again but she drew away from him.

'There's nothing to explain. I just thought you were being kind to me.' She turned towards him and in anger, told him she was not the kind of French woman who would give herself to a German for a few favours.

Her words cut him like a knife and he grabbed her again. 'Let me go!' Simone struggled again and in doing so, her bag fell on the car floor. The knife was no longer in reach. 'Let me go!' she screamed again.

'Martine – calm down. I love you. I would never hurt you.' His eyes bore a great sadness. 'You are not just some French whore. Never think that. I fell in love with you from the moment I saw you on the train.'

Simone laughed. 'You're married! This is ridiculous. Maybe in a few weeks or months, you will return to Germany – then what?'

'We can't think about tomorrow. This war has taught me that. It's now that's important. We have to grab what happiness we can.'

Simone wanted to laugh again, more out of relief that he wasn't going to kill her than anything else, but in a twist of fate, she realised she had him where she wanted him. If she played her cards right, she could lure him to his death. If not, she would probably never see him again and might even end up arrested and on the next train to Germany. He apologised and started the car. This time it was Simone who took the initiative. She leaned over and kissed his cheek.

'I'm sorry I laughed. It's just that this came as a shock. She reciprocated his kiss, this time with more passion. That moment of passion lasted for several minutes, and to her surprise and great relief, he did not try to make love to her.

'Your kisses tell me that you do feel something for me.' He swept away a few strands of loose hair from her face. 'So can I remain hopeful?'

Simone asked him to give her time. He pulled her hand to his lips. 'Time may not be on our side, but I respect your wishes.'

When he dropped her off at the hotel, she thanked him for a lovely evening, careful not to allow him to kiss her in case anyone was watching.

'Will you allow me to take you to dinner again?' he asked. 'Maybe at the weekend as I will be away on business over the next few days.'

'That would be lovely.' She was about to step away when she suddenly bent down and looked at him through the open window. 'You know, I don't even know where you live.'

'I will take you there the next time we meet.'

'I look forward to it.'

Albrecht watched her step inside the hotel before driving away. She caught sight of his car turn out of the square. The hotel manager was in his office when he saw her return. The reception was empty and he called her inside. 'I gave your envelope to Alexandre,' he said. 'And he asked that you meet him in the park tomorrow evening – eight o'clock sharp.'

CHAPTER 23

AT FIVE MINUTES to eight, Simone entered the park and walked along the pathway that meandered through lawns and clusters of shade trees, the fragrance of their blooms floating through the night air. There was no lamplight because of the blackout, but she had no difficulty in finding her way around in the moonlight. Every now and again she passed a couple – lovers in an embrace, grabbing what happiness they could amidst the horrors of war.

Simone barely recognized Alexandre. He was wearing a grey wig and beard and a dishevelled grey overcoat. He also had a walking stick, which she guessed contained a weapon of some sort. She sat on the bench next to him and in an instant, he knew something was wrong.

'What is it?' he asked.

'I don't think I can go through with this,' she replied.

There was a moment of silence while they waited for two people to pass. 'Explain yourself. What's happened between now and when I last saw you? You got the job at the Gestapo HQ which was the biggest hurdle.'

Simone began by saying she thought his information on Bruno Albrecht was wrong. 'It's Mueller who's behind all this – not Albrecht. He told me last night that Mueller wanted the Legrands executed as an example to the Resistance, but Albrecht talked him out of the idea saying it would only antagonize the Resistance even more. Mueller then came up with the idea of sending them to a concentration camp, which we know, would kill Madame Marie. Finally, it was agreed that they would be sent to some sort of detention centre in Germany where they could be used as a bargaining chip if the Allies won.'

'Do you know where this place is?'

'No, except that there are other VIPs there and it's well guarded. At least they won't suffer hard labour.'

Alexandre thought about it for a while and admitted it was some consolation, if indeed Mueller did keep his word. 'What else do you have to tell me? Your note said you memorized the names of those recently executed. Who were they?'

Simone tried to recall as many as she could. 'As it was my first day, I couldn't write anything down. In fact we are being watched all the time, suffice to say we're not talking about a handful of people; there were several hundred names. I was told to add my own version of their death in some cases.' She stared straight ahead for a while. 'It took me all my time not to walk out, but how could I? I am now classed as "one of them" and will be watched. To make it worse, there is a frightful woman called Olga Bauer who watches us like a hawk. Everyone is scared to death of her. What's more, she doesn't like me.'

Alexandre listened, taking in every word. He saw how distressed she was by the tears in her eyes and handed her his handkerchief.

'What also torments me is that they have given me Fifi's old desk,' she added.

'Anything else?' he asked.

'Isn't that enough?' she snapped. 'What more do you want me to say – that I am afraid of being found out as an imposter every second I am there.' She wiped her eyes. 'My God! What have I got myself in to?'

'Martine, have you forgotten that we worked closely together over the past weeks. I know you well – well enough to know you've not told me everything.'

His words were soft, caring, and inquiring. He was like Pascal and Jacques; too smart to be fooled.

'Alright – if you must know, Adler told me he's fallen in love with me.' She blurted it out feeling rather foolish. It was not what the leader of a largest Champenoise Maquis group wanted to hear.

'Did you…?'

'You mean did I sleep with him? The answer is no.' She perceived a

176

look of relief in his eyes. 'I told you I wouldn't, although I don't know how long I can string him along. That's what frightens me.'

They sat in silence for a while.

'Do you want to pull out?' he asked.

Simone knew it was the last thing he wanted. He was testing her. 'Of course not, but I will ask you again, all things considered, are you sure he is as bad as you make out?'

Alexandre took a deep breath. 'I didn't want to tell you this – at least not yet, but before Pascal's death, he was in touch with an agent from the OSS.'

'You mean the Office of Strategic Services – the Americans?'

'That's right. What the man told him was off the records, so it's for your ears only – understood!'

Simone nodded. 'Of course.'

'Apparently Mueller and Albrecht have been in touch with them. I am not sure who approached who as these sort of things can get extremely murky, although there are many dubious situations like this these days, especially with the Allies gaining ground. One never quite knows what to believe. It seems that in the event of an Allied win, a proposal was put to the Americans that they were to give evidence against the Reich.' He paused to let his words sink in and gauge her reaction. 'Here's the catch – in return for a pardon.'

'What! The murderers want a pardon?'

'Unbelievable as it seems, yes. There would be some sort of mock trial, of course; they may serve a few months, but the Americans will put pressure on the judiciary and they will be free – free to work for the Americans.'

Simone stared at him. 'Free to work for the Americans – I don't understand. They are criminals – at least Mueller is.'

'It seems complicated now, but they know the Americans are against the Soviets; they don't trust them because they are fearful of the spread of communism. This was told to Pascal in confidence because many resistants are communists and they wouldn't want to hear anything negative. The Soviets are our allies now, but there is still a deep philosophical mistrust about the rise of communism when we win the war. The Soviets have fought hard; lost a lot of men, and they will expect to keep whatever land they recapture. No-one wants an uneasy peace treaty as we had after the Great War.'

'If what you are saying is true, how many killers will escape justice?'

Alexandre shrugged. 'Who knows? The point is, Pascal told London about this. De Gaulle for one, wants true justice for the French, but is wary about the French communists in the Resistance. The British Government and MI6 have not made their thoughts clear to anyone outside the organisation, but Pascal knew SOE would want accountability.'

'Have they actually given the go ahead to assassinate them?' Simone asked.

'Not in so many words; that's where all this is murky, but Pascal knew SOE and MI6 well. There is competition between the Americans and the British when it comes to intelligence and Pascal left me in no doubt that we were not to give Albrecht and Mueller the chance to avoid justice.' Alexandre saw she was having a hard time digesting this information. 'Now you understand the importance of the mission.'

She shook her head and sighed. '*Merde*, what a mess. So what you're saying is, there is some plan to use the Germans for their own gain after the war.'

'It seems that way. So, Martine, this will be the last time I will ask you, do you want out or not?'

'Of course not.'

Alexandre declared it was getting late and they'd better be making their way back. 'Come on, I'll walk with you as far as the fountain.'

Acting like an invalid with his walking stick, Simone, held on to him as she would an old man. She had the distinct feeling Alexandre was enjoying the closeness. When it came time to part, he told her there were always people looking out for her and she shouldn't think she was alone. He also told her that she was the one who had to choose a time and place for the assassinations to minimize reprisals against innocent people, which, he assured her, would not be light in view of Albrecht and Mueller's importance.

'One more thing,' he said, before parting ways. 'You asked if we were wrong about Albrecht. The answer is no. We have evidence that he has personally executed Frenchmen or entrapped them for the Gestapo. Don't be fooled by his gentlemanly ways. He is a charmer and I don't doubt that he has fallen for you, but maybe not quite as deeply as he makes out. He's good at double-bluffing. Use his amorous ways to your advantage, but remember, the Gestapo have you on file and you will be under the watchful eye of their intelligence which makes you one of the first people they would suspect when something happens.'

*

Over the next couple of days Simone returned to her work at 18, rue Jeanne d'Arc with a sense of foreboding. Each day she was given a different ledger with different information to fill out. The latest ones were on train transports and the destinations varied from Auschwitz to Dachau and several places she'd never heard of before. Some of them, especially the unfortunate souls destined for Natzweiler Struthof in Alsace, bore an NN against the name; *Nacht und Nebel* – Night and Fog – which meant they were to disappear without a trace.

She developed a friendship with the woman at the next desk who imparted snippets of information during their breaks. The woman said she had got the job through her boyfriend, a Frenchman called Henri who supplied black market goods to the Germans. She also let slip that Henri worked for the Resistance. Simone professed to not knowing any resistants and the woman laughed. 'Surely you must know someone?' she said, and pressed her further. 'What about the old lady and her son who own the Champagne house?'

Simone was shocked. She had never mentioned the Legrands. How did she know that?

'I have no idea what you're talking about?' she said.

'I overheard Fräulein Olga discussing it with Obersturmbannführer

Hermann.' Simone refused to continue the conversation. 'Don't worry,' the woman whispered. 'Your secret is safe with me.'

However, this conversation *did* worry Simone. Something was telling her that the net was closing in on her. What else did they know? She had to get this assignment over with once and for all and resolved to tell Alexandre that it had to take place as soon as Albrecht returned. The same day she was due to meet up with Alexandre, Fräulein Olga asked her to stay behind after the other secretaries left for the day.

When they were alone, Fräulein Olga's frosty demeanour changed to one of insincere friendliness. She asked Simone to take a seat and offered her real coffee and cake. 'How are you settling in?' she asked with a caring soft voice and a warm smile. 'You may not be able to type, but your work is good.'

Simone was wary and reciprocated the same false friendliness. 'Thank you,' she replied.

Fräulein Olga started to chat like a friend – how did she like living at the hotel? Maybe she should move and find a place of her own; after all, her pay was enough to rent a modest one-room apartment. Little by little, the questions became more intrusive. How well did she know Herr Albrecht? Simone replied that she barely knew him but he'd been kind enough to help her because of his friendship with a mutual friend.

'Ah yes, the Legrands. They left for Germany. Surely he told you.'

Simone's blood ran cold. 'No. Why would he? I told you, I barely know him.'

Fräulein Olga offered Simone a cigarette and waited a few minutes to see how she took the news of the Legrands. 'You weren't aware they were aiding the Resistance?' she asked, her voice still clam and friendly.

'No. I never saw any evidence of it.'

'It says here in your file that you are from Paris.' She opened Simone's personal file. 'I have been to Paris, I have friends there. Where do you live? You might even know them.'

Simone could see the woman was as cunning as a fox, and as slippery as an eel and confidently reeled off the address Jacques had given her in the hope that would be the last of it.

'Are you aware that many resistants in Paris have been rounded up over the past few weeks?' The question came like a bolt out of the blue. Had they been checking into her resistance work there? Worse still, she worried whether Jacques was alright, but then remembered he'd gone to Normandy.

'No, I'm not aware of what's going on in Paris these days, except that people are suffering.' She paused for a moment. 'Can you tell me what the point of this meeting is?'

'It's just a friendly chat. I like to get to know my girls, that's all. Are you afraid I might ask you some awkward questions?'

'Of course not. I've got nothing to hide. If I had, I certainly wouldn't be working here, would I?'

Fräulein Olga noted Simone's demeanour when she responded to her questions. As abruptly as the "little chat" started, it ended. Fräulein Olga bade her a good evening and said she would see her again in the morning, bright and early.

Simone left the building and stopped at a nearby bar to order a drink to steady her nerves. Uppermost on her mind was Claude and Madame Marie. She prayed they would survive. About ten minutes later, she noticed Fräulein Olga walking down the street. She passed the bar without looking inside and Simone decided to follow her. Thankfully the streets were quite busy and she was able to shadow her without being seen. She followed her for about five minutes and to her great surprise, saw her turn into the same street Fifi had lived in – Rue Saint Julien. Halfway down the street, Fräulein Olga took out a key from her bag, unlocked the door and entered the apartment.

Simone couldn't believe her eyes. Did Fräulein Olga live opposite Fifi? Was she partly responsible for Fifi and Pascal's death? Her head was spinning. She would have to let Alexandre know as soon as possible. It was five-thirty and she wasn't due to meet him for another two hours. As she moved away, she noticed another woman turn into the street – the woman who sat next to her at work. The same woman who was trying so hard to be friendly; the same woman who had a boyfriend called Henri.

Simone slipped into the recess of a large doorway. A few people passed and she pretended she was looking at the names of those who lived there. When the woman failed to pass by, Simone peeked her head out and saw her standing by the door of Fräulein Olga's apartment. The door opened and the woman disappeared inside.

'*Putain!*' Simone mumbled to herself, angrily. The two were trying to trap her. Careful not to be seen, she left the street and went straight to the café in the Square des Jacobins. She was angry, upset, and frightened – a lethal cocktail for an agent. Serge had just finished serving a customer when he saw her. 'Good evening, Martine. What can I get you?'

'Something strong,' she said.

Serge realised something was wrong. He looked around and in a low voice asked if she wanted a quiet table inside. She followed him inside and he took her to a table away from prying eyes. He brought her vodka which he said he'd just purchased on the black market from a Ukrainian soldier.

'What is it?' he asked. 'You don't look well.' He leaned forward and gave her a half-smile. 'Don't tell me you've killed someone again?'

'That's not funny,' she replied curtly. 'Although I do feel like killing someone at the moment. Do you know of a man called Henri who is a black-marketeer? Someone who sells to the Germans?'

He laughed. 'Do you know how many men called Henri deal in the black market? Can you be more precise?'

'He has a girlfriend who is a secretary in Rue Jeanne d'Arc.' Simone went on to describe her.

He shook his head. 'Sorry, I can't help you.'

Simone finished her drink in no time and Serge brought her another. 'I know you mean well,' she said, 'but I really can't say any more – except that I may be in grave danger.'

'I gathered that much. You and a few thousand more, so I would say we're in good company.' Despite the gravity of the situation, his laissez-faire attitude made her laugh. 'That's better. Frowning doesn't suit you.' The café began to fill with customers. 'I wish I could sit and talk longer but I have work to do; I can't risk my customers frowning too. Just remember I'm here if you need me.'

The short time with Serge managed to cool her anguish for which she was grateful.

*

Alexandre was waiting for her in the park and to Simone's great surprise, he had someone else with him – Jean-Yves.

'And how is our little Parisian girl?' Jean-Yves gave her a warm embrace.

'Well, well, this is a wonderful surprise. I see the leg has healed well.'

'All thanks to you.' He gestured towards Alexandre, 'This time it's him that has the walking stick.' Alexandre gave him a playful prod with his stick.

'What brings you to Reims?' Simone asked.

'I'm needed here now. The farmhouse is too far away.'

She asked if that was wise as the radio detector vans were everywhere. 'It's dangerous here. You could be picked up at any moment.'

'I'm cautious. A few minutes are all I need, then I'm gone; from one safe house to another.'

'Well just be careful. I don't want to see your name in those files they give me.' She gave a little sigh. 'I've missed you. In fact I've missed you all. My time at the farmhouse was good, even if our *chef* did put us through our paces.' She smiled at Alexandre.

'That's why you're still alive,' Alexandre replied. Their light-hearted banter was cut short. 'What news do you have for me?' He was as direct as ever.

'I'm afraid what we feared has happened. Claude and Madame Marie have left for Germany.' There was a long moment of silence. 'I can't tell you where as it's not in the deportation files I've seen. They are being very secretive about it, so let's pray they survive.'

'What else?'

183

Simone proceeded to tell him about Fräulein Olga and the secretary. His response was the same as hers. 'She must go,' Alexandre said. He left them in no doubt what that meant. 'And the secretary.'

Simone thought it was too risky for her to do it because of her work. Her primary mission was to kill Albrecht and Mueller and she couldn't jeopardize that.

After a short discussion, it was agreed that Jean-Yves would do it.

'I don't want to waste time on this,' Alexandre said. 'Martine could be in danger as we speak. We'll act immediately.'

It was arranged that Simone would lead him to the apartment, check that Fräulein Olga actually did live there, and if she did, she would drop a handkerchief as a signal. From there, Jean-Yves would make his move. She described the two women in detail – their colouring, height, build, facial features: Nothing was left to chance.

The next point of discussion was about Albrecht. Jean-Yves told them a German radio transmission had been intercepted about a secret mission by Hitler to his command bunker near the city of Soissons, in the municipality of Margival in the northern French countryside, southeast of the region of the Somme – where the fierce offensive of the British and their Allies took place in 1916.

'You mean Hitler is actually in France!' Simone couldn't quite believe it. 'They certainly kept it quiet at Rue Jeanne d'Arc.'

Alexandre nodded. 'The meeting took place on the 17 June between the Führer and Field Marshals Rundstedt and Rommel. We believe Albrecht was there. Our intelligence tells us that Rommel and Rundstedt argued for either massive reinforcements or a withdrawal. Naturally Hitler would not hear of it. He views such ideas as treasonable. Things didn't go down well and Hitler has returned to Germany with the orders that they must not retreat.'

Jean-Yves said that *if* their intelligence was correct, Albrecht would return to convey the Führer's orders to his associates to dig in. They still had a long way to go before France was free.

'So when he does return, be aware of this. It could make him all the more unpredictable, so we have to act as soon as possible.' Alexandre added that all being well, it should be over soon. 'We cannot lose heart now. We must be strong. As soon as he returns, let the manager of the hotel know. I want an update. Then we act.'

The meeting ended. Alexandre went one way, Simone the other with Jean-Yves not far behind. The route took them via the Square des Jacobins and Simone stopped to look in a window. Jean-Yves stopped too.

'You see that café over there,' she said to him. 'If you get into trouble, go there. The waiter is called Serge. Tell him you're my friend. He'll look after you.'

She continued to walk ahead and soon turned into Rue Saint Julien. When she passed the door to Fräulein Olga's apartment, she checked the names to see if she did live there. There were two apartments and one was in the name of Bauer. Simone dropped the handkerchief as a sign that it was the correct address and walked on until she was a safe distance away. She stood in a doorway recess and from there, watched Jean-Yves. He picked up the handkerchief, put it in his pocket and rang the doorbell. At first it appeared as though no-one was there and he almost walked away. Then the door opened and Simone recognized Fräulein Olga's blonde hair. In an instant, she noticed Jean-Yves' swift arm movement and Fräulein Olga crumpled into his arms. He glanced towards Simone and disappeared inside the building, carrying the body in his arms.

Simone looked on, terrified something would go wrong, but a few minutes later, he exited the building and walked towards her. When he got closer, Simone stepped out of the shadows, looped her arm through his, and together they sauntered away, like lovers, oblivious to anyone but each other.

'It's done,' he whispered. 'Fräulein Olga didn't have time to see the knife. I carried her inside and luckily, she'd left the door to her apartment ajar. The secretary you described so well happened to be in the bedroom. When she heard the door close, she called out, "Olga, who was it?". When she saw me walk into the bedroom, she got more than a shock. She was naked in the German's bed. It appears the two were lovers. I shot her before she could scream.'

Simone gave a deep sigh of relief. A couple of streets away they decided it was best to part company.

'Take care, Martine,' Jean-Yves said. 'I saw the way Alexandre looked at you. He's more worried about you than he lets on.'

With those words ringing in her ears, they went their separate ways.

CHAPTER 24

WHEN BOTH FRÄULEIN Olga and the secretary failed to turn up the following day, rumours quickly started to circulate that something untoward had happened. Obersturmbannführer Hermann sent a woman from another department to take over Fräulein Olga's job until she returned. He was not in a good mood.

'There will be no breaks today,' he bellowed. The women looked at each other, fearful for their own safety.

At one point, Simone was allowed to uses the Ladies Room. Another secretary was just about to leave. 'I wonder what's happened?' she said to Simone. 'Did you know they were lovers?' She shrugged. 'Personally, I hope the Resistance killed them. Bitches – both of them.'

By the time it came to leave, the building was buzzing with more news. Someone had been sent to Fräulein Olga's apartment and discovered both her and the secretary had been murdered. 'One was knifed, the other shot,' the same secretary whispered to Simone. 'I think I will celebrate tonight!'

The Gestapo were on high alert and no one was allowed to leave before being questioned as to their whereabouts from the time they left the building the day before. Simone was interviewed by Obersturmbannführer Hermann himself. 'I went for a drink, then back to my hotel,' Simone said, confidently. 'Then I went for a walk and was in bed by nine-thirty.'

When she left the building, she saw Albrecht's car parked outside. She'd noticed that he often liked to drive himself, but this time his chauffeur was standing by the car. He recognized Simone and snapped his heels together. 'Good evening, Fräulein Dumont.'

She acknowledged him and walked on, wondering when – or if

– Albrecht would contact her after what had happened. Back at the hotel, she pulled the manager aside and asked him to give a coded message to Alexandre saying that Albrecht was back and she'd keep him updated. As usual, the manager's wife took over his duties while he delivered her message. Simone went to her room and lay down on the bed, deep in thought. In her mind, she was running through the various scenarios of how to kill Albrecht and it was making her feel ill. Even more so, was the worry about how to do it without getting killed herself or causing a repeat of an Oradour-sur-Glane reprisal. She drifted into a light sleep when there was a soft knock on the door. It was the manger's wife. Making sure no-one in any of the other rooms could hear, she told her that Albrecht was waiting for her downstairs.

'He particularly stressed that you should wear something beautiful,' she added. Simone blushed and was about to apologise when the woman stopped her. 'No need. I am aware of what's going on.'

Simone thanked her for her understanding. 'Please tell Herr Albrecht that I will be down soon.'

She spruced herself up, putting on her new dress from *Maison de Paris*. She thought about putting her pistol in her bag, but decided against it because Alexandre had specifically asked her not to do anything without his blessing. But she did place her retractable knife in her belt as she so often did.

Albrecht's face lit up when he saw her. When he took her hand and kissed it, she could smell alcohol on his breath. She glanced back at the hotel manager's wife as she left. Her eyes warned her to take care.

'Where are we going?' Simone asked as she got into the car. Thankfully Albrecht had given the chauffeur the evening off and she had him to herself without the fear of prying eyes watching her every move.

'You asked where I lived and that's where I'm taking you.'

Simone was apprehensive but acted delighted. Albrecht told her that he normally stayed at a variety of exclusive hotels and villas in Épernay, Reims, and various other towns and cities, all of which she knew were requisitioned.

'However there is one place I have that's quite special to me. You will love it – but it's never been a home. I've had no-one to share it with.' He reached out to hold her hand. 'You are the first woman I've ever taken there.'

'I'm honoured.' She gave him a warm smile.

His villa was about twenty kilometres southeast of Épernay. It was one Madame Marie and Alexandre had told her about, that was requisitioned from the family of a distinguished Champagne house who had fled France for America at the start of the Occupation. Although he didn't live there, it was still well guarded. An electric fence surrounded the five acre property and it was manned by German guards at all times. Simone recalled her first impression of Madame Marie's bourgeois villa, but this surpassed even that. The sign over the gate said Chateau Clarion. An armed guard opened the gate, saluted Albrecht, and after a brief chat, the car drove along the driveway to the white chateau with grey-slated rooftops and turrets. An elderly German-speaking French couple who lived in the servants' quarters greeted them outside the main entrance with the deference of a man of distinction. They addressed him in German.

'It's good to see you again, *Mein Herr*,' the man said. 'I hope everything is to your liking while you are here.'

Albrecht took Simone through to the salon, which doubled as a music room. 'It's simply beautiful,' she said, looking out of the window with its spectacular view across the grounds towards the vineyards. 'What a pity not to share it with someone.' It took a great deal for her to say that without feeling bad for the real owners. 'Is that the River Marne over there?'

'Yes. The few times I'm here, I often sit by the river. It's a tranquil place; a place for reflection because it reminds me that during the Great War, both Germans and French died side-by-side in this region; one vast cemetery.'

'Maybe you can show me,' Simone said. 'You always seem so busy. I would like to see this other side of you – the contemplative side.'

Albrecht pulled her to him and started to kiss her. Simone was prepared for this and returned his kisses. Strangely, it was as if her body and feelings were separate. After a few minutes, his hands began to explore her body, at first along her back, and then to her buttocks. He felt her tense and stopped.

'I'm sorry. It's just that you set my heart on fire. When I am with you, I am reminded that I have feelings once again. These last few years, I've conditioned myself to be someone uncaring – someone that is not me.'

She put her hand on his cheek and stroked it gently. 'Maybe you *can* show me who you really are.' She smiled; a soft caring smile that made him want to kiss her again. 'But not now, later. I'm famished. I haven't eaten all day.'

'Of course. Forgive me.' He rang the bell and the Frenchman appeared. 'Ask Madame to prepare dinner for us, please, Philippe. We will dine outside tonight. The weather is perfect.'

'That sounds like a wonderful idea, Bruno.' Her voice purred with affection. 'We can savour the stillness of a beautiful evening together.' She moved closer and touched his arm. 'And then you can show me the river.'

'Splendid. I would like that.'

While they were waiting for the food to be prepared, they sat outside in the garden. Albrecht opened a bottle of fine Champagne that he'd acquired when he requisitioned the house. It was at times like this, in the still of the evening that Simone thought about her time with Madame Marie. She even missed Ulysse and hoped he'd settled in with Olivier and wasn't pining for his mistress. She quickly snapped herself out of her nostalgic thoughts and asked about his trip.

'I missed you,' she began sweetly. 'I don't know if you're aware, but things have not gone well here. Fräulein Bauer was found dead in her apartment and I believe one of the other secretaries was with her.'

'Yes, Mueller informed me.' He bore a worried look. He seemed reluctant to talk about it but she pressed him further.

'They seem to think it was the Resistance? I heard talk that there would be reprisals.'

'I doubt if Mueller would order reprisals for two secretaries – lesbians at that!' Simone was shocked at the callous way he said that. 'Anyway at this point in time, reprisals wouldn't help.'

'What do you mean by that?'

'I've just come back from a very important meeting. I can't tell you where, except to say that it was not fruitful.'

'I'm not following you,' she replied.

'A week ago, I thought we might still have a chance. Now I don't believe it.' It was the first time Simone had seen him so vulnerable. Gone was his arrogance and the undefeatable might of the Reich, and in its place was a man reduced to fear – just like everyone else the Germans and collaborators had beaten into submission.

She sidled up to him, hoping he would say more. He did. 'Rommel and Rundstedt believe we can't win and must evacuate. Unfortunately...' He stopped short of mentioning Hitler by name. 'Unfortunately higher powers have overruled them.' He looked at her with a deep sadness in his eyes. 'So you see, my dear Martine, the deaths of two secretaries are unimportant in the scheme of things.'

Simone was careful to appear understanding rather than confrontational. 'Bruno, if you think all is lost, why don't you go back to Germany while you still have a chance?'

He burst out laughing. 'Do you realise what you are saying? I have been posted here and must remain until the end. If I return to Germany I will be shot as a traitor. No, that is not an option.' After a moment of silence, he perked up and put on a brave face. 'The Führer has secret weapons. Maybe they will save us.'

Simone had heard all about the rockets, but said nothing. If she and the Resistance knew, then the Allies would find a way to destroy them.

Philippe arrived to say that the food was ready and a table for two had been laid under the shade of a tree. The setting was beautiful. The table had been laid with a crisp white tablecloth with a fine dinner service decorated with pretty pastoral scenes in the style of a toile de Jouy. The spoils of war, Simone thought to herself. Philippe's wife had

191

thoughtfully placed a vase of roses on the table and placed lanterns around the table and from the boughs of the tree. It was a magical scene and quite took her breath away.

'Oh, Bruno, I am so glad you brought me here. It's an honour for me to share your little slice of Paradise. You must come more often.' Her comment pleased him.

Dinner was a salad of foie gras with cold cuts of meat, terrine and cheese. After years of rations and a near starvation diet, the richness was hard to take. 'Aren't you enjoying it?' Albrecht asked.

'Of course, it's just that I'm not used to such rich food – not since the last time we dined out. '

After they'd finished their meal, they lit up cigarettes and sat for a while in silence, enjoying the peacefulness of the night. A myriad of irregular, luminous bands of millions of stars stretched across the sky, the nightingales sang their beautiful song, and somewhere, an owl hooted. At that moment, they heard a low droning sound. The sound grew louder and they both looked up. Although they couldn't see them, they instinctively knew what it was – hundreds of Allied bombers were flying overhead towards Germany on another bombing mission. *Which town or village would lie in ruins? Who would lose a loved one tonight?* It was a sound she would remember till the day she died.

Five minutes later, the sound faded. 'I don't know what it is about you,' Albrecht said. 'I barely know you – which is not wise for a man in my position – yet I feel at ease with you.'

His words – *I barely know you* – resonated. 'There's not much to know. As I told you, I'm a nurse. I came here to get away from the turmoil of Paris, and apart from that, I haven't done much with my life. Surely the other women in your life, not to mention your wife, must be far more interesting.'

He frowned. 'Not another word about other women, especially my wife. I haven't heard from her in a long time.' He looked up at the sky wistfully. 'Maybe it was one of those bombers that took her away.'

Simone could see the combination of too much drink and the

bombers was making him melancholic and suggested they go for a walk. 'Take me to the place where you go to think,' she said. 'The place by the river.'

They picked up a lantern each and headed towards the vineyards. At a certain point, an undulating field of wildflowers interspersed with trees sloped gently towards the River Marne. Along the side of the bank were thickets of bushes and yellow marigolds. Colourful dragonflies hovered across the clear water as it ran past, splashing over the occasional rocks and pebbles that lined the bank.

'It's divine,' Simone said. 'I can see why you love it so much.' She set down her lantern, kicked her shoes off, pulled up her dress a little, and waded into the water until it covered her calves. 'The water is so cool,' she called out. Albrecht was bewitched by her playfulness. 'Come in,' she shouted. He refused, preferring to sit on the river bank and watch her.

Simone wasn't simply playing in the water; she was using this time to think. This was the perfect spot to kill him. Not a soul in sight. Even the guards couldn't see them here. They were completely isolated. There was one problem however, everyone would know she had been with him and she would be arrested immediately. All the same, it presented the best opportunity so far with minimal probability of civilian reprisals.

She came out of the water and lay down on the grass next to him. 'Why don't we come back here tomorrow evening? We could have a picnic, and afterwards, we could...' She pulled him to her.

He finished the sentence for her. 'And afterwards we could make love.' He kissed her. 'I want to make love now; tomorrow is a lifetime away.' His kisses became more passionate and he put his hand under the skirt of her dress, kneading her thighs sensuously, and as she thought, like a man who knew how to pleasure a woman.

Simone closed her eyes, gave a little sigh of delight, and at the same time, moved his hand away. 'Not now.' Albrecht was becoming too aroused and she needed to cool his ardour quickly. She pushed him over on to his back and leaned over him, returning his kisses. 'Tomorrow my love, I promise.'

He pressed her mouth to his. 'Martine, why do you make me wait? Can't you see I want you – now – this very minute – not tomorrow.'

She ran her hand over his cheek and lips, and then sat up, looking at the water glistening in the moonlight. 'You know what I want to do tomorrow?'

'What?'

'I want to bathe in that water – naked. *Then* we will make love.'

The idea appealed to him and he pulled her to him, kissing her with such intensity, she feared she would give in to him.

'And now I must go back to Reims. It's late and it's been a long day.'

'Aren't you going to stay the night? I can get my chauffeur to drop you off in the morning.'

Simone slapped his arm playfully. 'All good things are worth waiting for, you know.'

CHAPTER 25

IT WAS WELL after curfew when she was dropped off at the hotel. The place was unusually quiet but the manager was still up. 'I've been waiting for you,' he said. 'You have a guest. He's waiting for you in your room. Simone didn't need to ask who it was. When she unlocked the door, she saw Alexandre, his gun aimed in her direction. He had been lying on her bed flicking through one of her fashion magazines while he waited for her. She locked the door and sat on the side of the bed while she took her shoes off.

'The manager informed me of your rendezvous,' he said, his voice barely a whisper. 'I needed to see for myself that you were fine.' He looked her up and down. 'You look very pretty; that dress suits you.' He saw a section of the hem was still damp and asked what happened.

'I was hot and paddled in the Marne.'

He knitted his eyebrows together in a frown. 'Don't be smart.'

'I'm not.' She took a cigarette from the packet lying on the bedside table. He flicked his lighter and lit it for her. Their eyes met.

'I was worried about you, if you must know,' he said.

She smiled. 'As you see, I'm fine. In fact, I think I've found the perfect place to dispose of Bruno.'

He raised his eyebrows. 'Bruno now, is it? How touchingly close.'

'Sarcasm doesn't suit you,' she said, blowing out a curl of cigarette smoke. 'Do you want to hear what I have to say or are you going to make me feel bad for flirting with a man I detest?'

Alexandre apologised. 'I just don't like to think of him touching you.' He looked at her hair and pulled a blade of grass out of it.

She quickly picked up her hairbrush and brushed it several times. 'There! Now let's get down to business. As I said, I've found the perfect place.' She described Albrecht's villa and the grounds around it, particularly the area where the River Marne passed by this particular part of the property. She also told him it was Albrecht's favourite spot, and about the proposed evening meal and swim in the river.

'How do you plan to kill him? From what you say, a gun would be heard by the guards, unless it's the one Pascal used that has a silencer.'

'That wouldn't work,' Simone replied. 'It would look suspicious if I took my handbag to this spot, and the gun is not exactly small. My own gun would be heard, so that's out.' Alexander asked if Albrecht would have his gun with him. 'Unfortunately, yes. He's never without it. Killing him with a knife is also out of the question as it would leave a mark.'

'What then?'

'It must look accidental, possibly a drowning – that way there would be no wounds.'

'Albrecht is not exactly a small man and I would imagine he's a good swimmer, so how will you overpower him?'

'I've thought about that. There are rocks along the bank. I can catch him unawares when we go swimming. I will hit him on the back of the head with a rock and drown him.'

Alexandre flung the magazine aside and paced the room angrily. 'So you are telling me that a man like Albrecht will not notice you picking up a rock. It's a preposterous idea. NO!'

Simone continued. 'It will be an accidental death and I'll run back to the house to get help. This way there will be no reprisals.'

'No, I said.' He was still angry with her. She stood up to face him and in her distress, banged her fist on his shoulder. 'Don't you realise I can't keep stringing him along. He expects me to make love to him and he won't wait another night. I'll be forced to…'

Alexandre grasped her wrist to calm her down and drew her into his arms. 'My Martine, it's too risky. It could all backfire and I couldn't bear to lose you as well.'

She pulled herself from his arms and looked into his eyes. 'What are you trying to say?'

'Can't you see?' he replied.

'Then say it – tell me you love me!'

He let go of her and turned away. 'This war has dulled my senses –except one. Let's leave it that.'

Simone slumped down on the bed. He was in love with her and couldn't say it. Why? His heart bore a great pain and he couldn't let it go. They sat next to each in silence for a while. Finally, Alexandre said he liked the idea but he had a bad feeling about it. Simone assured him she was a capable woman and she would judge the situation as it arose. In the end, she promised him that if she had doubts about pulling it off successfully, she would not go ahead and they'd find another way.

It was almost three o'clock in the morning when he slipped out of the hotel. Simone was exhausted and fell asleep easily. When she woke in the morning, she was late for work and was chastised by the woman who had taken Fräulein Olga's place.

Knowing that she was meeting Albrecht again in the evening, the day dragged by slowly and she went over and over things in her mind to make sure nothing could go wrong. It wasn't easy to concentrate because even at this late stage, there were more deportations and more executions to be written in the ledger. In fact the executions that had once taken place in the privacy of the Gestapo yard before she got there were now taking place at various times of the day. Apart from the tap-tap-tap of the typewriters, and the occasional slamming of a car door outside the building, the silence in the room was now interrupted by screams or bursts of machine-gun fire in the Gestapo yard. The women dared not look at each other. After work, Simone walked part of the way home with another secretary.

'I've heard a rumour that they're getting ready to evacuate the building,' she whispered. 'Things aren't looking good.'

'How did you find that out?' Simone asked.

'My fiancé is a local truck driver. He disposes of the dead and transports the other poor souls to the railway carriages or other trucks to be taken to Germany.'

Simone wondered if this wasn't another trick to fool her, like the other secretary's imaginary lover in the Resistance, and she listened without commenting. Back at the hotel, she whispered this fact to the hotel manager and he said he would pass it on. That evening, Simone refreshed herself, put on her best dress from *Maison de Paris*, and dabbed a little perfume on her wrist and behind her ears. She wanted to look her best and knowing that she would be undressing, put on her prettiest lingerie; ivory silk, edged with lace. It had cost a small fortune.

She still kept her retractable knife hidden in her belt, just in case, but hoped she wouldn't have to use it. She looked at her watch. Albrecht was late and she began to worry something was wrong. She went downstairs and waited for him. The manager had gone out on "an errand" and his wife was behind the reception desk. She could see Simone was not her usual self.

'Would you like a glass of wine while you wait?' she asked.

Simone needed to keep her wits about her and refused. At that moment, Albrecht's car pulled up and this time the chauffeur was driving. 'How was your day?' Simone asked Albrecht as she cuddled close to him.

'I don't want to talk about work today. Tonight is our night.'

Simone saw the chauffeur was watching them through the rear view mirror. She had the distinct impression he was wary of her. A few kilometres from Albrecht's villa, they found the road blocked with German armoured vehicles lining the road.

Albrecht got out and wanted to know what was going on. The officer in charge recognized him and saluted. Simone looked on anxiously but couldn't hear what they said. After a brief discussion the officer ordered the men to allow Albrecht's car through.

'What was that all about?' she asked when he got back in the car.

'The Resistance were spotted in the area. It appears they thwarted an ambush, but it's all under control.' He turned to look at her. 'Who knows; maybe it was meant for me.'

The incident unnerved her and she felt her throat tighten. It meant everyone would now be on high alert. It was almost eight when they arrived at the villa and Philippe and his wife had already taken the basket laden with food to the allocated spot by the river.

'I hope you find everything to your liking, *Mein Herr*,' Philippe said. 'The finest food prepared by my Frau and the Champagne is on ice.'

'And the other things I asked for?' Albrecht asked.

'Yes, sir; there are towels too.'

Simone was careful to leave her handbag in the house and together she and Albrecht took a lantern each and headed to the river bank. Everything was laid out so beautifully that it took Simone a few moments to believe it was really happening. A large rug surrounded by more lanterns, a Champagne bucket with ice, the finest silverware, crystal and porcelain plates, and delicate napkins. It was a way of life so removed from her own that she had to pinch herself.

Albrecht took off his jacket and Simone noticed he still wore his holster and gun. She took the platters of food out of the basket while he poured them a drink. For the next ten minutes, they sat together in silence, watching the sun set over the tranquil countryside. With a flourish of a painter, nature herself painted the countryside ever-changing shades of blush pinks to intense reds and gold that deepened as the minutes passed by. She moved closer, so that he could feel her presence, wondering what was going through his mind. All too soon, the fiery reds and pinks were gone, and in their place was a palette of mauves and blues, darkening by the minute. For a brief moment, the war had disappeared for both of them.

Simone was careful not to drink her Champagne. When he wasn't looking, she tipped it away, a little at a time and asked him to pour another while she prepared the food. Philippe's wife had cooked a beautiful terrine in aspic and there were more cold cuts of meat. This was accompanied by an assortment of salads and vegetables. Albrecht was most attentive towards her, caressing the nape of her neck and reaching out to touch her while they were eating. Towards the end of the meal, he started to unbutton her dress and she was finding it harder to quell his ardour. In the meantime, she continued to ply him with drink, always refilling her own and pretending to drink it.

Finally they moved aside the remains of the feast and lay down on the blanket. By now, Albrecht's passion was rising to the point where she had to act. She stood up in front of him, unbuttoned the rest of her dress and slipped out of it. Seeing her standing there in her beautiful lingerie, the curves of her body silhouetted against the backdrop of the river, was more than he could bear. He grabbed her ankle trying to pull her back down beside him. She playfully went along with his desires as he caressed her breasts and tried to pull down her silken knickers. At the same time, she undid his shirt and trousers, coaxing him to take them off too. He did as she wished, removing his gun in the process.

As she continued to kiss him, she carefully slid his gun further away from the blanket out of reach. Finally, after Albrecht had removed the rest of his clothes, she arched her body and let him take off her knickers. The sight of her completely naked, devouring his body as much as he devoured hers, drove him wild and he tried to pin her down and enter her. His desire was making him more determined and she had to act quickly. She rolled over and jumped up.

'Come on,' she said, laughing. 'You promised we would swim together.'

'Later!' He reached out to pull her back down.

She moved quickly, picked up two of the towels, flung one over her shoulder, and the other she threw at him. 'No, my darling – now – then we will make love.' She took the Champagne bottle out of the bucket, picked up their empty glasses and ran towards the edge of the water. 'Come on.'

He sat up and called after her. 'My crazy darling, all right you win.'

She waved the Champagne bottle in the air as he sauntered towards her, refilled their glasses and put the bottle down next to the towel by the side of the bank. Holding the glasses, high, she started to wade into the water. 'It's perfect,' she called out.

The river flowed through the vine-laden countryside, swirling against the rocky bank and glinting brightly in the moonlight, and here and there, overhanging bushes and the branches of a fallen tree created eerie shadows along the riverbank. If Simone expected Albrecht to inch himself into the water, she was wrong. He arched his body into the air and dived into the river with the grace of an expert swimmer, disappearing for a few seconds under the water. When he re-emerged, he swam over towards her and took the glass from her.

'That was impressive,' she said. 'You could have broken your neck.'

'I've swum here many times before. I know this river well.'

His reply was not exactly what she wanted to hear. 'Come on, I'll race you to the other side.'

Even after all the Champagne, Albrecht was a strong swimmer and he reached the opposite bank well before her. She wrapped herself around his body telling him that deserved a kiss. At that moment, they heard the distinct thrumming sound of Allied bombers like the steady rumble of a drum roll heading towards them again.

'Oh, damn!' Simone said, and suggested they swim back again. When they reached the bank, the bombers were already overhead and they stood, immersed in the water watching them. The ack-ack guns could be heard in the distance and tracer bullets curved up into the night sky, ending in puffs of smoke. Albrecht looked up watching it all. It was now or never. Simone moved away a little and picked up the Champagne bottle. Mustering as much strength as she could, she brought it down on the back of his head. The bottle shattered.

Albrecht lurched forward and hovered for a few seconds trying to grasp the side of the bank. As he did, he stared at her for a few moments, wide-eyed with surprise. His mouth opened as if he wanted to say something, but she kicked out, knocking him further away from the bank. His body started to sink, and in one last gasp for life, he reached out his arm towards her. She backed away and watched him sink between the swirling water. In a matter of seconds he was gone and the surface of the water glinted in its usual peaceful and magical way, oblivious to the horror that had just taken place.

Simone could not let his body drift away or she would be accused of his disappearance. She slipped beneath the water and could just make out the dark shape of his body starting to move downstream.

Gathering all her strength, she swam towards him and caught him just in time, bringing him back to the river bank. Somehow, she managed to drag his body out of the water and arranged it in such a way that it looked as though he had slipped as he entered the water. Lastly, she placed the broken Champagne bottle and a glass nearby to make it look like an accident. Staring down at the body, she was deeply aware of the sweet perfume of the night drifting through her nostrils. Its beauty enveloped her, confusing her senses with the horror of what she had done.

The deed of killing Albrecht over, she now had to extricate herself from this terrible mess. She quickly wrapped a towel around her, picked up a lantern and ran back to the house, screaming for help. Within minutes the guards were on the scene, their flashlights shining in her direction. She pointed to the riverbank. 'There's been a terrible accident – down there – by the lanterns. Herr Albrecht! He's dead!'

One man took off his jacket and wrapped it around her shoulder, while the others ran towards the picnic area. The outside light went on at the villa and she could see Philippe and his wife heading towards them. Simone was crying, doing her very best to act like a distraught lover.

'What on earth's happened?' Philippe asked.

'Bruno – Herr Albrecht – he slipped on the rocks – Oh God – I couldn't save him.' She continued to cry.

By this time, the guards had discovered the body. Simone returned to the scene of the crime to help, when in reality, she wanted to make sure they didn't suspect foul play.

'How did it happen?' one of the guards asked, kneeling over the body.

'I was in the water and he was clambering down the rocks to join me when the bombers flew over. He looked up and slipped. I swam back but couldn't do anything. He must have hit his head here.' She pointed to a spot where shards of the Champagne bottle lay scattered about. 'Then he started to slip into the water. It was a struggle for me to stop him from going downstream.' She pointed to the same spot again. 'He was carrying the glasses and Champagne bottle at the time. It all happened so quickly.'

She began to sob again and Philippe's wife picked up another dry towel and covered her head and shoulders. Simone gathered up her clothes from the ground and glanced coyly at the men as she clutched her lingerie. The men eyed her with a mixture of suspicion and lechery.

'Come inside and get dry before you catch a cold,' Philippe's wife said. 'There's little more you can do here.'

As she was being led away, she heard one of the men call out to others to help remove the body and take it back to the house. 'Leave everything else as it is,' the man added. 'The police will want to investigate.' Their words sent shudders down her spine.

Back at the house, the police were called and Mueller himself was also notified. Simone, now fully dressed, sat hunched on the couch trembling like a leaf. The police and a Gestapo doctor from Épernay arrived shortly afterwards.

The police took copious notes while the doctor examined the body. The back of Albrecht's head had a bad gash, dried blood and swelling. Simone was worried he might find traces of glass in the wound, but if he did, he didn't say anything. After several hours, she was told she could leave, and Albrecht's chauffeur was called to take her back to the hotel. It was a harrowing drive as he refused to speak to her and viewed her with suspicion, even though she sobbed theatrically throughout the journey. It was four-thirty in the morning when she arrived at the hotel. The manager was half asleep in his office when he heard her return. He rushed into the lobby to see the chauffeur supporting her to a chair.

'My God, what happened?' he asked. 'You're as white as a sheet.'

'Fräulein Dumont has had a terrible shock,' the chauffeur said, matter-of-factly. 'Please take care of her.' He saluted and left.

'Martine,' the manager said. 'What's happened?' He went to the reception desk, called his wife on the house telephone and poured her a strong drink.

She took one sip and passed out.

CHAPTER 26

ALBRECHT'S ASSASSINATION HAD taken its toll on Simone and she spent the next day resting from nervous exhaustion. By evening she felt a little better and went downstairs to speak with the manager. The place was unusually quiet.

'Has anyone tried to contact me?' she asked.

He shook his head and in a low voice told her that the people she was probably referring to were out of town. He was careful not to mention any names. 'The Allies have taken Caen,' he said, 'and rumour has it there's been an assassination attempt on Hitler. It's all a bit hush-hush, but it looks like even the Germans have had enough. That's why there are few people around this evening.'

This news pleased her, but knowing that she'd undertaken such an important task for the Resistance and still no-one had tried to contact her, worried her immensely. What could possibly take precedence over whether she'd succeeded in her mission and was fine? She particularly worried about Alexandre as he'd been so concerned about her.

The manager assured her someone would make contact soon, but after thinking about it, she decided to go to his safe house. Alexandre stressed she could do that in an emergency, and to Simone, this was an emergency.

There were few people in the cafés that evening. The remnants of the once powerful Wehrmacht were trickling back from Normandy, many on horseback or walking, and the Gestapo and Milice were on the prowl, constantly stopping people and examining their papers, looking for any excuse to haul people into Rue Jeanne d'Arc.

When she reached his apartment, she noticed that the blue pot of bright red-geraniums was not on the window sill, a sign telling her it was not safe to enter, yet she ignored it. She rang the doorbell and the same middle-aged woman who had greeted her before appeared. She looked anxious when she saw Simone, and like before, peered up and down the street to check no-one was following her. She pulled her inside.

'You should not come here,' she said, in an off-hand manner. 'The Gestapo were here a few hours ago. That's why there's no plant pot on the window sill.'

'What happened?'

'Luckily, the monsieur was not here – nor his friend.' The woman took her to Alexandre's apartment and showed her what they'd done. The whole place had been ransacked; furniture all over the floor, and the fillings of cushions and his mattress, slashed. Simone was shocked.

'They questioned me for hours,' the woman said, 'but I told them I had no idea about the man they were looking for. I just rented out the apartment. I also gave them a false name and identity, which confused them even more as that name didn't correspond with the person they were looking for, so I cannot tell you anymore.'

'Do you think the monsieur knew they were on to him?'

The landlady shrugged. 'Maybe. He usually kept to himself, except for the occasional visitor, but there *was* another man who came here quite often over the past week or so. He disappeared beforehand too.' After a brief description, Simone thought that might be Jean-Yves. There was no evidence of the transmitter, which was a relief. 'I think you'd better not stay any longer,' the woman said. 'They might come back.'

Shaken by this latest news, Simone left quickly. She had no idea why the raid had taken place, but it must have something to do with why Alexandre had not come to see her.

The following day, she went back to work at Rue Jeanne d'Arc. It was something she dreaded, but if she didn't show up she was convinced the Gestapo would come for her. She made her way upstairs and bumped into Obersturmbannführer Hermann.

'You didn't come to work yesterday. What happened?' he asked.

'I was ill and stayed in bed all day.' She was about to step into the secretarial room when he told her that Herr Mueller wanted to see her.

'What – now?' She realised that sounded ridiculous.

Obersturmbannführer Hermann looked at her in a disapproving manner. 'Do you expect him to wait while you powder you nose?' His voice was curt and filled with sarcasm.

'I don't know where his office is.'

He called someone to take her. Simone's heart started racing again. This was not going to be easy. The man knocked on Mueller's door. A voice called out "Herein". The man stepped inside to say Fräulein Dumont was here. She heard Mueller tell him to show her in. The man clicked his heels, gave a Hitler salute and Simone stepped inside the large office, her heart hammering in her chest.

Mueller sat back in his black leather chair and smiled. 'Take a seat, Fräulein.' His cold eyes surveyed her for what seemed like an interminably long time – the intimidation tactic which she still hadn't quite got used to, and probably never would.

'I gather you were with Herr Albrecht, when his unfortunate death occurred.' It was more of a statement than a question.

Simone took her handkerchief out of her bag in readiness to mop her tears in a moment of grief. 'That's right.'

'How did it happen?' he asked, in a calm and caring voice that belied his frosty exterior.

Simone went through the story, carefully pausing to appear saddened and distressed at the appropriate places. She concluded with the statement that she had become close to him over the past few days.

'What will happen to his body?' she asked. 'Can I see him before they bury him – for one last time?' She fidgeted nervously with her handkerchief.

'I'm afraid that won't be possible. On orders from the Führer himself, his body was sent back to Germany today. He was well-respected and will be given a proper Reich farewell, which he deserves. His family has also been notified – especially his wife.' Simone couldn't bear to look at him and instead, stared at the large oriental carpet on which his desk and the chairs were placed. 'You do know he had a wife, don't you?' Mueller asked.

'Yes, but he refused to talk about her.'

Mueller grinned – a dark and dangerous grin. 'I bet he did.' He gave a heavy sigh. 'What I find puzzling, Martine – do you mind if I call you Martine?' She shook her head. 'What I find puzzling, Martine, is that you would become the mistress of a man who sent your employer and her son to Germany. I would have thought you'd despise him.'

Simone knew he was trying to trick her. 'Firstly, he was *not* my lover. For what it's worth, we never made love. Bruno was a gentleman with me. I grew to love his kindness.'

Mueller laughed. 'I think I know Herr Albrecht – or Bruno – as you came to call him, rather better than you. But my dear, we will not go into that now.' When he saw her start to sob he cracked his knuckles together angrily. 'I am in two minds whether to send you on the next transport to Germany, but I have too many other important things on my mind at the moment.'

He stood up, walked around the desk, and stood over her. 'Stop that snivelling immediately and stand up.' Simone did as she was told. His face was so close to hers she could smell his cologne. 'Get out of my sight, French whore. Don't let me ever see you here again – or anywhere for that matter. If I do, I may be tempted to…' He didn't finish the sentence, instead calling a guard outside.

'Take away Fräulein Dumont's work Identity Card and escort her from this building immediately.'

Five minutes later, she found herself, unceremoniously dumped into the street like a piece of old furniture. The guard told her to stay away or she would be shot on sight.

On the one hand it was a relief not to have to go back to 18, rue Jeanne d'Arc again; on the other hand, she knew Mueller probably suspected foul play. Obviously he had no evidence to prove it, but since when did the Gestapo need evidence for anything they did? Wondering what to do next, she went to the square to have a drink with Serge. Maybe he had snippets of news to impart.

He was pleased to see her. 'I heard about Bruno Albrecht's death,' he said. 'Good riddance, if you ask me. Under that gentlemanly exterior, he was a nasty piece of work.'

'Besides being German, why do you say that?' Simone asked.

'He was responsible for sending many Jews to Poland.'

'How do you know that?'

'Working for the Abwehr, he made lists of them prior to the German Occupation. Of course, he had a few favourites who paid him a small fortune for their freedom. As for the Legrands, it's believed he actually liked them.' He shrugged. 'That's what they say anyway. I personally believe he was behind Pascal and the blonde woman's death.'

It was the first time, she'd heard him mention Pascal's name. 'How do you know Pascal?' she asked.

'He used this place as a safe house. We got weapons from him. It's better if you don't ask any more questions. That's why I didn't mention it before.'

Simone knew he was right. The less people knew, the better. 'I'm thinking of going back to Paris,' she said.

'Paris is a mess at the moment. It's expected it will be liberated soon so the Germans are doing their best to get revenge. Maybe you should wait a while longer.'

'It's not safe here either, and I need to work.'

'There's always work for you here. You could help my mother behind the bar. She needs a rest.'

The thought made Simone smile. 'Thanks, but I'd make a lousy barmaid.'

Serge always had a way of making her laugh. 'The offer is there in case you change your mind.'

Two days passed and still there was no news from Alexandre, or anyone for that matter. In the end, she decided they must have important Resistance work to attend to and bought a ticket back to Paris. The hotel manager and his wife were disappointed to hear she was leaving.

'I can't hang about any longer and I'm running out of money,' Simone said. 'I leave in two days' time.'

With the Allies gaining ground, Reims was becoming more dangerous by the hour due to ever-increasing sporadic shootings by the

Resistance of collaborators and Milice. There were more heavy-handed Gestapo roundups and she decided to stay in her room until the day of her departure, which looked like it might be delayed due to constant sabotage on all train lines in and around the area. Getting a lift to Paris by other means was virtually impossible, as most remaining cars and trucks had been requisitioned and there was no fuel to be had anyway. Even the horses were needed for the German Army because of abandoned vehicles.

Just before dawn on the day of her departure there was a soft knock on her door. By now, Simone's nerves were so frayed that she thought it was the Gestapo. She grabbed her gun in readiness to shoot. If it was the Gestapo, she would rather die fighting than suffer torture in the basement of Rue Jeanne d'Arc. She opened the door a little to see who it was.

'Baptiste! What are you doing here? Come in quickly.'

'There's no time to talk. Pack your things and get out of here – now. I'll meet you outside the side entrance. I borrowed a milk cart.' He left immediately. Simone hurriedly threw everything into her suitcase and quietly went downstairs. There was no-one at the reception desk and the manager's office was locked. She hated the idea of leaving without saying goodbye, but it couldn't be helped.

The side door to the hotel was unlocked and Baptiste was waiting for her next to the horse-drawn milk cart. He took her suitcase from her, jumped up on the cart and hid it behind the large milk cans. There were also several bales of hay at the back. He pulled her up and handed her a blanket. 'Wrap yourself in this and lie down here.' Without uttering a word, she did as she was told. He covered her with the hay before setting off through the deserted streets.

The milk cart clattered loudly on the cobblestones and Simone was sure they would be stopped. Before long, a combination of mental exhaustion and the rhythmic clip-clopping of the horse's hooves lulled her to sleep. Sometime later, she awoke as the hay was lifted away and Baptiste pulled back the blanket.

'Where am I?' Simone asked, her body stiff from the ride.

'Somewhere safe,' Baptiste replied.

CHAPTER 27

SIMONE WAS RELIEVED to find herself back at the old farmhouse surrounded by her friends from the Maquis who welcomed her with open arms. She scanned their faces, but there was no sign of Alexandre. One of the Spaniards, Enrique, jumped up onto the cart, lifted her up and passed her into the arms of another maquisard.

'Welcome back,' they called out.

'Where's Alexandre?' she asked, brushing away the hay clinging to her dress and in her hair.

The men's smiles instantly disappeared. 'Inside,' Baptiste said. The look on their faces alarmed her. Something was terribly wrong. She followed him inside the building, and there lying on a mattress was Alexandre, his eyes closed and his bullet riddled body covered in a bloodied sheet. He was being tended to by Sonia, the woman from the Troyes Resistance, and a doctor.

'Oh God! No!' This was the last thing Simone had expected. For a brief moment, it was as if her heart stopped, her face paled, and she felt as if her legs would give way.

'Is he...?'

'Dead?' replied the doctor. 'No. He's in a coma, but its touch and go. We need you to help us. There are two others in the next room who also need our attention.'

Simone knelt down by his side and examined his injuries. He had eight bullet wounds from an automatic rifle covering the area from his thigh to the nape of his neck. Luckily the one in the neck just missed his jugular, exiting the other side, and the others missed his vital organs. Most of the bullets had been removed, except for one which was embedded millimetres away from his right lung. It was clear that if that bullet was not extracted, he would die. The doctor had done what he could, but there was also the possibility of gangrene if the wounds weren't kept clean. Sonia emptied a bowl of bloodied water and brought over another fresh bowl of hot water and a clean cloth. Simone noted how tenderly she bathed his forehead.

'What happened?' she asked.

'It took place the other night,' Baptiste replied. 'He was adamant that he wanted to ambush Bruno Albrecht's car and finish him off as he was driving back to his villa. We tried to persuade him against it as those roads are patrolled by the Germans all day now. He took six others. One was killed, the others managed to escape. How they managed to carry Alexandre back here is a miracle as two were hit themselves, although not as badly as this.' There was a pause and one of the maquisards said they'd heard Albrecht died anyway – a drowning they thought.

Simone put her hand gently on Alexandre's cheek. 'Oh you foolish man,' she said in a soft, caring voice.

The others looked at her, as if waiting for an explanation.

She turned to them and told them he knew she was going to kill Albrecht that night and tried to dissuade her. 'He didn't like the way I planned it. We disagreed because he thought I would get killed.' Tears filled her eyes. 'That must have been why he planned the ambush – to stop me.'

The men all looked at each other. 'Are you are telling us it was *you* who killed Albrecht?' Baptiste said.

'Yes. It was meant to look like an accident and I got away with it.'

She continued to stroke Alexandre's cheek. Sonia put a sisterly arm around her. 'We are proud of you, Martine.' She looked up at the men. 'We are *all* proud, aren't we?'

The men started to clap and the heaviness in the room, momentarily lifted. One by one, they approached her and shook her hand. Baptiste was the last. 'Well, Martine, you are definitely a hero. Alexandre would be proud of you.'

There was little time for celebration. She accompanied the doctor to the next room and checked out the other two men.

'You'll pull through just fine,' she assured them. 'You were very brave, knowing how bad the situation is now.'

'We couldn't let him go on his own could we?' one of them said and gave her a wink.

After a brief discussion with the doctor, they agreed that if Alexandre had any chance of survival, they had to get that last bullet out. The men were given the task of scrubbing the kitchen table down with boiling hot water until it almost gleamed and they laid him on it, while Sonia prepared cloths and sterilized their instruments. The doctor and Simone then set about opening Alexandre's chest. The incision was deep, but there was no other way to get at the bullet. Working as swiftly as possible, they finally removed it and Simone sutured the wound. It was agreed that they could not return him to the same mattress for fear of infection so he was to remain on the table for a few days, until they considered it safe to move him.

The doctor apologised but he had too much to do to stay any longer. He was exhausted but there were injured maquisards everywhere, and they needed him. 'I'm leaving these men in your capable hands,' he said to her. Baptiste left with him.

After two days, Alexandre still remained in a coma. Throughout this time, she sat by his side, only leaving to get some sleep when Sonia took her place. The atmosphere at the farmhouse was oppressive and Sonia urged her to get some fresh air before she fell sick herself. She went outside and sat on a rock, recalling the first time she had come here. The men had viewed her with suspicion – a mere young woman – a Parisian at that, yet she had proved to be an expert shot with enough courage for them all.

Enrique came out with something to eat. 'We are lucky to have you, Señorita Martine. You are a brave woman.'

Over the next few days, a sense of despondency set in and despite constant medical care, Alexandre's health deteriorated. The men gathered around, saying prayers and urging him on. Enrique sat beside him playing his guitar and singing his favourite Spanish songs, but it was no use. Alexandre passed away almost a week later. They gave him a hero's burial in the woods where he'd trained Simone to be a sniper. His grave was marked with a rudimentary wooden cross and painted with the Cross of Lorraine. The Maquis gathered around, someone started to beat a drum, and Simone began to sing the first line of "Le Chant Des Partisans".

'Ami, entends-tu le vol noir des corbeaux sur nos plaines? Ami, entends-tu les cris sourds du pays qu'on enchaîne? – My friend, do you hear the dark flight of the crows over our plains? My friend, do you hear the dulled cries of the country put in chains?'

At first her voice was low, almost a tremble, but after the first two lines, it became stronger and she encouraged the others to join in. Their voices grew louder and louder, Enrique strummed his guitar and the men raised their fists defiantly in the air, and by the time the song ended, they felt strong and emboldened again.

The first few evenings after Alexandre's death, Simone found solace by sitting by his graveside, talking to him. She told him her life story, about Pierre who had been sent to Germany and whose face she could no longer remember, about joining the Resistance and working with Jacques, about the Legrands. She even spoke about Ulysse and vowed to get a dog like him when the war was over. Finally, she said she wished he'd been able to say those words – I love you – but she knew he did. That's why he died – for her – for France. The maquisards felt her grief and left her alone.

After a few days, she realised the time for grieving was over. She picked up his sniper's rifle and with a determined walk, went outside and started to practice again. The men came to watch her. One after the other, she delivered accurate shots into her targets.

She turned to face them. Without Alexandre and Pascal, they were like a rudderless ship. 'Enough of this misery,' she said. 'We have work to do; the people need us.'

A long meeting ensued and the Maquis filled her in on what they'd been doing and what was still needed to do. Instinctively, she took charge and started to give them missions, making sure they acted as a co-ordinated group. Jean-Yves came from his safe house in Reims and she told him to let London know what she was doing – and also those in charge of the French Liberation Army. He informed her that since the Allies' invasion of southern France, officially the Resistance groups were now called the *Forces Françaises de l'Intérieur* – French Forces of the Interior.

'I don't care what we're called,' she said. 'Advise them that I'm coordinating things here.'

She also wanted to know if there was any news of anyone from Verzenay. 'Olivier, Father Thomas; are they okay?'

'They are doing fine. Olivier keeps a check on Madame Marie's house and I believe the wine cellars are still used.'

'What about the manager and his wife at the Hôtel De La Cathédrale? Do you have news of them?'

'They are fine too. They don't know you're here. They think you caught that train back to Paris. It's best that way.'

'What about the Gestapo? How many more people has Mueller tortured?'

He sighed. 'There are raids constantly. Anyone walking the streets after curfew is shot on sight.'

She fingered Alexandre's sniper's rifle. 'Keep an eye on him. I want to be informed of everything he does, where he goes, who he meets, etc.'

Jean-Yves saw the look of hatred on her pretty face. 'I'll inform you, but promise me you won't do anything stupid. He's not like Albrecht you know. He has a retinue of bodyguards.'

Simone gave a little smile. 'Everyone lets their guard down at some time or another. It's a matter of patience – waiting for that moment. That was one of the first things Alexandre taught me as a sniper.'

CHAPTER 28

August 1944

In August, the combined French Forces of the Interior mounted an anti-German insurrection in Paris, and the Free French 2nd Armoured Division under General Jacques-Philippe Leclerc drove into Paris to consummate the liberation. On 26 August, Simone, together with members of the Maquis, gathered around the radio and cheered as de Gaulle entered Paris in triumph.

'It's only a matter of days now before Reims is liberated too,' Baptiste said. He also told her there were strong rumours that the Gestapo were starting to destroy documents.

'Take me back to Reims with you,' she said. 'We must keep an eye on Mueller. We can't let him go into hiding.'

'You will be recognised and shot,' he told her. 'Just leave it. He'll get what's coming to him.'

'I can't take that chance. The information Alexandre gave me was that he will try and give himself up and make a deal with the Americans. It's what he's been banking on. He aims to escape justice and we can't allow it.'

Simone called Sonia into the room. 'Can you help me dye my hair and make it blonde like yours.'

'This is not my natural colour,' she said with a smile. 'It's from a bottle and I only have one left.'

'Can you spare it? When the Allies arrive, I will treat you to the finest hairdresser in Reims.'

'Of course I can spare it. It's for a good cause.' They all laughed.

Within a few hours, Simone had gone from dark-haired shoulder-length hair to a short platinum blonde with a fringe. 'I look like a flapper, but I like it.' She smiled. 'Maybe I'll go into the movies when the war is over.' The maquisards came inside to give their seal of approval and all agreed she looked like a Hollywood film star. 'I don't want to look too glamorous or I'll attract attention. 'I need a pair of glasses and a change of clothes, preferably something more dowdy.'

With the addition of these little extras, she had transformed herself. 'Where is our pretty little Parisian Señorita?' Enrique asked. He gave her a cheeky grin.

There was one more thing to do. She needed to change her identity in case she was checked. One of the forgers looked for a similar photograph to match her new look and she became Marthe Lucas. She packed her suitcase, making sure she had her two guns safely hidden in the compartment, and asked Baptiste to hide Alexandre's sniper rifle in a bundle of long twigs. After leaving a list of things for the Maquis to do, she said goodbye and hid under the hay on the milk cart as she had done before.

'Bon courage,' the men said. 'Take care.'

'Where are you going to stay?' Baptiste asked as he hid her under the hay. 'You can't exactly go back to the hotel. They'll be watching the place and taking note of the guests.'

'I'll tell you when we get there,' she replied.

The roads into Reims were clogged with retreating Germans from further south and the cart was stopped, searched, and allowed on. If it had not been for the fact that it was a milk cart, it would have been confiscated. As it was, the soldiers took several cans of milk and if they'd removed one more row, Simone would have been discovered.

'We're here,' Baptiste said eventually. 'Where do you want me to drop you off?'

She gave him the address of the café in the square and asked him to pull up in a nearby quiet side street.

'I already know it. Pascal and I have used it as a safe house. Serge is a good man.'

His comment heartened her. The streets of Reims were swarming with retreating Germans and finding a quiet street was virtually impossible. In the end, Baptiste steered the horse and cart through an open gate into a yard, hoping that the owners wouldn't make trouble for him. As she got out, he noticed a lace curtain move. An old woman came out to see what was going on. 'I won't say anything,' she said. 'Just don't stay here too long.'

'Thank you, dear lady.' Baptiste gave her a tin of milk and a piece of dried sausage wrapped in a cloth for her kindness. The woman looked surprised and showered him with gratitude.

'Wait here while I check that everything's okay.' Simone said. She wrapped Sonia's grey shawl around her shoulders, pulled down the tatty felt hat covering half of her face, put on an old pair of wire-rimmed glasses through which she could barely see, and headed in the direction of the café.

Serge was outside wiping the tables when she arrived. Not recognising her, he thought she was another of the many homeless victims of war he now saw on a daily basis, and pointed to the end of the street. 'The priest there will help you,' he said, and returned to cleaning a table.

'Serge, it's me – Martine.' Her words were barely audible.

He stood back and stared at her for a few minutes, but there was no doubt about the voice. 'What's going on? Why are you dressed like this?'

'I need your help. Can you hide me? I'll explain later.'

He took her inside and after explaining to his startled mother who she was, showed her to their private quarters.

'I need you to get some things for me. There's a man with a milk cart in the yard with the big black double doors in the next street. I believe you already know him. He'll give you my things. Hurry! He can't hang around.'

Serge scurried away to collect her suitcase and the faggot of sticks. Luckily for them all, he already knew that Baptiste hid weapons in the faggots. 'Look after her,' Baptiste said. 'She's headstrong.'

'You don't have to worry. I'll take care of her.'

Serge's mother looked nervous when she saw her son return with a suitcase and bundle of sticks. 'If that's hiding something,' she said, referring to the sticks, 'you'd better put them in the broom closet in the washroom.'

In the safety of their private quarters, Serge demanded to know what was going on. 'I don't expect you to tell me everything, but for the sake of my mother especially, you need to give us a reason as to why you're here – and dressed like this.'

'I know I can trust you, so you have to trust me. I've heard the Gestapo are destroying documents. They will try to flee any day now. I need to know where Mueller is. I can't tell you anything else, except that it's imperative he doesn't go into hiding or flee back to Germany. Do you have any idea where he's staying? I know he has an apartment at the Hotel Regina, but he's like Albrecht, he moves about between there and his other fine villas too.'

'I'll put the word out and get back to you. In the meantime, stay put – and keep away from the window.'

'Thank you – and your mother.'

She overheard them discussing the situation in hushed voices outside the door. The next minute, he put on his jacket and cap and headed into the square. The time dragged slowly. Occasionally his mother brought her a drink and something to eat, but never stayed to talk, as she needed to keep an eye on the customers. Simone knew it was because she'd rather not know what she was up to.

Sometime later, Serge arrived back with the news that the situation was not going well at 18, rue Jeanne d'Arc. 'The French employees have all been sacked, and it's as you said, they are destroying documents. They're burning them in the yard where they execute the prisoners. My sources also told me that some of the Gestapo have already left for Germany.'

'What about Mueller?' Simone asked, anxiously.

'I've been told by a waiter at the Hotel Regina who works for us that he's still there, but he did say there's a lot of unusual activity. Some of the men have moved on. Wehrmacht officers in the next hotel have already moved out too. We're not sure if they've moved to other villas or simply gone back to Germany. From what I hear, they are mining their other villas, so I would say it's the latter.'

Simone was relieved. 'Well at least Mueller's still here. Tell me, is there any place nearby where I can hide and keep watch on the hotel?'

Serge thought about it. 'I'm not sure. Let me check it out.'

She grabbed his arm. 'I know I'm imposing on you and putting you at risk, but I can't afford to wait. Can you do it now?'

He sighed. 'You're a difficult woman, but I can't resist that smile of yours.' At that moment, they heard a huge explosion from the direction of the railway station. It was followed by sirens, armoured vehicles filled with Germans, and fire trucks. 'My God!' he called out. 'That was loud. They must have destroyed an ammunition dump too.'

Simone gave him a knowing look. 'Probably the Resistance again.' Further away, there was another, smaller explosion. 'You'd better get going while you can.'

It was almost midnight when he returned. The streets had quietened down and the café was closed. Not even the Germans wanted to be out after dark knowing they were targets for the Resistance. Simone was eagerly awaiting his return with his mother.

'Thank God, you're safe, son,' his mother said, pushing a plate of food towards him. 'Please eat something or you will collapse.' The strain was etched on her face.

'I only just managed to evade a group of Waffen SS youths shooting angrily at anything that moved. Only God knows what harm they've done,' he said, tucking into his food.

Serge's mother crossed herself. 'I pray everyone has the good sense to stay behind locked doors.'

Serge told Simone that there were several grand apartments in the same street as the Hotel Regina, but none of the owners were known to be in the Resistance. There was, however, a shoemaker's shop on the corner of the street. 'The man and his teenage granddaughter are sympathetic to us and he's willing to let you stay in his attic. It's not the best accommodation, but there's a small window with a good view of the street and the Hotel Regina. There's also a trapdoor which leads out onto the roof should you need to hide at a moment's notice, especially any weapons. I checked that out too. The slate roof is fairly steep, so you wouldn't want to be going out there if you can help it.' He shrugged his shoulders. 'It's the best I can do I'm afraid.'

He paused while Simone absorbed this information. 'There's something else. The retreating Germans have blown up the bridges over the Marne. It means the Allies are almost here.'

He tuned the radio from the Vichy propaganda channel to the BBC. The reports were optimistic, but this only served to make Simone more concerned. 'Can you get me into that house straight away?'

Serge mopped up the last piece of food from his plate with his bread and gave a deep sigh. 'Can't we simply ambush him and blow up the cars up with a grenade and be done with it?'

'No! Look what happened when the Czechs tried that with Heydrich. Look what happened at Oradour-sur-Glane. We cannot risk another whole village being burnt to the ground. Please, Serge, can we go now? If the situation in Rue Jeanne d'Arc is as bad you say, Mueller may go into hiding at any time.'

Serge thought about it. He was adamant that she could only carry what was absolutely necessary. 'You can't take your suitcase; it will slow us down. He gave her a small backpack. 'Put a change of clothes in this and I will carry the rifle.' She did as he asked and put her two guns inside her shirt.

It took a while for them to weave their way safely through the back streets to the shoemakers. In the darkness of the night, danger lurked in every shadow. Fortunately there were more Allied bombers making their way to Germany again, which kept most Germans off the streets. The shoemaker was waiting for them and showed her to the attic. The first thing she did was check the window. From there she could see the whole street.

'An excellent view,' she said to them.

Simone looked around the tiny room. It was barely large enough to accommodate little more than a bed, table and washstand. It had a strong musty smell of leather, gum, and paints. The shoemaker saw her inhale the smell and apologised. 'It was used as a workshop ages ago,' he said.

She assured him it was fine and thanked him for his kindness. A small girl dressed in a white cotton nightdress stood in the doorway watching her. 'I've made the bed for you, Mademoiselle,' she said, her voice soft, yet all-knowing for one so young, 'and given you an extra blanket.'

After the man and his granddaughter left the room, Serge said he would keep her informed of what was happening as much as possible. 'I'd better get going now, or my mother will start to worry.'

'Thank you for everything,' she replied.

Alone in the claustrophobic room, Simone had nothing to do but wait. When she first joined the Resistance, patience and waiting around for things to happen was something she was not good at. Until then, she had been impetuous, but after seeing what impetuousness did to people in the Resistance, she soon changed.

She placed the chair by the window and took a good look at the street, now bathed in moonlight. Then she loaded the rifle and watched the street, grabbing little naps every now and again. In the morning Serge returned with the rest of her things and the good news that the U.S. 5th Infantry Division had liberated Épernay.

'Patton's army is unstoppable,' Serge proclaimed. 'They've repaired the bridges destroyed by the retreating Germans.' The news lifted Simone's spirits, but she did not stop watching the street, especially the Hotel Regina, noting who was coming and going. In the middle if the night, Serge returned again. The Americans were about to enter Reims. A few hours later, the news they had been waiting for finally arrived: Reims was liberated. He threw his cap in the air, picked her up and kissed her. It was the spontaneous kiss of an excited friend rather than a lover, and she was only too happy to have him by her side at such a momentous time.

'The Resistance were there to greet them,' he told her. 'The French flag is everywhere.' With those words ringing in her ears, he left once more to join the throng.

Outside, the sounds grew louder. French civilians were flooding into the streets singing and crying out in joy, welcoming the Americans with a huge fanfare. The shoemaker came upstairs to inform her that the French flag now covered the bronze statue commemorating WWI near the Place de la Republic. Towards the late afternoon, jubilation was turning to anger and mobs of hot-tempered civilians started to gather outside the Hotel Regina, throwing stones and sticks at the windows. They wanted revenge and Simone feared a bloodbath. She steadied her rifle on the attic windowsill and looked through the telescopic sight. Minutes later several American jeeps and trucks drove into the street, the crowd parted and watched as armed Americans entered the building. One by one, the remaining Gestapo, Wehrmacht, and other Germans officials staying there were led outside at gunpoint, their arms in the air, and loaded into the waiting vehicles.

Simone's senses were on high alert as she aimed her rifle at the doorway of the hotel. She counted them all – fifteen in total, several of whom she recognised from her time at 18, rue Jeanne d'Arc, including the strange-looking man she'd seen in the breakfast room at the Hôtel De La Cathédrale. So he was a collaborator after all. She had been so careful to look at each person, yet the one man she wanted was not with them. Neither was his associate, Obersturmbannführer Hermann. After all this time, she was forced to admit Mueller might have evaded them after all. Tired and exhausted, she felt deflated. Had all this cat and mouse game been for nothing?

CHAPTER 29

A few hours later, Serge arrived with Baptiste and she told them what had happened. 'I can assure you that neither are at the Allied Headquarters,' Baptiste said. 'I've just come from there myself, so I know who they've picked up. They're being interviewed at the moment and all will be imprisoned. Quite a few had false Identification, but there were enough of us to know who is a Gestapo agent and who isn't.'

Simone told him she thought Mueller had a French mistress. 'Do you think he's hiding out at her place?' she asked.

'I doubt it. Her home was in the country and from what we know, she left around the time the Allies took Caen. The place had been mined too. We know that because someone was blown up as they entered the building. If he's gone, it's possible she went with him.'

All they could do was put out an alert for him with the Resistance.

'Are you going to come and join us now?' Baptiste asked. 'The men would love to see you.'

Simone declined. 'I'd love to, but I think it's best if I stay here a while longer, just in case he's still hiding in the hotel.'

'You'd better get some sleep then,' Baptiste said. 'You look drained.'

When they'd gone, she took his advice and lay down for what she thought would be a light nap, but within minutes fell into a deep sleep. She awoke a few hours later to find the shoemaker's granddaughter standing beside her with a bowl of hot stew. 'Please eat Mademoiselle, or you will get sick.'

The next minute, her grandfather entered the room with a radio. 'I've brought something to cheer you up. You can listen to the BBC and de Gaulle's speeches without hindrance now.' He placed it on the table, gave it a good wipe, and tuned it to a French station which was playing music rather than Vichy propaganda. Edith Piaf was singing *L'accordeoniste*. Simone grabbed the little girl's hands and they started to dance in a circle, laughing happily. When it finished, she picked her up and hugged her. 'Your granddaughter has a future,' she said to the shoemaker with tears in her eyes.

The little girl kissed Simone's cheek. 'That's because of brave people like you. My pappy told me.'

Over the next few days, the streets continued to fill with happy French civilians, but there was a darker side. Collaborators were being shot or strung up from lampposts rather than face justice, and women who'd had German lovers were marched through the streets, their hair shorn and abuse hurled at them. Just when she'd almost given up on Mueller, something unexpected happened. A man wearing civilian clothes slipped out of a blue-painted door two buildings away from the Hotel Regina. Simone had admired this particular building from the first moment she saw it because of its architectural beauty. Over the door was a beautifully carved stone lintel, decorated with bunches of grapes, and in the centre was the head of a weeping angel. Because of the grapes, she wondered if it had been built by the owners of a Champagne house. The man walked with a slight hunch, his collar upturned, and wearing a fedora pulled down in such a way that it partially shaded his face. His demeanour told her he didn't want to be noticed. She looked through her telescopic sight and instantly recognised him – Obersturmbannführer Hermann.

Simone was elated. It was obvious he had been hiding there, and if that was so, it was highly likely Mueller was with him. She watched him until he was out of sight. The building he'd just left was much closer to her than the Hotel Regina. She watched it for several minutes. Seeing no movement in the windows, she ran downstairs and asked the shoemaker to get a message to Serge and Baptiste.

Serge was the first to arrive. Baptiste came an hour later. 'You were right about him,' Baptiste said. 'It was Hermann and he went for a meeting with someone associated with OSS. They met in an apartment next to the American HQ. It's guarded so he must have had some sort of arrangement to get in.'

'Then Pascal and Alexandre were right all along. I just didn't realise Hermann was involved in this too. Maybe he's the go-between.'

'If he is, he will want immunity too. He was still there when I left.'

'He came out of that building,' Simone said, pointing to the blue door. 'I suspect that's probably where Mueller is too.'

'You keep watch here,' Serge said. 'I'll go downstairs and keep a lookout from the shop.'

Baptiste decided to return to the American HQ to ask a couple of trusted associates in the Resistance to keep an eye out for them. He would also post someone at the either end of the street. 'If he's in there, he won't escape,' he told her.

Later that day, Obersturmbannführer Hermann returned to the building. He still maintained the same cautious manner, but had no idea that he was being watched. As instructed, no-one approached him. Simone prepared her sniper's rifle, going over Alexandre's instructions carefully in her mind: *never shoot at a target unless you have identified him. When it happens, move away quickly.* All the time, it went through her mind that she was killing someone in cold blood, just as she had in the disused warehouse in Paris.

At that moment an American jeep came into view and drew up outside the building. A man in an American army uniform got out and knocked on the blue door while the driver waited. Keep your nerve, she repeated to herself over and over again. Taking deep breathes to compose herself, she aimed at the door. It opened and the man entered.

'Merde' she hissed to herself. Moments later a light went on in an upstairs room. She strained her eyes through the sight and saw who it was – Mueller, his red-haired mistress and Obersturmbannführer Hermann, speaking to the man from the jeep. The room was at such an angle that if they stood in the window, she could get a clean shot, but they didn't do that. She saw them move about the room and put on their coats. The woman covered her head with a scarf.

Simone ran to the top of the stairs outside her room and called out to warn Serge they were leaving. Within seconds, she was back in her position, rifle steadied and taking deep breaths. Downstairs the shoemaker poked his head into the street, a sign to the others that something was about to take place, and she noticed someone immediately stride down the street in their direction.

In her mind, she heard Alexandre's voice. *Okay, Martine, show them what you're made of.* The blue door opened and the occupants started to leave. Just as the American was about to open the jeep door for them to get in, there was a crack – the split second crack of the sniper's bullet. She had aimed at Mueller's heart and the shot found its target. In a split second, she reloaded and shot Obersturmbannführer Hermann, this time in the throat. As the two men hit the floor, the woman screamed. Her headscarf slipped off, showing her glossy red hair. The American officer and his driver looked shocked. One look at the bodies told them they were dead and that this was a professional hit job. Mueller's mistress continued to scream and the officer hurriedly attempted to help her into the jeep, but at that very moment, a woman on a bicycle wearing a brown felt cloche hat, rode by and at the moment she passed them, took a gun out of her jacket and shot Mueller's mistress in the back. She fell into the officer's arms.

By now, the street was quickly filling with onlookers, and realising who the victims were, rushed towards the jeep shouting abuse. Knowing exactly who the three were they were intending to take away, the American let go of the woman, jumped back in the jeep and quickly drove away, leaving the bloodied bodies on the pavement.

Hours later, the three dead bodies were strung up from lampposts, pelted with stones and spat on. Mueller's mistress had been stripped naked and her hair cut off. Her red locks lay in a bloodied tangled mess on the cobblestones underneath her hanging body. The next day, the Americans ordered their bodies taken down. They were put in the back of a truck and driven away, just as they had done to their own victims. It was over.

The months and weeks of planning had taken its toll on everyone and there was a massive outpouring of grief and anger. Traitors who had dishonoured France were hunted down like wild animals, and the

Allies and the Free French Army, now under de Gaulle's wing, were unable to stop it.

Over the next few days, the maquisards came down from their hideout in the countryside and together with the rest of the Resistance, they celebrated their freedom. Serge's café was one of their favourite hangouts. Enrique and Carlos serenaded them with Spanish songs; the men danced tangos with the women in the street; there was lots of lovemaking, lots of drinking, and most of all, lots of tears. The more they drank, the more they felt a deep sorrow at the loss of their comrades and loved ones. It was a time of mixed emotions.

Dressed in her plum-coloured dress from Madame Blanche – who had been charged with collaboration and her dress shop ransacked – Simone joined her friends in their celebrations.

'Tell me, one thing,' Simone asked, as she sat outside enjoying the warm September night with Serge, Baptiste, and Olivier, who had ridden all the way from Verzenay to be with them. 'Who was that woman in the brown cloche hat that shot Mueller's mistress?'

The men looked at each other. 'Why, that was Sonia. She volunteered to help.' Sonia was some distance away, dancing to an Edith Piaf number with an attractive maquisard. 'She was the reason Alexandre came to this area. They were once lovers, but something – probably the war – got in the way.'

Simone felt a tingle down her spine. Sonia! Of all people! Why had no-one bothered to say anything?

Baptiste saw the shocked look on her face and grabbed her hand. 'Come on little Parisian girl, let's dance.'

As they danced, he assured her it was over with Sonia long before she arrived at Verzenay. 'You know, Martine,' he said, 'Alexandre was a man who kept to himself most of the time, but we all knew he'd fallen in love with you. I'm sorry it ended the way it did, but please don't be angry with Sonia. She's also a heroine – and if it helps, she knew he was in love with you too.'

Simone looked across at the pretty woman dancing under the stars wrapped in the arms of her handsome maquisard, and for a fleeing minute, they caught each other's eye and smiled. Both recognised what that smile was about. Life had to go on.

CHAPTER 30

PARIS, OCTOBER 1944

SIMONE STEPPED OFF the train at the Gare de l'Est with her suitcase, still wearing the same suit she'd left in, months earlier, except now, it was at least two sizes too big. The platforms were crowded with people jostling each other to welcome their loved ones home. One thing was immediately noticeable – the absence of the swastika, German uniforms, and that ever-constant look of fear on the civilians' faces. Now people smiled. La Marseillaise blared from loudspeakers and the French flag flew once again. Outside the station, she put down her suitcase and breathed in the familiar Parisian air. It was so good to be back.

The ride back to her apartment was tinged with a combination of happiness and sadness. Under the hazy, cloudless skies of an Indian summer, fire-bombed buildings and vehicles were still being cleared up, and smoke hung in the air overpowering the distinctive autumn smell of decaying leaves that lay in pools of golden yellow and orange around the base of the trees.

68, rue Octave Feuillet was exactly as it had been when she left several months earlier. It was as if time stood still. Even the light in the stairway still hadn't been fixed. She unlocked the apartment, vividly recalling the evening Jacques had let himself in and was waiting for her. Now the apartment was empty and it was as if the past few months had been a dream. She turned on the radio, put her clothes away, and started to make the place lived in again. There was no food so she went for a walk and purchased what few items were still available with her ration cards, and with the last of her money, bought a bunch of flowers to cheer herself up. Tomorrow she would try and get her old job back, but before she did that, she needed to find Jacques.

The next day, she went to the kiosk opposite the church in Clichy; the place where Jacques had said she could always contact him. The owner had changed and didn't recognize her coded sentence, but she did realise Simone was after someone or something.

'Look, dear, why don't you go and see the priest at Église Saint-Vincent-de-Paul. Maybe he can help you.'

Simone made her way to the church with a sinking feeling that something bad had happened. She pushed open the church door and the priest appeared out of the vestry.

'I was looking for someone – a man. He said I could find him via the kiosk, but the owner can't help me.'

The priest asked her to take a seat and told her that the previous owner was taken away just weeks before Paris was liberated. 'The whole family was accused of helping the Resistance and shot,' he said. 'Many around here were taken.' He paused for a moment. 'Who were you looking for?'

There was a time when she wouldn't have said the name, but now the Germans had gone and it was different. 'Jacques – a friend.' She started to describe him.

'I know exactly who you mean. He went to Normandy. The last I heard, he'd joined up with de Gaulle's men and was somewhere in Alsace, chasing the Germans away.'

Simone felt a surge of joy. 'You mean he's safe?'

'As far as I know, yes.'

'If only you knew how happy that's made me,' she replied.

'I'm glad to be the bearer of good news for a change,' the priest said with a smile.

Simone returned to her nursing position at Lariboisière Hospital. She didn't contact anyone from the Resistance in Paris, or in Reims, but never forgot them. Their faces would appear when she least expected it and occasionally she found herself talking to them, telling them about the progress of the war; how the Russians were on the outskirts of Vienna and Berlin. Sometimes she thought the war had traumatized her in ways that she couldn't explain and feared her life would never be back to what it was. She had killed in cold blood and that stain was impossible to wipe away.

It was six months later when she left the hospital and saw people cheering in the streets. 'Hitler is dead,' they told her. She rushed home to listen to the news. Apparently the news came from the Germans themselves. *Reichssender Hamburg* radio station had interrupted their normal program to announce that Hitler had died that afternoon – 30 April 1945. His successor was President Karl Dönitz, who called upon the German people to mourn their Führer, whom he stated had died a hero defending the capital of the Reich. It wasn't long before the world realised this was a lie and that he'd committed suicide.

Two days later, Simone was just about to enter her apartment building, when she heard a voice call out, 'Mademoiselle Dumont.' It had been so long since she heard her code name that she thought she was imagining things, yet she recognised the voice instantly. She spun around and there behind her stood Jacques. At first, she barely recognised him, he'd lost so much weight and his hair was greyer than she remembered it.

'Oh, God, Jacques; is it really you?' They embraced for what seemed like an eternity while passers-by smiled, happy to see another couple reunited again. 'I can't believe it,' Simone said, wiping away her tears. 'Tell me I'm not dreaming.'

He laughed. 'Come on. I'm taking you out for a drink. We've got lots to talk about.'

That evening Jacques told her what had happened since she left: the people in the Paris Resistance who'd been caught, the people they'd managed to save, his trip to Normandy to work with the Resistance there after he heard his son was with the French Forces on D-Day.

'Thank God my son survived,' he said. 'He went to fight in Belgium after that. He's still fighting. As for me, I've just come from Lüneburg where there has been a partial surrender of German forces to General Montgomery. Admiral von Friedeburg has been ordered by Admiral Dönitz to attempt to negotiate a similar agreement with the Americans. I'm in touch with them and that's why I'm here now. General Eisenhower has cabled the Soviet Army Chief of Staff General, Alexei Antonov, and informed him that he intends to demand an unconditional surrender on all fronts from the Germans. As you know, the Supreme Headquarters Allied Expeditionary Force is in Reims. I want you to go there with me.'

'This is the best news I've had in a long time,' Simone said. 'First, knowing that you are alive and well, and now this. Of course I'll accompany you. When do we leave?'

'Tonight.'

She burst out laughing. 'You're not one for wasting time are you? I should have expected that answer.'

'The Americans have given us a car. We'll be travelling in style for a change and staying for a few days, so you can introduce me to some of your friends.'

They travelled through the night telling each other what they'd been doing – the highs and the lows of working undercover and how they were glad to have survived. Jacques already knew of Pascal's death and the assassination of Albrecht and Mueller and congratulated her on a job well done.

'Now you understand why I couldn't tell you everything at the beginning of the mission,' he said. 'There was only a handful who knew. You rose to the occasion and I'm proud of you.' Just before they entered Reims, he said he wanted to mention one important thing. 'Don't expect any of the Allied top brass to congratulate you for killing Albrecht and Mueller. The fact that they've considered using Germans for their own ends when the war is over is not something they will admit to.' Simone understood all too well. 'We'll be entering a new phase soon; things will become murky again.'

On entering Reims, Simone was surprised to find that they were staying at the Hotel Regina. Walking through the entrance gave her goosebumps and she hoped it wouldn't open a Pandora's box of negative emotions. One look around the lobby decked out in Allied flags, told her something important was about to take place and she felt honoured to be there.

'You'd better get some sleep,' Jacques said. 'Tomorrow's going to be a big day.'

Simone was shown to her room and the first thing she did was go to the window and check the street. The shoemaker's shop was still there, and she intended to pay him a visit. That night, as she slipped between the covers of her large, soft bed, she found it hard to believe she was back in the city that meant so much to her. The following day, Jacques introduced her to important members of the Allied Expeditionary Force who thanked her for her work with the Resistance. She was informed that a reply from President Dönitz had been received and that General Jodl, along with his aide, Major Oxenius, were flying to Reims to join von Friedeburg to sign the surrender. At first it appeared the Germans were stalling for time, saying that the surrender terms were unacceptable. When Eisenhower was informed, he repeated his demand for total capitulation or all negotiations would be broken off. Faced with this ultimatum, in the early hours of the 7th May 1945 General Jodl received a message from Dönitz: "Full power to sign in accordance with the conditions as given."

Everyone at Supreme Headquarters swung into action. The Germans taking part in the negotiations were housed at 3 Place Godinot, a building normally used to accommodate officers visiting SHAEF, picked up in the early hours of the morning, and taken to the "war room" at General Eisenhower's Headquarters where there was a large number of press and observers waiting, including Jacques. An interpreter read out the terms of the surrender document before General Jodl signed it at 02:41 hrs on Monday, 7th May.

Jacques hurried back to the hotel and told Simone that Eisenhower was not at the signing but remained in a nearby room and was represented by Lieutenant General Walter Bedell Smith. The capitulation went into effect at 23:01 hrs Central European Time on Tuesday the 8th May 1945. The next day, Field Marshal Keitel and other members of the German High Command travelled to Berlin, and shortly before midnight, signed another document of unconditional surrender, again surrendering to all the Allied forces.

'It's over,' Jacques said. 'It's finally over.'

Over the next few days, Simone caught up with members of the Maquis and Resistance, including, Jean-Yves, who was still in Reims reporting to SOE; Baptiste, who had been nominated for a medal from de Gaulle; Serge and his mother, who still ran the café in the square; the shoemaker and his granddaughter, who showered Simone with kisses, and finally Olivier in Verzenay, who still tended Mme Legrand's garden and took charge of the vineyards as he'd always done. Simone and Olivier showed Jacques the hidden tunnels under the wine sheds and he commended them on their ingenuity and bravery. There was still no news of Claude or his mother.

On the day before they returned to Paris, Simone took a drive out to the farmhouse to visit Alexandre's grave. All the maquisards had gone; the place which was once full of activity was now deserted. Walking through the ruined building, with its upturned rudimentary furniture, rusty cooking pots, and the odd piece of clothing, was like being surrounded by ghosts. She walked to his grave, kissed her fingertips and touched the cross on his grave, telling him he had contributed to this day as much as anyone. A soft breeze blew through the trees where he'd trained her, and in that moment, she heard music and the maquisards singing in unison just as they had when they buried him.

Friend, do you hear the dark flight of the crows over our plains?
Friend, do you hear the dull cries of our country in chains?
Hey, Partisans. Workers and farmers, this is the warning.
Tonight, the enemy will know the price of blood and tears.

A strange sense of peace enveloped her. She took one last look at the place and returned to Verzenay.

Jacques and Olivier could tell the visit had upset her and Jacques tactfully suggested they get going. 'Come on. If we leave now, we'll get back to Paris before sunset.'

'You will notify us if Claude or Madame Marie return won't you?'

Simone said.

'Don't worry. You will be the first to know,' Olivier replied.

*

In Paris, Simone carried on with her nursing work. She still saw Jacques, but as time went on she saw less and less of him until one day, quite out of the blue, he arrived at her apartment. She could tell by the look on his face that it was serious. With never-ending revelations about the horrors of mass graves and concentration camps, she wondered what it was.

'It's bad news, isn't it?'

He nodded. 'I'm afraid so. I've been asked to accompany you to Épernay.'

Simone instinctively put a hand to her mouth. 'Is it Claude and Madame Marie?'

'There's no easy way to break the news. Claude has returned, but he's in a bad way. As for Madame Marie, she never made it. I'm so sorry Simone.'

Jacques drove Simone to Claude's villa in Épernay. There they were met by his nurse and doctor, and a man who introduced himself as the Legrand family solicitor. Simone was shown to Claude's bedroom where another nurse was tending him. She gasped aloud when she saw the state he was in. He was skin and bones. She had a hard time recognising the handsome man she'd known over a year earlier.

'Oh Claude, what have they done to you?' Her voice was breaking with sorrow.

Claude was still having trouble speaking but his eyes lit up when he saw her. The solicitor told them that he and his mother had been held captive in a castle in Bavaria and although they hadn't been mistreated, they and other VIPs intended to be used as bargaining chips, had been left with barely any food and no care the whole time they were there. It was the Americans who found them and transferred those who were still alive to an Allied hospital until they were able to return home.

Mme Legrand died shortly after arriving at the castle.

'With the right care, Monsieur Claude will pull through,' the solicitor said. 'There's something else I need to discuss with you.' He asked if she would accompany him to Claude's office. He picked up a file inside which were several papers.

'Claude asked me to read this to you. It's Madame Legrand's will.' Still deeply upset, Simone asked what that had to do with her. 'A part of it concerns you,' he said. 'If you will allow me...' He started to read. 'It states that in the event of her death, in agreement with her son, Claude Legrand, having no surviving heirs, the vineyard belonging to the Legrand Champagne House would be split between the two of you. Claude keeps his property here in Épernay and two others that he owns – one in the South of France and another in Switzerland – and the house in Verzenay, with all its furniture and accoutrements, she leaves to you.' He handed her the papers to read through. 'So my dear, you are now the proud owner of a beautiful home in a prestigious area of the Champagne region. Congratulations.' He shook the stunned Simone by the hand.

Simone was so overcome that she burst into tears. The solicitor called Jacques into the room. He wondered if there had been more bad news.

'Not at all, Monsieur. Mademoiselle has had a shock, that's all – but a good shock.'

When Simone told him, he was shocked too. 'What did I do to deserve this?' she asked. 'It should be Claude's not mine.'

They went to his room to see him.

'No,' Claude said. 'My mother and I spoke about it before we went to Germany. 'I agreed with her. She knows how much you loved the house. Besides, I already have this place.'

'I don't know what to say. I don't know anything about viticulture.'

Claude smiled. 'You'll soon learn. Besides, you'll have Olivier to help you.'

Two weeks later, Simone said farewell to Jacques in Paris, and moved to Verzenay. 'You will come and see me won't you?' she said.

He laughed. 'Do you think I would pass up the opportunity of all that Champagne?'

Simone was glad to be back with her old friends again. Serge and Baptiste became regular visitors to the house, as did Sonia, who moved from Charmont-sous-Barbuise to marry her maquisard. Not long after she'd settled in, there was one thing she needed to do. She made arrangements with Father Thomas for Alexandre's body to be moved from the farmhouse and reburied in the churchyard next to the tomb which the Resistance had used when accessing the hidden tunnel. Now he was among friends.

On many a quiet evening, as the sun set over the vineyards, Simone sat on the terrace with Ulysse by her side, recalling the day she'd told him that one day after the war, she would have a black Labrador just like Ulysse. The war had finished; it had been fought for with blood and tears, but now she had a new life to look forward to and she intended to make the most of it.

POSTSCRIPT

The idea of writing a novel set in the Champagne region came to me a few years ago after visiting the area and spending a few days in Reims. There I visited the Museum of Surrender (*Museum de la Reddition*). The surrender took place in secret in the early morning hours of May 7, 1945, around 3am, in a redbrick schoolhouse – *Collège Moderne et Technique* – that functioned as the headquarters of SHAEF (the Supreme Headquarters Allied Expeditionary Force). There is a film room on the first floor where an intro movie is played. The surrender room and two large display rooms are on the second floor.

In his last book in his series on The Second World War entitled *Triumph and Tragedy*, Winston Churchill describes these events simply:

Friedeburg went on to Eisenhower's headquarters at Reims, where he was joined by General Jodl on May 6. The Germans played for time to allow as many soldiers and refugees as possible to disentangle from the Russians and come over to the Western Allies, and they tried to surrender the Western Front separately. Eisenhower imposed a time-limit and insisted on a general capitulation. Jodl reported to Doenitz: "General Eisenhower insists that we sign today. If not, the Allied fronts will be closed to persons seeking to surrender individually. I see no alternative: chaos or signature. I ask you to confirm to me immediately by wireless that I have full powers to sign capitulation."

The instrument of total, unconditional surrender was signed by General Bedell Smith and General Jodl, with French and Russian officers as witnesses at 2:41am on May 7. Thereby all hostilities ceased at midnight on May 8. The formal ratification by the German High

Command took place in Berlin, under Russian arrangements, in the early hours of May 9.

Because of these two different dates, Europeans and the United States celebrate Victory in Europe (VE day) on May 8, while Russia notes May 9 as Victory Day. The actual room where the signatures were signed is as it was on that very day. The chairs are labelled to denote who sat where, and large maps cover the walls. It was quite a moving experience to be there.

By accident, I also came across a plaque on one of the platforms at Reims railway station, a few minutes' walk from the museum. On that particular day, there happened to be a gathering of members of the Reims Resistance and their families who had worked for the railway and who lost their lives. After playing the Marseillaise, there was a speech and wreaths were laid. That also was a moving experience. I later learnt that the railway workers all over France played an important role in the Resistance and there are plaques to commemorate their bravery at many railway stations, including Caen.

The Gestapo Headquarters in Reims was located at 18, rue Jeanne d'Arc. The building was demolished but the façade was left in place in 1986 and turned into a memorial, which was inaugurated in 1987. *Des Victimes de la Gestapo* is a quiet space which pays tribute to those who were victims of the Gestapo. The stone for the monument came from the demolition of the Gestapo Headquarters. Sculpted bronze plates depicting the plight of the victims, covers the façade of the stone. Behind the monument is a garden area with benches and a small fountain. Numerous plaques inscribed with names, dates of birth, and dates of death of those who were victims are displayed on the wall.

It is now quite a well-known fact that after the devastation of the Champagne region during WWI, the Champenoise and particularly the Champagne houses, were well-prepared for the German Occupation in WWII and deliberately tried to prevent them from stealing the Champagne by blocking off wine cellars. In the first weeks of the Occupation, more than 2 million bottles of wine were stolen by the Germans. Moët suffered more than most. The Chandon château on the grounds of Dom Pérignon's abbey was burned down and many other buildings were requisitioned by German troops. To stop the looting, the Nazis appointed a *weinführer* to each wine region. They were often from the German wine trade and knew both the French producers and their wines, thus ensuring that the Germans got all the best wine available. The *weinführer* for the region of Champagne was Otto Klaebisch.

In 1943 the Resistance Movement became stronger in Champagne and the situation with the Germans began to deteriorate. The Germans arrested or deported several merchants, high ranking employees, and growers. Count Robert-Jean de Vogüé, who ran Moët during that time, struggled bravely, but unsuccessfully, to protect the company from German control and was arrested and accused, along with the other executives of Moët, of actively helping the Resistance. He was charged with obstructing trade demands and sentenced to death. The sentences brought outrage and resulted in a region-wide strike. Ultimately de Vogüé's sentence was suspended, and he spent years in prison (along with the other Champagne executives) while Moët was placed under direct control of the Germans. One can read more about de Vogüé in his memoirs.

"To be a Frenchman means to fight for your country *and* its wine."
— Claude Terrail, owner of Restaurant La Tour d'Argent

The village of Verzenay was chosen as a setting for part of the story, purely because it is a classic Champenoise village. The events and persons in the novel are purely fictional. Verzenay is 17 km from Reims and 19 km from Épernay.

ALSO BY THE AUTHOR

The Viennese Dressmaker

The Secret of the Grand Hôtel du Lac

Conspiracy of Lies

The Poseidon Network

Code Name Camille

The Blue Dolphin: A WWII Novel

The Embroiderer

The Carpet Weaver of Uşak

Seraphina's Song

WEBSITE:

https://www.kathryngauci.com/

To sign up to my newsletter,
please visit my website and fill out the form.

The Viennese Dressmaker

From USA TODAY Bestselling author, Kathryn Gauci, comes a powerful and unforgettable story of one woman's incredible will to survive and protect those she loves against insurmountable odds.

"In the half-light of a new day, the city resembled a macabre scene from hell. The gay Vienna of her youth had disappeared – vanished as utterly as if it had never existed."

Vienna 1938: Austria's leading couturier, Christina Lehmann, sits at the pinnacle of Viennese society. Her lover, the renowned painter, Max Hauser, is at the height of his career. But Max harbours a secret, and it is only a matter of time before the Gestapo finds out. The situation takes a dramatic turn on Kristallnacht, when the pogrom against the Austrian Jews escalates and one of Christina's Jewish seamstresses is brutally murdered.

In order to protect both Max and her couture house, Christina begins a double life, plunging her into the shadowy world of Nazi oppression, fear, and mistrust fuelled by ancient hatreds.

As Vienna descends into chaos, hunger and disillusionment, will her deception be enough to save Max – or will it end in tragedy?

Based on actual events, this is an epic story of courage and resilience. It is the kind of book that wraps around your soul and leaves an impression.

"Brilliant and moving, The Viennese Dressmaker is a compelling and vivid portrait of wartime Vienna; a story of human relationships, and the will to survive under the shadow of the most evil power the world has ever known." — JJ Toner, author of *The Black Orchestra*

"Filled with suspense from the first chapter to last, *The Viennese Dressmaker* is a nail-biting story masterfully crafted to show the oppressive reality of life in Vienna during the dark days of WWII. I feared for Christina at every turn as she confronted threats and dangers lurking in every corner to help the victims and those she loved. For WWII resistance fiction fans, Gauci never disappoints." — Alexa Kang, USA Today bestselling author of the *Rose of Anzio series*.

"Triumphs, defeats, and loss. Kathryn Gauci's characters bleed from the pages in this perfectly paced novel set in Vienna. This great historical novel transported me to Austria and allowed me to see, smell and feel the streets beneath my feet as I walked alongside the characters." — Jana Petken, the #1 bestselling author of *The German Half-Bloods Trilogy*.

"With *The Viennese Dressmaker*, Kathryn has once again created a page-turning story based on well-researched historical detail. Searing and heart-breaking, Christina's story will stay with you long after you finish the final page. I loved it." — Eoin Dempsey, bestselling author of *White Rose, Black Forest* and *The Longest Echo*.

"*The Viennese Dressmaker* is a WWII novel in all the best traditions of the genre. Deeply touching and captivating, this is a powerful tale of courage and self-sacrifice under the pressure of unrelenting terror. The brilliantly portrayed characters, breathtaking twists of fate, and a surprise ending will take you on a journey you won't soon forget." — Marina Osipova, multi-award-winning historical fiction author of *How Dare the Birds Sing*.

The Secret of the Grand Hôtel du Lac

Amazon Best Seller in German

and French Literature (Kindle Store)

From USA TODAY Bestselling Author, Kathryn Gauci, comes an unforgettable story of love, hope and betrayal, and of the power of human endurance during history's darkest days.

Inspired by true events, *The Secret of the Grand Hôtel du Lac* is a gripping and emotional portrait of wartime France... a true-page-turner.

"Dripping with suspense on every page" — JJ Toner
"Sometime during the early hours of the morning, he awoke again, this time with a start. He was sure he heard a noise outside. It sounded like a twig snapping. Under normal circumstances it would have meant nothing, but in the silence of the forest every sound was magnified. There it was again. This time it was closer and his instinct told him it wasn't the wolves. He reached for his gun and quietly looked out through the window. The moon was on the wane, wrapped in the soft gauze of snowfall and it wasn't easy to see. Maybe it was a fox, or even a deer. Then he heard it again, right outside the door. He cocked his gun, pressed his body flat against the wall next to the door, and waited. The room was in total darkness and his senses were heightened. After a few minutes, he heard the soft click of the door latch."

February 1944. Preparations for the D-Day invasion are well advanced. When contact with Belvedere, one of the Resistance networks in the Jura region of Eastern France, is lost, Elizabeth Maxwell, is sent back to the region to find the head of the network, her husband Guy Maxwell.

It soon becomes clear that the network has been betrayed. An RAF airdrop of supplies was ambushed by the Gestapo, and many members of the Resistance have been killed.

Surrounded on all sides by the brutal Gestapo and the French Milice, and under constant danger of betrayal, Elizabeth must unmask the traitor in their midst, find her husband, and help him to rebuild Belvedere in time for SOE operations in support of D-Day.

Amazon Reviews

"Enthralling. This is a page-turner." Marina Osipova

"A historical fiction masterpiece." Amazon Top 100 Customer Review

"Incredible book." Turgay Cevikogullari

"Author paints wonderful pictures with her words." Avidreader

"Great storytelling of important historical time." Luv2read

"Complex characters and a compelling storyline." Pamela Allegretto

"An SOE mission to German occupied France fraught with danger" Induna

Conspiracy of Lies

A powerful account of one woman's struggle to balance her duty to her country and a love she knows will ultimately end in tragedy. *Which would you choose?*

1940. The Germans are about to enter Paris, Claire Bouchard flees for England. Two years later she is sent back to work alongside the Resistance.

Working undercover as a teacher in Brittany, Claire accidentally befriends the wife of the German Commandant of Rennes and the blossoming friendship is about to become a dangerous mission.

Knowing thousands of lives depend on her actions, Claire begins a double life as a Gestapo Commandant's mistress in order to retrieve vital information for the Allies, but ghosts from her past make the deception more painful than she could have imagined.

A time of horror, yet amongst so much strength and love Conspiracy of Lies takes us on a journey through occupied France, from the picturesque villages of rural Brittany to the glittering dinner parties of the Nazi elite.

Amazon Reviews

"My heart! What a fabulous story." Amazon Top Customer

"Gripping and Charismatic." B. Gaskell-Denvil

"This novel should be made into a movie." Wendy J. Dunn

"Beware, this story will grip you." Helen Hollick for *A Discovered Diamond*

"Well-written and emotional." Pauline for *A Chill with a Book Readers' Award*

The Poseidon Network

A mesmerising, emotional espionage thriller that no fan of WWII fiction will want to miss.

"One never knows where fate will take us. Cairo taught me that. Expect the unexpected. Little did I realise when I left London that I would walk out of one nightmare into another."

1943. SOE agent Larry Hadley leaves Cairo for German and Italian occupied Greece. His mission is to liaise with the Poseidon network under the leadership of the White Rose.

It's not long before he finds himself involved with a beautiful and intriguing woman whose past is shrouded in mystery. In a country where hardship, destruction and political instability threaten to split the Resistance, and terror and moral ambiguity live side by side, Larry's instincts tell him something is wrong.

After the devastating massacre in a small mountain village by the Wehrmacht, combined with new intelligence concerning the escape networks, he is forced to confront the likelihood of a traitor in their midst. But who is it?

Time is running out and he must act before the network is blown. The stakes are high.

From the shadowy souks and cocktail parties of Cairo's elite to the mountains of Greece, Athens, the Aegean Islands, and Turkey, The Poseidon Network, is an unforgettable cat-and-mouse portrait of wartime that you will not want to put down.

The Embroiderer

A richly woven saga set against the mosques and minarets of Asia Minor and the ruins of ancient Athens. Extravagant, inventive, emotionally sweeping, The Embroiderer is a tale that travellers and those who seek culture and oriental history will love

1822: During one of the bloodiest massacres of The Greek War of Independence, a child is born to a woman of legendary beauty in the Byzantine monastery of Nea Moni on the Greek island of Chios. The subsequent decades of bitter struggle between Greeks and Turks simmer to a head when the Greek army invades Turkey in 1919. During this time, Dimitra Lamartine arrives in Smyrna and gains fame and fortune as an embroiderer to the elite of Ottoman society. However it is her grand-daughter Sophia, who takes the business to great heights only to see their world come crashing down with the outbreak of The Balkan Wars, 1912-13. In 1922, Sophia begins a new life in Athens but when the Germans invade Greece during WWII, the memory of a dire prophecy once told to her grandmother about a girl with flaming red hair begins to haunt her with devastating consequences.

1972: Eleni Stephenson is called to the bedside of her dying aunt in Athens. In a story that rips her world apart, Eleni discovers the chilling truth behind her family's dark past plunging her into the shadowy world of political intrigue, secret societies and espionage where families and friends are torn apart and where a belief in superstition simmers just below the surface.

The Embroiderer is not only a vivid, cinematic tale of romance, glamour, and political turmoil, it is also a gripping saga of love and loss, hope and despair, and of the extraordinary courage of women in the face of adversity.

Amazon Reviews

"The Embroiderer is a beautifully embroidered book." Jel Cel

"Stunning." Abzorba the Greek

"Remarkable... even through the tears." Marva

"A lyrical, enthralling journey in Greek history." Effrosyne Moschoudi

"A great book and addictive page-turner." Lena

"The needle and the pen create a masterpiece." Alan Hamilton

"The Embroiderer reveals the futility of way and the resilience of the human spirit." Pamporos

"A towering achievement" Marjory McGinn

The Blue Dolphin: A WWII Novel

From Amazon Bestselling author of *The Secret of the Grand Hôtel du Lac*, Kathryn Gauci, comes a powerful and unforgettable portrayal one woman's struggle to balance a love she knows will ultimately end in tragedy, and of the hardships of war combined with the darker forces of village life. A real page-turner.

'I saw him everywhere: in the brightest star, in the birds that came to my window — he was there. After a love like that, you can endure anything life throws at you.'
Set on a Greek island during the German Occupation of Greece, *The Blue Dolphin* reads like a Greek tragedy. Rich with loyalties and betrayals, it is a harrowing, yet ultimately uplifting story of endurance and love.

1944 Greece: After Nefeli loses her husband during the Italian invasion of Greece in 1940, she ekes out a meager living from her Blue Dolphin taverna with the help of her eight-year-old-daughter, Georgia, their small garden, and Agamemnon the mule.

Four of Nefeli's close friends, who belong to the Greek Resistance, ask her to hide a cache of weapons, placing her in mortal danger from the enemy. When the Resistance blows up a German naval vessel filled with troops, three of them are killed, and the Germans start to make regular visits to the island.

With the loss of her friends, Nefeli's dire circumstances force her to accept a marriage proposal arranged by the village-matchmakers, but what happens next throws everyone on the island into turmoil and changes the course of Nefeli's and Georgia's lives forever.

"Kathryn Gauci is a storyteller who possesses a phenomenal ability to make her readers fall in love with her characters."
Extravagant, inventive, and emotionally sweeping, this is a novel that lovers of Nikos Kazantzakis, Louis de Bernieres and Victoria Hislop will not want to miss.

Amazon Reviews

"It doesn't matter in which country or century they take place, all of them are impossible to put down. Five stars for this masterpiece for sure!" Amazon reviewer

"Set on a tiny quiet Greek Island, this incredible and credible WWII drama by Kathryn Gauci has beautiful descriptions of the landscape and lifestyle to feed and calm all the senses." Pamporos

"Kathryn Gauci is a storyteller who possesses a phenomenal ability to make her readers fall in love with her characters, equally real and rounded, whether sympathetic or abominable. In this story, I rooted the most for Nefeli and Martin." Marina Osipova

"The ability to write sympathetically, with impressive details in atmosphere and fact, rising to a crescendo as the story develops is all part of Gauci's style." Suzi Stembridge

The Carpet Weaver of Uşak

A haunting story of a deep friendship between two women, one Greek, one Turk. A friendship that transcends an era of mistrust, and fear, long after the wars have ended.

"Springtime and early summer are always beautiful in Anatolia. Hardy winter crocuses, blooming in their thousands, are followed by blue muscari which adorn the meadows like glorious sapphires on a silk carpet."
Aspasia and Saniye are friends from childhood. They share their secrets and joy, helping each other in times of trouble.

When WWI breaks, the news travels to the village, but the locals have no idea how it will affect their lives.

When the war ends the Greeks come to the village, causing havoc, burning houses and shooting Turks. The residents regard each other with suspicion. Their world has turned upside down, but some of the old friendships survive, despite the odds.

But the Greeks are finally defeated, and the situation changes once more, forcing the Greeks to leave the country. Yet, the friendship between the villagers still continues.

Many years later, in Athens, Christophorus tells his grandson, and his daughter, Elpida, the missing parts of the story, and what he had to leave behind in Asia Minor.

A story of love, friendship, and loss; a tragedy that affects the lives of many on both sides of the Aegean, and their struggle to survive under new circumstances, as casualties of a war beyond their control.

If you enjoyed Louis de Berniers' *Birds Without Wings* then you will love Kathryn Gauci's *The Carpet Weaver of Usak*. "As she weaves her poignant story and characters with the expert hands of a carpet weaver."

Amazon Reviews

"An unforgettable atmospheric read." Amazon Top Reviewer

"So beautifully written." Elizabeth Moore

"Broken homes, broken lives, and lasting friendships." Sebnem Sanders

"Hooked from page one!" Francis Broun

Seraphina's Song

"If I knew then, dear reader, what I know now, I should have turned on my heels and left. But I stood transfixed on the beautiful image of Seraphina. In that moment my fate was sealed."

Dionysos Mavroulis is a man without a future: a man who embraces destiny and risks everything for love.

A refugee from Asia Minor, he escapes Smyrna in 1922 disguised as an old woman. Alienated and plagued by feelings of remorse, he spirals into poverty and seeks solace in the hashish dens around Piraeus.

Hitting rock bottom, he meets Aleko, an accomplished bouzouki player. Recognising in the impoverished refugee a rare musical talent, Aleko offers to teach him the bouzouki.

Dionysos' hope for the future is further fuelled when he meets Seraphina — the singer with the voice of a nightingale — at Papazoglou's Taverna. From the moment he lays eyes on her, his fate is sealed.

Set in Piraeus in the 1920's and 30's, Seraphina's Song is a haunting and compelling story of hope and despair, and of a love stronger than death.

A haunting and compelling story of hope and despair, and of a love stronger than death.

Amazon Reviews

"Cine noir meets Greek tragedy, played out with a Depression era realism. Gauci creates in this novel the smoke, songs and music of Papazoglou's tavern so convincingly one can almost hear the strings through the tobacco-fuelled murk. " Helen Hollick *A Discovered Diamond*

"A very beautiful novel, I couldn't put it down." Pauline *A Chill with a Book Award*

"A book like no other." Jo-Anne Himmelman

"Dark and emotionally charged." David Baird

"The Passion That Ignited Greek History." Viviane Chrystal

"Where there is love, there is hope." Janet Ellis

Code Name Camille

Originally part of the USA Today runaway bestseller, The Darkest Hour Anthology: WWII Tales of Resistance. Code Name Camille, now a standalone novella.

1940: Paris under Nazi occupation. A gripping tale of resistance, suspense and love.

When the Germans invade France, twenty-one-year-old Nathalie Fontaine is living a quiet life in rural South-West France. Within months, she heads for Paris and joins the Resistance as a courier helping to organise escape routes. But Paris is fraught with danger. When several escapes are foiled by the Gestapo, the network suspects they are compromised.

Nathalie suspects one person, but after a chance encounter with a stranger who provides her with an opportunity to make a little extra money by working as a model for a couturier known to be sympathetic to the Nazi cause, her suspicions are thrown into doubt.

Using her work in the fashionable rue du Faubourg Saint-Honoré, she uncovers information vital to the network, but at the same time steps into a world of treachery and betrayal which threatens to bring them all undone.

Time is running out and the Gestapo is closing in.

Code Name Camille is a story of courage and resilience that fans of *The Nightingale* **and** *The Alice Network* **will love.**

AUTHOR BIOGRAPHY

Kathryn Gauci is a critically acclaimed international, bestselling, author who produces strong, colourful, characters and riveting storylines. She is the recipient of numerous major international awards for her works of historical fiction.

Kathryn was born in Leicestershire, England, and studied textile design at Loughborough College of Art and later at Kidderminster College of Art and Design where she specialised in carpet design and technology. After graduating, she spent a year in Vienna, Austria, before moving to Greece to work as carpet designer in Athens for six years. There followed another brief period in New Zealand before eventually settling in Melbourne, Australia.

Before turning to writing full-time, Kathryn ran her own textile design studio in Melbourne for over fifteen years, work which she enjoyed tremendously as it allowed her the luxury of travelling worldwide, often taking her off the beaten track and exploring other cultures. *The Embroiderer* is her first novel; a culmination of those wonderful years of design and travel, and especially of those glorious years in her youth living and working in Greece. It has since been followed by more novels set in both Greece and Turkey. *Seraphina's Song, The Carpet Weaver of Uşak, The Poseidon Network*, and *The Blue Dolphin: A WWII Novel.*

Code Name Camille, written as part of *The Darkest Hour Anthology: WWII Tales of Resistance*, became a **USA TODAY** Bestseller in the first week of publication. *The Secret of the Grand Hôtel du Lac* became an Amazon Best Seller in both German Literature and French Literature, and *The Poseidon Network* received The Hemingway Award 2020 – 1st Place Best in Category – Chanticleer International Book Awards (CIBA) . Both *The Secret of the Grand Hôtel du Lac* and *The Blue Dolphin* received **The Hemingway Finalist Award 2021**

Made in the USA
Las Vegas, NV
30 September 2022

56284871R00144